Reviews

"Letter from a Dead Man is a deligh[...] [...]stery in an 18th century setting." Historical Novel Society.

"Letter from a Dead Man has a similar wit to Pride and Prejudice, and Harris holds up a mirror to society in the sort of way that Austen did." Margot Kinberg, whose Confessions of a Mystery Novelist have brought her many awards in America.

"This story has everything: excitement, mystery, humour and romance. Great stuff!" Sheila Norton, popular award winning author.

"The book sits well within the historical mystery genre, and I have no hesitation in recommending The Fat Badger Society as an enjoyable historical read." Historical Novel Society.

Website:- **www.dawnharris.co.uk**
Follow me on Instagram at **historicalfictiondawn**

CHAPTER ONE

Summer 1794

It was close to midnight when the messenger arrived from the Alien Office in London. No courier had ever come this late before. Nor had one stood swaying with exhaustion as this poor young man was. That alone made me uneasy. And with good reason. For the letter he carried was one I would never forget.

Messengers had become commonplace ever since Downing Street had asked if a highly secret operation could be run from Westfleet Manor, my home on the Isle of Wight. I had willingly agreed to Mr. Pitt's request, for I was very much involved in the operation and that made it easier for me to play my part.

The letter was addressed to Lord Elvington, the man in charge of the secret operation. As he read it I urged the messenger to be seated and poured him a good measure of brandy, which he accepted with a grateful, 'Thank you, Lady Drusilla.'

Elvington passed the letter to his assistant, Louis Gauvan, who sat at the card table with Gisele, his stunningly beautiful wife. Gisele, who had no part in the operation, was tidying the table where the four of us had enjoyed a riotous game of lottery tickets. As I rejoined them, Elvington took the letter back from Louis, but instead of handing it over to me, as I'd expected, he slipped it into his pocket, and carefully avoiding my eyes, told the messenger, 'Fenton, I want you to leave for France first thing tomorrow.'

'Yes, sir. Of course.'

'Good man.' He took the empty glass from his hand, and said, 'There's a bedchamber waiting for you once you've eaten.' Aware that I'd sent the servants to bed after my aunt and uncle had retired for the night at ten, he reluctantly turned to me and asked, 'Lady Drusilla, could you find Mr. Fenton some supper?'

Gisele took one look at my face and immediately got to her feet, 'I'll do that, Jago.'

I was seething at the letter being kept from me, but I managed to control my feelings long enough to thank Gisele, and to ask Louis if he would kindly show Mr. Fenton into the breakfast parlour. If I was going to lose my temper, I preferred to do so in private.

Elvington and the Gauvans, being old friends, were on Christian name terms, and as I was now working closely with the two gentlemen, it made sense for me to be too. But on this occasion, the instant the Gauvans left the room I addressed him with icy formality. 'Lord Elvington, I would be obliged if you would allow me to read the letter.'

He gazed at me in the superior manner he invariably adopted when addressing me or, indeed, any woman. 'I really don't think that would be wise.' We were of the same height, a fraction under six feet, but his good looks were marred by a pair of forbidding dark brown eyebrows. As a gentleman of only four and twenty summers he was remarkably stuffy, for he believed no woman should play any part in the war against France.

Catching a measure of concern in his voice, I relented a little and assured him, 'I promise I won't faint.'

He sat down opposite me, pursing his lips primly. 'Drusilla, believe me there is nothing you can do about this – er - problem.'

I looked him straight in the eye. 'May I remind you Jago, Mr. Pitt gave strict instructions that you were to inform me of everything that happened in your secret operation. It was on that understanding that I allowed Westfleet to become your headquarters.' The great man had also told him I'd recently unmasked a double agent, but I didn't remind him of that. Nor could I tell him the other task Mr. Pitt had given me. An assignment I could not do unless I *was* kept fully informed of every tiny detail.

Inclining his head in reluctant agreement, he murmured. 'Well --- ye-e-s, but......'

'As Mr. Pitt runs this country, I do feel you should do what he says,' I declared in as pleasant a manner as I could manage, hiding my clenched fists under the card table.

Heaving a long drawn out sigh, he muttered, 'Very well, ma'am. If you put it like that.'

'I do,' I reiterated firmly. And with great reluctance he took the letter from his pocket and gave it to me.

It was from William Wickham, the recently appointed head of the Alien Office, a comparatively new government department in London.

This office organised the activities of all our secret agents in France, and also dealt with the flood of French émigrés fleeing from that country's violent revolution.

And I began to read the letter in some trepidation.

My dear Jago,

I'm afraid I have some very bad news concerning your secret operation. An hour ago I received information from a highly reliable source, that the turncoat who organised the recent attempt to start a French-style revolution in Britain, has just betrayed all our Paris agents to the French authorities. The French now possess a list of their names and where they were lodging. I am told they will all be arrested at daybreak on the same day. The date is not known, but is thought to be soon.

If they succeed, not only will we lose these fine young men, but obviously we cannot replace them until the turncoat is put out of action. Until then we will have no knowledge whatsoever of what is happening in Paris.

My informant does not know the traitor's name, but learnt of his treachery through a member of the Committee of Public Safety in Paris, with whom he has managed to become very friendly. Furthermore, he was told this turncoat is not a Frenchmen working for us, as we had believed. That he is, in fact, English.

This appalling act of betrayal, coming so soon after the failed attempt to assassinate the King, makes it even more vital that you identify and catch this traitor with all possible speed. For, he may try again, and next time he might not fail.

Mr. Wickham ended the letter in the usual manner and I handed it back to Lord Elvington with as steady a hand as I could manage, for arrested agents could expect a quick trial followed by a ride in a tumbril through the crowded streets of Paris to the guillotine.

'Thank you,' I said. Stuffy he might be, but he was no fool, and had not been at Westfleet more than a few days before realising that one agent in Paris meant more to me than I was prepared to admit. That was why he hadn't wanted me to read the letter. Perhaps he expected me to swoon, or have hysterics on reading those terrifying details, but I could never see the point in indulging in such reactions, for it solved nothing. I believed in finding solutions to difficulties that occurred, no matter how impossible that might seem.

Jago laid the letter on the card table, but before he could say any more, Louis came back into the room and announced that Fenton was eating like a horse. 'I've shown him where his bedchamber is and he will leave for France at first light.' He sat down, smoothed his rather dashing black moustache, and informed us that Gisele had gone to bed.

3

Picking up Mr. Wickham's letter from the table, he asked in a worried tone, 'What will you do about this, Jago?'

Elvington, normally a calm man, suddenly burst out angrily, 'Warn them, of course.'

'Yes, but how?' Louis demanded. 'We don't know which one is the traitor. If we warn them all, the traitor will.....'

I cut in, 'You're forgetting Mr. Reevers. He's the right man to deal with this situation.' Radleigh Reevers was already in Paris, sent there by Mr. Wickham two weeks ago to seek out the turncoat.

Louis suggested eagerly, 'Radleigh might have discovered who the traitor is by now. If he has, he can warn the others.'

'Ever the optimist, Louis,' Jago said, a faint smile hovering on his lips. 'But I agree Radleigh is the one man we can safely warn about the betrayal. Fenton will sail for France on the "Arabella" on the early morning tide and go straight to Paris.' Lord Elvington, a very wealthy man, used his own schooner to convey agents and messengers to and from France, insisting that a fast and reliable vessel was essential if this secret operation was to succeed. The schooner was currently moored at Yarmouth, some five or six miles from Westfleet, and the captain, Edgar Barr, was leaving for France in the morning to pick up two of our agents from Normandy.

With the decision made Louis left to get some sleep, as he had an early meeting in Cowes with Mr. Arnold, the Island's Customs Officer. Meanwhile Jago and I went into the library, where he wrote to Mr. Reevers giving him carte blanche to do whatever he thought right, while I made a copy of Mr. Wickham's letter to go with it. Then he wrote a quick note to Captain Barr explaining why Fenton was joining him, although the captain was accustomed to last minute passengers.

I finished first and as I used the silver sand shaker to dry the ink, Jago casually suggested, without looking up, 'Drusilla, if you wish to write to Radleigh, it can go with-----'

Cutting in quickly, I thanked him, but politely declined the invitation, accompanied by a firm shake of my fair curls. I'd made my decision regarding Mr. Reevers, and I meant to stick to it. It was the hardest thing I'd ever had to do, for although I had refused to marry him, I had not found a way to stop loving him. Yet I simply could not bear the thought of him not being alive somewhere in the world.

Quickly changing the subject, I asked, 'Jago, do you think it wise to send Mr. Fenton to Paris? The poor fellow is exhausted.'

4

'Yes, but he's the best man for the job. He left London at four this morning and......'

'Today?' I gasped. This involved a seventy mile ride from London to Portsmouth, a sea trip across the Solent, and then another long ride over the Island. No wonder he was worn out.

'He was told to reach us with all possible speed. I think you will agree he succeeded. He can catch up with sleep on the yacht.' That gave me great faith in Mr. Fenton. Such a man would do everything in his power to reach Paris as quickly as possible. I prayed he would get there in time.

It was after one when I finally climbed into bed, but I lay awake, my heart thumping with fear. I couldn't stop thinking about Mr. Reevers, alone in his lodging in Paris, unaware that the entire French revolutionary government, the infamous Committee of Public Safety, now knew his name and where he was living.

Mr. Reevers was a highly experienced agent, accustomed to difficult and dangerous situations, but I was terrified his luck was about to run out. Nor did he know that the turncoat he'd gone to Paris to seek out was now thought to be English, not French. Frenchmen who chose to work for us did so because they were strongly opposed to the revolution in their own country. There was, however, always a risk of a double agent hiding amongst such men. But it was even harder to believe that an English agent would ever go over to the French. Yet, I knew one who had, and the thought of him made me shudder.

Toby East was that agent, and the turncoat put him in charge of the treacherous Fat Badger Society. The society's aim was to assassinate the King and start a French-style revolution in Britain. But the plot failed, and we simply had to capture the turncoat before he tried again. For, as Mr. Wickham said in his letter, next time he might not fail.

On the very day Lord Elvington was given the task of catching this turncoat, there had been a breach of security at the Alien Office. As a consequence, Jago had categorically refused to run his operation from there. Insisting that, if he was to succeed, his headquarters must be set up in a place where there was no chance of any secret information leaking out.

He wanted to be in a quiet coastal area, as near to France as possible. Where, with the aid of his schooner, he and Louis could keep in contact with Mr. Reevers and our other agents. That was when Mr. Pitt had asked me if I would allow my home to become their headquarters, and I had willingly agreed. For, surely, no-one would ever expect such a highly secret operation to be run from the remote and tranquil Westfleet Manor. The house was over two hundred years old and I loved every inch of it, from the beautiful mellowed stones to the elegantly furnished rooms, mullioned windows, strong oak doors and the wide sweeping staircase.

With all my fears for Mr. Reevers preying on my mind I thought I'd never get to sleep that night, but I must have eventually, for I woke up with a start and could see daylight coming through a tiny gap in the curtains. I prayed Mr. Reevers was still alive to see the start of this day.

I got up and as I drew back the curtains, I saw Louis set off on horseback in a northerly direction for Cowes, where he was to meet up with Mr. Arnold. I liked Louis, for he was of a good-natured cheerful disposition. Slim in stature, his laughing eyes and handsome moustache made him highly popular with women. Although born in France, his family had moved to London when he was two, and he was very English in his outlook and ways, having been educated at Eton and Oxford.

The clear blue sky and a pleasant breeze gave me hope that Mr. Fenton would enjoy a swift passage across to France. Early though it was, I wanted to be sure he left in good time. For Mr. Reevers' life, and that of the other agents, depended on him sailing on this morning's early tide. I put on a pale blue dress, brushed my hair, and as I went outside I was very relieved to see Mr. Fenton was already down by the stables, talking to Jago. As I began to walk towards them, they shook hands, and Mr. Fenton climbed straight onto his horse and set off for Yarmouth.

Like any other agent or messenger sailing to France, he would leave his horse at the Dog and Duck inn, which stood about a hundred yards from where Jago's schooner was moored. Louis had arranged with the innkeeper that hired horses could be stabled there at any time of the day or night. These horses were later collected by Roche, the Gauvans' groom, who returned them to the inn from where they had been hired. Usually that was in Cowes, which was around twelve miles from Yarmouth, and it was a system that worked very well.

On reaching Jago I said how pleased I was that he'd taken the trouble to see Mr. Fenton on his way. 'It was the least I could do,' he responded, and murmured enviously, 'I only wish I could have gone with him.'

But as I knew only too well, that simply wasn't possible. Not in his present circumstances. And they would never change. Not now. I tried to take his mind away from it by talking about the weather, and in response he glanced up at the sky and pronounced in his customary reassuring way, 'Yes, it couldn't be better for crossing the channel. With luck, Fenton will be in Paris in a few days.'

We walked round to the terrace, where we sat talking for a while in the early morning sunlight, until eventually he suggested it was time we had some breakfast. We strolled indoors to the breakfast parlour, where we enjoyed a long leisurely meal. It was far too early for my aunt and uncle, or Gisele, to put in an appearance, and afterwards I went up to my bedchamber and rang for my maid to see to my hair properly.

As I waited I stood for a moment looking at the portraits of my parents. Sadly my mother died when I was three, and my father had suffered a fatal seizure eighteen months ago. I had inherited my mother's lovely hazel eyes, but in looks I strongly resembled the rather ordinary features of my father. I did not mind that at all, as I had loved him dearly and still missed him enormously.

Once my maid had worked wonders with my hair, I joined Jago in the library, where we dealt with some routine matters concerning our secret operation.

Early that afternoon Luffe came in to inform Jago that Roche wished to see him. Jago looked up from the papers he was studying and said absently, 'Send him in, Luffe.'

Roche entered cap in hand and addressed Jago in his usual brusque manner, 'Mr. Fenton's horse is back at the Rose and Crown, sir.' Louis, who kept a meticulous record of hired horses used in our operation, had ordered Roche to inform him immediately after he'd returned a horse to Cowes. And if Louis wasn't there, he was to report to Jago or myself.

Jago nodded. 'Any problems?'

'No, sir.'

'Was the horse in good shape?'

'Yes, sir.'

'Good. Thank you, Roche.'

As the groom left and shut the door behind him, I commented in amusement, 'Roche seems to be a man of few words.'

'True. But that can be a blessing for a groom. Some of them talk far too much.'

Later that afternoon, when we had finished working, I went for a ride over the Downs accompanied by John Mudd, my groom, and thought how lucky I was to have a groom who knew when to speak, and when to keep quiet.

Mudd had come to Westfleet at the age of fifteen, when I was three, and he had been my devoted servant for four and twenty years. Being of average height and build, with wavy brown hair, he was inconspicuous in appearance, but there was a great deal of intelligence in his warm brown eyes. He'd taught me to ride, and when I was investigating the Saxborough murders, he had saved my life.

Since I started working for Mr. Pitt earlier in the year, I'd kept nothing from Mudd, and nor did I now. As a servant he sometimes heard or saw things that I didn't, things that had already proved invaluable. Thus, when we stopped to rest the horses, I told him about the message from London, and that Mr. Fenton had gone to warn Mr. Reevers.

I could only guess at how long it would be before that brave messenger returned from Paris. Much depended on the weather, for if a bad storm seriously delayed his return, it could be weeks before I knew whether Mr. Reevers was alive or dead. In the meantime I would help with the secret operation and continue with the extra task Mr. Pitt had given me. A task of which no-one else was aware.

That was all I could do to keep myself busy. Or so I thought. But I couldn't have been more wrong. For what happened the following morning was so heartbreaking, it even forced my fears for Mr. Reevers' safety to the back of my mind.

CHAPTER TWO

My aunt and uncle were not early risers, nor were my guests, except when work made it necessary. Consequently I sat alone in the breakfast parlour the following morning, my thoughts entirely with Mr. Fenton, who was risking his life by going on a mission deep into a country with whom we were at war. Where the slightest mistake, or careless word, would see his life end on the guillotine. I was just finishing my meal with a second cup of coffee, when my butler, Luffe, came back into the room. 'My lady, Mr. Hamerton's groom wishes to see you on an extremely urgent matter.'

Glancing at the clock I saw it was only half past seven. Bridge, the groom, had not been with Mr. Hamerton for long, but I already knew him to be a sensible man, who would not bother me at such an hour on a trivial matter. Setting my cup down I said, 'You had better show him in then, Luffe.'

Bridge was ushered in, cap in hand, and before I could speak, he said, 'Mr. Hamerton sent me, my lady. He's at the Hokewell Inn and......'

'The smugglers' inn?' I queried, rather taken aback, for there was only one inn near the small hamlet of Hokewell. But no respectable gentleman ever went there, and Mr. Hamerton was extremely respectable. A widower of thirty, he'd only recently moved to the Isle of Wight. During his search for a suitable house he'd stayed at Westfleet for a few weeks, albeit under a cloud.

'Yes, my lady. He's just got back from France and------'

'France?' I gasped. 'I thought he'd gone to Portsmouth for a few days.'

'That's what he told everyone, my lady,' he said, twisting his cap in his hands. 'But the truth is he paid Jackson, the boss of the Hokewell smugglers, to take him to Normandy to rescue his sister. Only he's come home with a bullet in him. He's desperate to speak to you, my lady, and there isn't a moment to lose. I'm afraid he's dying.'

'Dying?' I whispered, my mouth suddenly going dry. 'Oh no----'

'Very agitated he is too. He won't die happy unless he gets what's worrying him off his chest.'

His master, a quiet, kindly man, was not given to exaggeration, thus I instantly ordered my favourite horse, Orlando, to be saddled. Then I hastily scribbled a note to my aunt and uncle explaining why I'd gone out, deliberately omitting to mention where, and gave it to Luffe to pass on to them when they came down to breakfast. Hurrying to my bedchamber, I quickly changed into a riding habit, and set off for the inn, accompanied by Bridge and John Mudd, praying I'd get there in time.

The Hokewell Inn was a notorious smugglers' haunt, which stood beside a cluster of fishermen's cottages on a low cliff overlooking the sea. I knew it well by sight, but had never crossed the threshold in all my twenty-seven years. It was about a mile from Westfleet Manor and just as I reached it, a huge ominous black cloud blotted out the sun, making me shiver. Quickly dismounting, I handed the reins to Mudd, and greeted the rotund, middle-aged, balding innkeeper, who was waiting outside.

Respectfully he opened the door for me. 'He's still hanging on, my lady.' And he added, 'You won't be disturbed. There's no-one else here.' Thanking him for his thoughtfulness I hurried inside, ignoring as best as I could the overwhelming smell of stale beer and tobacco, and the fact that if my aunt could have seen me, she'd be reaching for her sal volatile.

The innkeeper showed me into a room made dark by the smallness of the windows and beams that were so low I had to duck my head. John Hamerton lay on the settle in front of the inglenook fireplace, and I fell to my knees beside him, thankful to see that some kind soul had put a coat under his head. His face was a deadly shade of grey, his breathing came in short ragged bursts, but when he saw me, his eyes filled with relief. Recognising how frail his hold on life was, I urged him to tell me what was troubling him.

'Warn Pitt,' he whispered. 'The --- Frenchies ---- mean --- to----'

Each word left him gasping for breath, but his need to tell me what he'd learned in France had kept him alive this long, and I had no intention of letting him fail now. 'Go on,' I begged loudly, as a sudden heavy shower made the room even gloomier. 'What do the Frenchies mean to do?'

'Seize Pitt --- and -----take him --- to Paris. To the ---- guillotine.'

Despite keeping my ear close to his lips, I only just caught the words, yet I knew I hadn't misheard. That bunch of bloodthirsty revolutionaries governing France planned to capture the man running our country, and take him to France for a show trial and public execution.

France had declared war on us over a year ago. Their King and Queen had perished on the guillotine, and ever since Maximilien Robespierre, the most feared man in France, announced Terror to be the Order of the Day, thousands of innocent people, of all classes, had been executed. Robespierre had declared he aimed to purge France of the enemies of the revolution, and protect it from foreign invaders. To think they were actually planning to guillotine Mr. Pitt too made me choke with anger.

Aware I must learn every detail I could, I took a deep calming breath and implored the dying man to tell me where and when they planned to capture Mr. Pitt. I felt his lips move against my ear as before, but I could not hear a single word he said. Squeezing his hand, I begged him to repeat it. He didn't respond and in desperation I urged him again. The rain was thrashing against the window so loudly that, at first, I didn't notice there was no longer any other sound in the room. When I did become aware of it, I realised that John Hamerton, believing he'd told me all I needed to know, had given up struggling to hang on to life, and gone to meet his maker. Unaware that, although his mouth had framed those last few vital words, no sound had come out.

His passing filled me with immense sadness, and closing his eyes, I brushed away the tears trickling down my cheeks. In the short time I'd known him I'd come to like him a great deal, and had hoped to enjoy his company for many years yet.

I understood why he'd tried to rescue his sister, of course. It was what any decent Englishman would do in those circumstances. John Hamerton was well aware of the risks in such a venture, but he had never lacked courage.

The shower having passed, sunshine began to stream through the windows, and glancing down at him again, I saw he was totally at peace. His expression was that of a man who had done his duty. He'd warned me about the threat to Mr. Pitt's life, because he knew I would be able to speak to the great man personally, and make sure he realised the very real danger he was in. It wasn't hard for me to guess how he'd come by this knowledge, and that alone told me it was the absolute truth. This really was what the villainous revolutionary French Government planned to do.

I did not want to think of what would happen if they succeeded. But how much time did I have to warn Mr. Pitt? I wished with all my heart that I'd heard Mr. Hamerton's last few words. But I hadn't, and not knowing when and where the French meant to carry out their devilish plot, it was vital that I saw Mr. Pitt with all possible speed.

Unfortunately, as an unmarried woman, I could not go to London on my own. My uncle would escort me if I asked him, and he'd accept the need for secrecy as I'd worked for Mr. Pitt before. But my aunt would demand to know why I had to go and she wasn't easily fobbed off.

Westfleet Manor and its estates belonged to me, and my aunt and uncle had been my guests since they lost their small French estate to the revolutionaries. Uncle Charles had been born in Paris, but when his French father died a few months later, his English mother had brought him back to London. Where he remained until his French Godfather left him that small estate in Normandy. Despite their difficult situation, and the fact that they were guests in my house, my aunt still believed I should be advised by her in all things. And she strongly disapproved of women working for Mr. Pitt. A view shared by Lord Elvington.

To be fair, she worried about me being in danger, therefore I kept things from her whenever I could, as I had no desire to cause her that kind of distress. She would, however, be most upset about Mr. Hamerton, as she had taken a strong liking to him.

It was clear to me that Mr. Hamerton had gone to great lengths not to mention to anyone, except myself, that the French were plotting to capture Mr. Pitt. And that's how I intended it to stay. For, if it got out, the French would abandon the idea and set about organising some other fiendish scheme, of which we would then know nothing. Whereas now, as soon as I'd told Mr. Pitt of this conspiracy, he could take every possible precaution to ensure it did not succeed.

Just then I heard footsteps, but I thought it was the innkeeper going about his business, until an all too familiar voice pronounced in shocked tones, 'Lady Drusilla. What----'

'Good morning, Mr. Upton,' I broke in quickly, suppressing a groan at the sight of the short, rather scrawny, middle-aged local parson. 'If you have come to see Mr. Hamerton, I'm afraid you are too late. He died a few minutes ago.'

Ignoring what I'd said he declared, 'Ma'am, this is no place for a lady.' Glancing round the room, he went on, 'Surely you did not come here *alone*?'

'What I do is no concern of yours, Mr. Upton,' I retorted in rising anger. From the day my father, who I'd loved dearly, had died, some eighteen months ago, this insufferable little man had taken it upon himself to reprimand me firmly whenever he'd decided I had infringed the rules of propriety. 'It so happens Mudd and Mr. Hamerton's groom accompanied me.'

'That is all very well, but you do not have a gentleman to protect you,' he informed me in his usual pompous manner, 'Your uncle should.......'

'My uncle was still in his bedchamber when I left.'

'Then you should have waited for him, ma'am. The proprieties must be adhered to in all circumstances.'

Clenching my fists, I muttered, 'Don't be ridiculous. Mr. Hamerton wanted to see me before he died. As it was, I only just got here in time.'

Ruffled though he was, he forced himself to respond in a calm manner. 'I will ignore your rudeness, ma'am. You are naturally upset.' He proffered his arm, 'Allow me to escort you outside.'

As I'm only a shade under six foot and his head barely reached my shoulder, the vision of how absurd we would look did at least dent my anger a little, and I retorted, 'I do not need your escort.'

'Very well, ma'am,' he retorted huffily. 'What your father would have said I.........'

'My father taught me to use my common sense. I would be obliged if you would use yours.'

The parson, who believed in having the last word on any subject, had almost reached the door when he turned to inform me, 'Mr. Hamerton's funeral will have to take place on Monday. My.........'

'But that only leaves two days to make the arrangements.'

'Nevertheless it must be so. On Tuesday my wife is going to spend two weeks with her sister in Bembridge.' A journey by carriage across to Bembridge, right over on the island's east coast, on poorly maintained roads, was not something to be lightly undertaken. In fact I strongly suspected her sister and husband had moved there so that Mr. Upton would barely intrude in their lives. 'I shall, of course, escort her there myself,' he went on. 'I won't be home until Saturday as I am spending a couple of days with a friend in Shanklin, and I'm sure you won't wish to leave the funeral until the following week.'

I agreed I would not, and once he'd ridden off I went in search of the innkeeper, to tell him I would have the body removed as soon as possible. Then I went outside to where the grooms were waiting and when I told them Mr. Hamerton had died, Bridge asked, 'Was he able to tell you what was troubling him, my lady?' I put his mind at rest and inquired if he knew why Mr. Hamerton had gone to rescue his sister. 'Yes, my lady. He said she'd married a Frenchman, but was very unhappy and wanted to come home.'

This was true, for a few weeks ago Mr. Hamerton had told me in confidence that his sister's husband was a close confidant of Maximilien Robespierre. His sister had managed to smuggle a letter out to him, in which she said her husband had become as ruthless as Robespierre and she was desperate to escape from him and get back to England. I'd known John Hamerton had planned to rescue her, but believed he would make the attempt in August, during her annual visit to her husband's sister in Normandy. So why had he gone in July?

'I take it his sister wasn't on the boat?'

'No, my lady.' When John Hamerton bought his house on the Island, he'd told me he'd left everything he possessed to his sister. But was she still alive?

Bridge did not know, but thought that Jackson might, and he went on to ask a little awkwardly what he ought to do now, as he'd brought horses to the inn for Mr. Hamerton and his sister. I advised him to take them back to their stables, and inform the butler what had happened. 'I'll come over later today and tell everyone what the situation is.'

'Very good, my lady.' He was a neat and tidy man, who in the few weeks he had been with Mr. Hamerton had become a much valued servant. 'I must look for another position now,' he said, in a rather worried voice. I understood his concern. Mr. Hamerton's death put him in a most unfortunate situation, for his previous employer had also died at a young age, earlier this year. Two such deaths within a few months might well put off other people, even though it was no fault of his.

He left to attend to the horses, while I went to find Jackson, the leader of the Hokewell smugglers. A man I knew well. He lived in the tiny hamlet of Hokewell, some two hundred yards from the coast, in one of the cottages by the village green. In the short time it took to ride there, I told Mudd what Mr. Hamerton had said, and he was as horrified as I was.

'Those Frenchies call Mr. Pitt the enemy of all mankind,' he said in disgust. 'But there isn't a better man living than him, my lady.'

'I couldn't agree more,' I said, as we reached Jackson's cottage.

As Jackson must have been up all night, bringing Mr. Hamerton back from France, I thought he might have gone to bed, but he answered the door himself, holding a baby in his arms. He invited me in, and once I was seated by the fireplace, he settled into the rocking chair opposite. The room was spotless, the windows were clean, and the furniture well polished. I apologised for intruding and admired the child, who had pretty blue eyes and auburn hair. 'She's very beautiful.'

'Takes after her mother,' he said with a grin. His wife was outside putting the washing out to dry, while their three sons played in the garden. 'Our first daughter. After three boys we wondered if we'd ever get a girl.'

Jackson was about six foot, muscular, and boasted a fearsome black beard that was enough to frighten anyone. Perhaps it did at sea, but at home he was one of the most gentle men I'd ever met. Glancing contentedly out the window at his family, he said, 'You'll be wanting to know what happened, my lady.'

'I would be grateful.'

'Well, when we got to Normandy, Mr. Hamerton insisted on going ashore alone. The house where his sister was staying was only half a mile from the coast and I begged him to let me go with him, and I wish I had now, I can tell you. But he said he wasn't prepared to risk any life but his own. He had a pistol with him and said if he wasn't back within two hours we were to sail for home.' He gazed tenderly at the baby, whose eyes were starting to close, and went on, 'Well, when he came back he had blood on his shirt from a bullet wound, but we stopped the bleeding and he didn't seem to be in a particularly bad way. We made a fast passage home and he kept saying he had to see you, my lady.' He paused for a moment, and I saw genuine sadness in his eyes as he said, 'It was when we got him out of the boat and onto the shore that he took a sudden turn for the worse. So we carried him into the inn, that being the nearest place. To be honest, my lady, I thought he was going to die there and then, but he rallied enough to send Bridge to fetch you.'

'I see. Did he tell you why he wanted to see me?'

'No, my lady. But, once we were safely out at sea on our way home, he did say what had happened to his sister. She was alone in the house when he got there, as her relative had gone out. They talked while gathering her belongings and were about to leave when there was a loud knock on the door, and a voice shouted, "Open in the Name of the Republic." That made his sister tremble, for it usually meant soldiers had been sent to make an arrest, and she feared they would both end up on the guillotine. They ran out the back way, only the two soldiers gave chase. Shots were fired and his sister was hit. He turned and shot one of the soldiers. Then, he and the other soldier hurried to reload, and fired at the same time, hitting each other. He said both the soldiers were dead, but so was his sister. He was very upset, my lady.'

I thought back to what Mr. Hamerton had told me about his Will, for his sister's death changed everything.

Jackson went on wistfully, 'I wish we'd brought him home safe and sound, my lady. We would have too, if he'd let me go with him.'

'I don't doubt it. But he wouldn't risk your life, not when you have a family to keep. He was too good a man for that.'

'That he was, my lady.' The baby had fallen asleep against his arm and he gently kissed the top of her head. 'I sent a man for Dr. Redding but he had to leave a message. The doctor had been called out.'

'I'm grateful to you,' I said, and stood up to take my leave, insisting he stayed put so that he didn't disturb the baby.

It was obvious from what Jackson had told me that Mr. Hamerton had seen no-one in France except his sister. Therefore only she could have told him of the plot to capture Mr. Pitt. And she must have learnt of it from her husband. He, being so close to Robespierre, would certainly have known about it, and might even have been involved in the planning. So this wasn't some wild rumour. The revolutionaries planned to take Mr. Pitt to France for a public show trial, followed by an even more public mounting of the steps to the guillotine.

If they succeeded it would be one of the greatest disasters in our country's history. And it had to be stopped, no matter what it cost in lives and money.

CHAPTER THREE

I left Jackson's cottage and had just rejoined Mudd, who was waiting by the village green with the horses, when I saw a carriage heading in our direction, bowling along at a spanking pace, heedless of the poor state of the road. I recognised it at once, for it belonged to Julia and Richard Tanfield, two of my dearest friends, who had also become very close to Mr. Hamerton. They believed, as I had, that he'd gone to Portsmouth for a few days to see an old friend. Now I had to tell them the truth, and my heart sank at the prospect.

As I searched in my mind for the right words, Mudd said, 'Why, there's Mr. Frère, my lady.' I swung round and saw my uncle riding towards us from the opposite direction. I had no doubt that after my aunt had read my note she'd sent him to find me. And I groaned, for now she was bound to discover I had gone into the Hokewell Inn alone.

Her views on propriety were entirely in accord with Mr. Upton's. Even though I was twenty-seven years of age, she expected me to be chaperoned under all circumstances when alone with any man. Even one on his deathbed, as poor Mr. Hamerton had been.

As we all gathered together by the village green, I guessed my aunt must have sent a message to the Tanfields, being well aware of their friendship with Mr. Hamerton. My uncle reached us first and as he gave his horse into Mudd's care, the Tanfields' carriage came to a halt. Richard Tanfield was still recovering from his incredible act of bravery a few weeks earlier, when he'd hurled himself at Toby East, at the precise moment Mr. East fired a shot at me. The bullet struck Richard instead and he was fortunate to survive. Thankfully he was well on the road to recovery now, although he still found some things rather difficult. Such as climbing down from the carriage, which he did very slowly, before assisting his wife, Julia, who expected their second child in November.

Richard, who was wearing his favourite blue coat, took one look at my face and groaned in despair. 'I'm too late, aren't I?'

'I'm sorry, Richard. He died about an hour ago. I was with him at the end.'

My uncle shook his head sadly. 'He was a good man, a real gentleman.'

'Where is he, Drusilla?' Richard asked abruptly, his rugged good looks pale with shock. 'I want to see him.'

'He's at the Hokewell Inn.'

'The Hokewell Inn?' my uncle repeated, and demanded rather anxiously, 'Drusilla, you didn't go into that thieves' den, did you?'

'I had to, Uncle. But it was empty, apart from the innkeeper.' He grunted, which suggested that while he was not happy at what I had done, he understood why I had gone ahead. But my aunt would not be so easily silenced. Nor was Richard, who asked in a puzzled voice, 'Yes, but why did Hamerton send for you? Why not me?'

'Well, he was brought ashore just after seven this morning, and everyone knows I like to be up early. Besides, Doctor Redding told you to take plenty of rest.'

'That's true,' he acknowledged with a wry smile. 'But tell me, was Hamerton able to say what happened to him?'

Choosing my words carefully, I explained how his sister had died, and how he came to be shot. Richard ran a hand across his eyes, trying to overcome the pain he felt at the loss of his friend, and burst out, 'But why did he go now, in July? He said his sister went to Normandy every August, and that's when we planned to rescue her. Together.'

I pointed out kindly, 'You couldn't have gone, Richard. You're not well enough.'

He snorted in disgust. 'Nonsense. I'm well enough to sit in a boat, well enough to walk half a mile to the house where his sister was staying. And well enough to shoot any damn Frenchie who got in our way.' And he added wistfully, 'I wish Hamerton had told me what he meant to do.'

'I believe he always meant to go alone,' I said, 'He didn't want you to risk your life again.'

'Stuff and nonsense. If I had......'

'Richard, a man must be able to live with himself,' my uncle broke in. 'Think of the anguish he would have suffered all his life, if he'd survived and you hadn't.' Richard tried to interrupt, but my uncle persisted, 'No, Richard, hear me out. The anguish I speak of is the kind

18

of soul-destroying grief and sorrow Drusilla and I would have gone through if you had died when you saved our lives last month.'

Julia put her hand on Richard's arm. 'Mr. Frère is right,' she affirmed gently.

The expression on his face told me that he had not given a single thought as to how we would have suffered if he had not recovered, let alone what his death would have meant to Julia. In the silence that followed, as he digested what my uncle had said, I noticed that several women had come out of their cottages, under the pretence of cleaning their windows, or attending to their children. I quietly nudged Julia, using my eyes to point out our growing audience. She reacted with a wry smile and immediately suggested we would make less of a spectacle of ourselves if we all got into their carriage and drove to the inn where the gentlemen could see Mr. Hamerton for themselves. Adding, 'If Mudd could take your horses home Drusilla, we'll drop you and Mr. Frère off at Westfleet later.'

That being agreed to, we set off again, and during that short drive my uncle explained he'd gone directly to Mr. Hamerton's house, assuming that was where he'd been taken. 'Your note didn't mention where you were going, Drusilla.' I had deliberately not done so, but excused my lapse by saying I'd written it in a great hurry.

On arriving at the inn, the gentlemen went inside, while I stayed in the carriage with Julia, as Richard did not think it wise for her to see the body in her present condition. 'Richard will miss him dreadfully,' she said as we sat waiting. 'It's such a shame, Drusilla. Mr. Hamerton had so much to live for.' Julia was a fairly tall attractive redhead, whose sparkling green eyes were now filled with sadness. 'But I understand why he went. Life in France must have been terrifying for his poor sister.' She gave an involuntary shudder. 'No-one in Paris is safe any----' Her voice tailed away and she turned to me in horror. 'Drusilla, forgive me. I forgot --- about Mr. Reevers, I mean. Have ... have you heard from him at all?'

I shook my head. 'Nor do I expect to.' And I quickly changed the subject, asking after Edward, her three year son, who was my godson. She loved talking about him and I enjoyed hearing of his antics. Even so I couldn't get Radleigh Reevers out of my mind.

I'd met him once as a child, and our paths had not crossed again until spring of last year, when I was riding alone in Ledstone woods and saw Mr. Upton, the parson, approaching. I wanted to avoid this pompous little man, for he was so incredibly boring and irritatingly long winded in conversation. Therefore I'd gone deeper into the woods, to wait until he'd ridden past, when the sudden deafening sound of a gunshot, fired very near to me, upset Orlando, my horse, and I'd ended up being thrown into a bed of stinging nettles. It was Mr. Reevers who had fired the shot, unaware of my presence nearby. But, of course, he'd assisted me out of the nettles, and as we became better acquainted I had grown to love him.

It was when he'd told me that he'd had to sell his family home in order to settle his deceased father's gambling debts that I began to doubt the real reason for his interest in me.

This doubt was made infinitely worse when I learnt that, two years earlier, Mr. Reevers had offered for Sophie Wood, the only child of doting wealthy parents. They wanted her to marry for love, as they had done themselves, and therefore had sent him packing, realising he did not love her, and that her fortune was the real attraction. He'd admitted to me that it was true, but pointed out such marriages were not uncommon. At that time he said he had never met a woman he'd wanted to marry, and feared he never would. Although he liked Sophie immensely, he did not love her. He admitted that she believed he did, because he'd told her he did. Later, he very much regretted it, realising she deserved to marry someone who truly loved her.

I hadn't known what to believe, but I had greatly feared that he was behaving towards me as he had with Sophie, and for the same reasons. When, much later, Mr. Reevers made me an offer of marriage, I'd refused to consider it, as I had very good reason to believe he was only after my fortune, for my father's death had left me a very wealthy woman. Mr. Reevers had returned to France at the end of June, but I hadn't been able to put him out of my mind, no matter how hard I tried.

It was useless to pretend I didn't care for him when, night after night, I lay awake terrified of what would happen to him if he was caught spying in a country with whom we were at war, and where hundreds of innocent people were being guillotined every day. Even though I had decided not to marry him, the thought of him being caught by those revolutionary cut-throats and then executed, sent waves of icy shivers up and down my spine.

When the gentlemen came out of the inn they thanked the innkeeper for his help and climbed back into the carriage. As we drove off my uncle told us, 'The innkeeper said Dr. Redding had examined Mr. Hamerton now, so we can.......'

Richard interrupted, 'I should like to make the necessary arrangements, if you are agreeable, Drusilla.'

'Of course,' I said, for there was nothing he could do for his friend now except organise the funeral and deal with his affairs. 'But I'm afraid Mr. Upton insists the funeral must take place on Monday.'

When I explained why, he saw no objection. 'Hamerton hadn't been on the Island long enough to make many friends, so it will be a small affair. I'll look in at the parsonage on the way home.'

Julia agreed that would be sensible, and said, 'After the service people can come back to us. It's the least we can do.'

Richard took her hand in his and squeezed it. 'I hadn't thought about that, but you're right. They should come to us. Can you organise it in time?'

'Naturally,' she assured him with a loving smile.

'I wonder who will inherit the house,' my uncle remarked thoughtfully, as the carriage turned into the road leading to Westfleet.

As there was no reason now to conceal what Mr. Hamerton had told me only last week, I explained that he'd left everything to his sister.

'That I would expect,' my uncle acknowledged, 'but did he make provision in case she pre-deceased him?'

I was able to assure my uncle that he had, but when I didn't elaborate, Richard demanded a little impatiently, 'Who will inherit it now, Drusilla? I'd like to know who I'll be dealing with.'

'That won't be a problem. He left it to you and Julia, and your children.'

Julia's mouth dropped open in astonishment. 'Are you sure? What about his cousins in Scotland? They must be his only other living relatives now.'

'Yes, but he hasn't seen them since he was a small child.' She was still amazed and I said, 'It's what he wanted, Julia. He feared his sister might not get out of France alive and that's why he gave his Will such a lot of thought.'

'A man of sense,' commented my uncle.

Richard was clearly stunned by the news, but said, 'I knew he'd made a Will, but I never imagined for one minute that he'd.....' Overcome with emotion, he turned his head away from us and gazed out the carriage window in silence.

To give him time to recover his composure, I repeated in some detail what Mr. Hamerton had told me. That he did not see the sense in leaving his possessions to relatives he wouldn't even recognise, and who his parents had lost contact with over twenty years ago. 'He made bequests to his servants, of course.' And I went on, 'That reminds me, I promised Bridge, his groom, that I'd ride over to the house later and tell the servants what the situation is.'

By this time, Richard had his emotions under control again, and said, 'If the house is to be ours, Drusilla, I think I should do that.'

'Yes, of course,' I said, agreeing willingly.

'Good. I'll go this afternoon.'

When the coachman brought the carriage to a halt outside Westfleet, my uncle and I got out, and once the carriage had set off again we walked straight into the hall. Where my butler informed me that Lord Elvington and Mr. Gauvan had gone to Cowes after breakfast to assist Mr. Arnold with the émigrés who had arrived at first light this morning. This was the official reason the Alien Office had given for their presence on the Island, and they did what they could to help. My butler then went on to say how sorry he was about Mr. Hamerton. 'He was a most pleasant gentleman.'

The whole household had come to know Mr. Hamerton earlier in the summer, when he'd stayed at Westfleet while looking for a suitable house for himself. I wondered how Luffe had learnt of his death so quickly, except that servants always did seem to know what was going on. But, as I soon discovered, my aunt had questioned Mudd when he brought the horses home.

Aunt Thirza was in the blue room, which faced south, and had been my mother's favourite room, built with large windows to gain the most benefit from the sun. My aunt, who was a little over forty, had a trim, elegant figure, and her choice of clothes said much for her great sense of fashion, making up for her rather plain features.

When Uncle Charles and I walked into the room, she was sitting by the window in the sunshine, reading a letter. My uncle was not as trim as his wife, and his white hair made him look older, but he was the kindest of men. He instantly recognised the handwriting, and asked eagerly, 'Is that from Lucie? When are they are coming home?'

'Next week,' she informed him happily.

Lucie, their only child, had married Giles Saxborough the previous October. He owned Ledstone Place, a large estate some four miles from Westfleet Manor. Giles was of my own age and we had been great friends all our lives, and I was also very fond of his widowed mother, Marguerite, who was my godmother. They had all attended a family wedding in Yorkshire, and then taken the opportunity to tour that beautiful county, before ending their trip with a stay of several weeks in London. Naturally my aunt and uncle had greatly missed their daughter.

Suddenly Aunt Thirza gave a little cry of delight and looked up from the letter. 'Charles, we're going to be grandparents! Isn't that wonderful?' And she gave him the letter.

He read it eagerly and exclaimed, 'In January, I see.' And reading on, said, 'Ah, but she's suffering from sickness.'

'Just as I did, if you remember, Charles. But I'm sure she'll soon get over that. Giles wants to bring her home in his yacht, rather than have her suffer the journey in the carriage.'

'That's very sensible. Lucie likes sailing. She'll be much more comfortable.' I sat on the window seat, smiling at them, and once he'd finished reading the letter, he passed it to me, saying, 'Giles wants me to tell Leatherbarrow to take the yacht to London as soon as possible, so I'll ride over to Ledstone straight after nuncheon.'

I didn't want to put a damper on my aunt's joyful mood by declaring I must get to London quickly in order to see Mr. Pitt, but when I read the letter, I began to see a way out of this dilemma. I smiled as I handed it back to my aunt, commenting matter-of-factly, 'I see my godmother refuses to come home by sea.'

My uncle frowned. 'Yes, that is a pity.'

'She does suffer rather badly from seasickness,' I pointed out.

'Nevertheless,' my aunt put in, 'I think it's very selfish of her to expect Giles to go all the way back to London just to escort her home.' My aunt and godmother had never got on, and probably never would. For Aunt Thirza had no time for frivolous women who did not act their age, while my godmother detested women who had no sense of humour and who always took everything far too seriously. Yet I had no doubt they would both become doting grandmothers. Nevertheless, the letter gave me an idea for an excuse to go to London. The kind of excuse that would stop my aunt worrying about me.

CHAPTER FOUR

Aunt Thirza was genuinely saddened by Mr. Hamerton's demise and urged me to tell her what had happened to him. I did so at once, without mentioning where he'd actually died, allowing her to assume it was at his own home, praying that Lucie's wonderful news would take her mind off the finer details.

'Yes, but why did he want to see you?' she demanded.

'To tell me when his sister died, as her death affected his Will.'

She accepted this explanation without a quibble, but my uncle looked a trifle puzzled, although he said nothing. Upset as she was by their deaths, she was also intrigued to learn that the Tanfields would inherit Mr. Hamerton's house, and talked of it at some length, speculating on what they would do with it. This took her mind away from my part in the tragedy and while she would undoubtedly hear, eventually, that I'd gone into the Hokewell Inn, I hoped that, by then, it would be old news, and would have less of an impact.

Sensibly my uncle said nothing, and they went for a short stroll in the garden before joining me for our midday meal. It was rather quiet without Lord Elvington and the Gauvans, for Gisele had gone shopping in Newport, accompanied by her groom, Roche, and the two gentlemen were still in Cowes assisting Mr. Arnold with the émigrés. Now that Mr. Fenton was well on his way to Paris, they were able to concentrate on their official reason for coming to the Island.

Robespierre's Reign of Terror had seen a huge rise in the number of executions in France, resulting in an enormous increase in émigrés fleeing for their lives. Mr. Arnold had spoken to me about the problems those émigrés created. Not just the numbers, but the difficulty of spotting the inevitable spies amongst the genuine refugees. This was where Jago and Louis were of the greatest assistance, being highly experienced in recognising such men. When my uncle began to speak of this over our meal I commented, 'Mr. Arnold told me the Alien Act had given him a great deal more work to do. It seems every émigré must be properly registered.'

'Well, I think that is a good thing,' my uncle said.

'Yes, but Mr. Arnold will be fined ten pounds for every émigré he misses.'

'He won't miss anyone,' Aunt Thirza pronounced. 'He's far too conscientious.' And she immediately changed the subject to the only topic she wanted to discuss. The coming of their first grandchild, and my uncle was very happy to talk about that too.

'I hope it's a girl,' he said.

'Oh, no, Charles,' Aunt Thirza chided. 'Giles needs an heir first.'

I'd never seen her happier, and wishing to avoid any chance of returning to the subject of Mr. Hamerton, I casually remarked, 'I wonder what names they will choose.' As I'd expected, she started to go through all the family names, for both boys and girls, and that kept her very happy throughout the rest of our light meal.

A little later we set off for Ledstone on horseback rather than in the carriage, that being easier and quicker. My aunt was eager to give the servants their orders for preparing the house for the returning travellers, and my uncle needed to speak to Leatherbarrow about sailing Giles's yacht to London. My excuse for joining them was that I wished to do something pleasant and normal after the shock of the morning. That was absolutely true, but I also wanted to tell my uncle why I had to see Mr. Pitt. This I hoped to do while my aunt was busy dealing with the indoor servants.

When we reached Ledstone, the servant who came out to attend to the horses informed us that Leatherbarrow was working on Giles's yacht in Yarmouth, and that made my task even easier. I elected to go with my uncle, of course, and we set off at once, while my aunt went into the house.

Giles had bought a magnificent new yacht soon after his marriage, something he could easily afford now he was Mr. Saxborough of Ledstone Place, and a very wealthy man. In the sixteenth century Queen Elizabeth bestowed Ledstone, which is now one of the largest estates on the Island, on William Saxborough in recognition of his daring exploits against Spain. The imposing house stood in the midst of pretty undulating country, a short ride from the coast and the fishing villages of Dittistone and Hokewell. Giles had unexpectedly inherited the estate a year ago, and the manner in which that came about still filled me with sadness.

Leatherbarrow, his groom, kept the yacht in tip-top condition, and when we reached Yarmouth we found him cleaning the cabin.

Leatherbarrow, a tall, wiry man with greying hair and a kindly disposition, had taught Giles to ride and was his most trusted servant. When we told him why Giles and Lucie wanted to come home by sea, he stood grinning from ear to ear, and said how happy he was to hear such good news.

'Well, the sooner they arrive home the better,' my uncle commented. 'When can you leave, Leatherbarrow?'

'On the early morning tide, sir.'

'You mean tomorrow?'

'Yes, sir. If the weather stays fair,' he replied, casting an anxious eye at some black clouds in the distance. 'The yacht is completely ready to sail.'

My uncle complimented him on his efficiency, and with that happily settled, we rode back to Ledstone rather leisurely, which gave me the perfect opportunity to tell my uncle I had to go to London. 'I must see Mr. Pitt as soon as possible. Would you be so kind as to escort me?' He didn't answer at once, but brought his horse to a halt by some trees that were gently swaying in the breeze, and as I drew up beside him, I said, 'I hate to ask you now that Lucie's coming home, but it truly is a matter of life and death.'

He gazed at me in a puzzled fashion. 'This is all rather sudden, Drusilla.'

I never liked to lie to my uncle, nor did it serve any useful purpose to try, for he always saw straight through me. Therefore I sensibly told him as much of the truth as I could. 'The reason Mr. Hamerton asked to see me was that, when he was in France he had learnt of an appalling French conspiracy. He wanted me to inform Mr. Pitt of it. Unfortunately he died before he could explain how he came to be shot, or how his sister had died. But, he'd told Jackson what happened when they were on their way home, and this morning Jackson repeated it all to me.'

'Ah, I wondered why you went to see him,' he remarked. 'How long did Hamerton stay in France?'

'Only an hour or two.'

His eyebrows rose in surprise and he went on thoughtfully. 'That's not long. How did he learn of this conspiracy in so short a time?'

I shook my head at him. 'It's better that you don't know.'

As a rule, he didn't like to be burdened with secrets, but in this instance curiosity clearly got the better of him. He gazed at me for a

26

moment or two, working it out. 'Someone must have told him,' he said. 'But he only saw-----' And his eyes widened in sudden realisation. 'Of course -- it must be his sister. If her husband is one of Robespierre's closest friends she's bound to know what that maniac is up to. That's why you want to see Mr. Pitt.'

'You ought to be in the Secret Service, Uncle,' I teased.

'Oh, no,' he retorted, shaking his head vigorously. 'Not me. Far too worrying. I'd hate to have to watch every word I say. However do you manage it, Drusilla?'

'I don't find it difficult,' I said cheerfully. 'I've always been good at keeping secrets.'

He smiled and said, 'So I've noticed. But couldn't this secret be conveyed in a letter?'

I shook my head. 'I cannot take the chance of someone else reading it.'

'I see,' he murmured slowly, as he gently patted his horse's neck. I saw from his face that he understood how serious this was and then another thought struck him. 'But what about your guests, Drusilla? You can hardly go off and leave them.'

'I can, if Aunt Thirza remains at Westfleet. After all, they are here to work. And, in any case, Louis is like a son to you, so they're not like normal guests.'

'That's true. We are very fond of Louis. His parents were great friends of ours when we all lived in London. Nevertheless that still leaves Jago and Gisele.'

'They're not a problem. Aunt Thirza really likes Jago, because he always behaves exactly as he ought, and Gisele makes herself useful fetching and carrying. Nothing seems to be too much trouble for her. Why, when my aunt discovered she'd left her parasol at the Tanfields last week, Gisele immediately sent Roche, her groom, to fetch it.'

'Yes, but it was Roche who did the actual work,' he pointed out with a grin.

'True. Nevertheless Gisele was kind enough to think of it.'

'She does seem to be a thoughtful young lady. Rather shy, though. I find conversing with her a little hard going.'

I had to agree with him, but I felt sure she would improve as she grew older. 'Still my aunt can call on her for assistance if needs be. Besides, Aunt Thirza won't want to leave the Island now Lucie is coming home. If you offer to escort Marguerite home, so that Giles needn't return to London, I can go with you on the pretext of replenishing my wardrobe.'

He laughed. 'You have thought it all out, haven't you.'

'As a woman, I have to.'

'Well, I can't leave until Tuesday. I must attend Mr. Hamerton's funeral on Monday.'

'Yes, I realise that.' He asked if I would be taking my maid with me and I shook my head. 'We'll only be there a few days and I'm sure Marguerite's maid will do whatever I need.' As he knew, my maid was marrying a local farmer in two months time, and I said, 'It's a good opportunity for Gray to see to her wedding arrangements while I'm away.'

He nodded and inquired, 'Have you found someone to take her place?'

'No, not yet. There's plenty of time.'

We headed back to Ledstone then, joining my aunt in the library, where my plan went without a hitch. In fact she greeted the idea with enthusiasm, grateful that Giles needn't go back for his mother, and pleased I intended to do some shopping. 'You could do with some new gowns, Drusilla. I wish I could go with you, but I want to be here when Lucie arrives home.'

'Yes, of course, Aunt,' I said, smiling in understanding.

With that settled, my uncle wrote a letter for Leatherbarrow to give to Giles and Lucie, explaining what we planned to do. At the same time I wrote to Marguerite, asking if we might stay with her during our few days in London, before escorting her home, and I mentioned that Gray would not be with me. Mudd took the letters to Leatherbarrow, and later I wrote to the George Inn at Portsmouth bespeaking rooms for Tuesday night.

Fortunately, the weather remained favourable for sailing and Leatherbarrow left on the early morning tide as planned. I prayed that the good weather would make Mr. Fenton's journey easier too. Even so, I thought it likely I would be back from my trip to London before he returned. He had to reach Paris, see Mr. Reevers, find out the situation, ride back to the coast, and then sail across the channel. Those circumstances were not conducive to speedy journeys; and involved a significant amount of danger.

There was, as usual, a great deal to see to before we left the Island, and I had to find a suitable time for Mudd to see his ageing father.

Mudd senior had been involved in smuggling in his younger days but now lived a quieter life in his cottage at Dittistone. In the end I decided to give Mudd the whole of Sunday off, as he would be driving us from Portsmouth to London on Wednesday, and would have much to do in London too. After church on Sunday I spent the rest of the day preparing for our journey, conscious I would have little time to do anything on Monday, for Aunt Thirza and I had promised to help Julia attend to those mourners who came back to Breighton House after the funeral.

As expected, that turned out to be a small gathering, yet there was sincere heartfelt regret at Mr. Hamerton's passing, even though none of us had known him more than a few months. Despite that short acquaintance, people still spoke of him as being "the salt of the earth" and "a dashed fine Englishman."

In a quiet moment I told Julia that I was going to London with my uncle the next day, and although she was rather taken aback at us leaving so soon after the funeral, she understood my desire to escort my godmother home, and save Giles the trouble of returning to London. As I pointed out, 'If we leave tomorrow and stay in Portsmouth overnight, we should reach London on Wednesday.'

She nodded in understanding. 'How long will you be in London?'

I hadn't given that a thought, for my mind was concentrating entirely on warning Mr. Pitt that the French planned to capture him. In answer I said, 'A few days ---- no more than a week, anyhow. Provided my godmother is ready to leave.'

That made Julia laugh. 'I'll be surprised if she is. You know what---'

Aunt Thirza, who had been talking to Richard, interrupted at that moment. Neither of us had seen her approaching and we were totally unprepared for her outburst. 'Richard says Mr. Hamerton has left all his servants thirty pounds each. He must have taken leave of his senses. What can any servant possibly want with such a large sum?'

Julia, as always, remained perfectly calm, and explained, 'Mr Hamerton stated in his Will that he wanted them to have money to fall back on while they looked for another situation. After all, they had only been with him a few weeks, and won't have expected to be searching for another position so soon.'

'Well, I consider it a shocking waste. The women will fritter it away and the men will waste it on drink.'

My aunt's views on servants never changed, and I raised an eyebrow at Julia, who immediately had to stifle a giggle. My aunt believed all servants were out to feather their own nests, and refused to accept that many genuinely had their own high standards. When I asked Julia if the servants knew of their good fortune yet, she said Richard had spoken to them this morning.

'You see, we've decided to let the house, and......'

'That's an excellent idea,' I said.

'Well, we thought it might be just right for Edward when he's grown up. All the servants have agreed to stay, except Mr. Hamerton's valet of course, who wishes to return to London.'

My aunt sniffed. 'Once they get their hands on the money you won't see them for dust.'

Ignoring her outburst, I asked Julia, 'What will happen to Mr. Hamerton's horses?'

'Richard means to sell them. And Bridge has agreed to come to us.'

'Oh, that's good,' I said, thankful that he had a new position to go to so quickly.

'Well, he's a first class groom, and we need someone reliable to teach Edward to ride, to be his personal groom, and to keep an eye on him as he gets older. As Mudd did for you, and Leatherbarrow for Giles.'

A statement that made my aunt frown. 'Are you sure that's a good idea, Julia? He seems a bit of a Jonah to me. He'd only been with Mr. Hamerton for a month, and his previous employer, Mr. George Jenkins, drowned a couple of months after taking Bridge on. Both gentlemen were young, and both died violent deaths.'

'That's hardly Bridge's fault,' I pointed out.

'No, but some people seem to bring bad luck,' she warned darkly. She was about to go on when she saw her friend, Mrs. Woodford, was no longer talking to the parson's wife, and excused herself by saying she must have a word with her.

Watching her go, I said to Julia, 'You don't believe some people bring bad luck, do you?'

'Of course not. People make their own luck. Besides, we both like Bridge.'

I was in total agreement with her, yet I found myself praying we were right. I couldn't bear the thought of anything going wrong in the Tanfield family. Even as that notion crept into my head, I reminded myself forcefully that such beliefs were nothing more than silly superstition. Bridge was far more likely to be a godsend to them.

Before we left, Julia told us that one of her sisters was coming to stay for a few weeks. 'Lizzie's had a nasty bout of influenza and Mama thought some sea air would do her good.'

I knew Lizzie was her favourite sister, but I had yet to meet her, and I asked, 'When are you expecting her to arrive?'

'Hopefully in two days time. She's nineteen now, and I am so looking forward to seeing her.'

Later that day I went for a good long ride over the Downs, accompanied by Mudd, this being my last chance to do so until we returned and, as always, it lifted my spirits. I couldn't help thinking of Mr. Fenton, as it was the third day since he'd left for Paris, and I felt sure that, by now, he would at least be on French soil. Perhaps in one of the safe houses, and I prayed he would get to Paris without any difficulty.

On the way back, riding through Ledstone woods, the meandering path was perfect for letting the horses slow down to a walk when, as now, they needed a rest. We were about half way along it when I saw something glittering in the dappled sunlight some way off the path. I almost didn't bother with it, as I was already going to be a trifle late in dressing for dinner, but some instinct made me say, 'What the devil is that, John?' I pointed in the direction I'd seen it, and said, 'Take a look, would you?'

He rode through the undergrowth, dismounted, threw some fallen branches aside and stood staring down at the ground. I instantly urged Orlando forward, and Mudd, hearing me coming, swung round and came hurrying towards me. His eyes were wide with shock. 'It's a body, my lady. I'm afraid it's Mr. Fenton.'

'Fenton?' I gasped. 'Are you sure?'

'Yes, my lady. He spoke to me when I looked after his horse the other night. It's not a pretty sight, my lady. He's been stabbed.'

CHAPTER FIVE

Mudd's search of Mr. Fenton's pockets produced nothing except Lord Elvington's letters to Captain Barr and Mr. Reevers. The large sum of money he'd carried to help our agents escape from Paris had gone. As had his watch. Nor did we find the knife that killed him. His body had been left about fifty yards from the bridleway, and Mudd said that, although a good covering of branches had mostly hidden him from view, the silver spur on one of his riding boots had been just visible. If I hadn't seen the sun glinting on that spur, he might have been there for weeks without being found.

I was absolutely devastated. Not only by the death of this brave and honourable young man, but by the fact that Mr. Reevers was still unaware that he and every other agent in Paris, stood in imminent danger of arrest. He was accustomed to dealing with dangerous situations, but if the French arrested all our agents at daybreak, he would not escape the guillotine. And I shuddered with fear.

For a moment I couldn't seem to think straight, and then I reminded myself that if anyone could find a way out of a tight corner, it was Mr. Reevers. I tried to put my fears out of my mind and concentrate on what I had to do about poor Mr. Fenton. I told Mudd to cover up the body and mark the nearest tree clearly, to make it easy for Lord Elvington to find, as I guessed he would send his messengers to remove the body.

The very nature of Jago's work meant he required messengers to take letters to London and France, to Mr. Arnold at Cowes, to Captain Barr, or any other place that was necessary. As I did not have room at Westfleet to house these messengers, they stayed at the "Five Bells," the inn by the village green, when awaiting orders. If Jago had an urgent message for Captain Barr, and no messenger was available, Mudd would take it. He enjoyed going on the schooner and talking to the men about life at sea.

I rode home still in shock at the murder, and fearing what could happen to Mr. Reevers. On entering the hall I saw from the clock that it was later than I had thought, and I was not surprised when Luffe informed me everyone had gone to change for dinner. I hurried up to my bedchamber, where Gray, my maid, was waiting.

'Oh there you are, my lady,' she exclaimed in relief, 'I was afraid you'd had an accident.'

I forced a smile and assured her, 'No, I simply rode further than I'd intended.' I could have sent a message to Jago, but I didn't want to create a furore over the situation, as nothing could be done to resolve it today. His schooner had not yet returned from France, and until it did, a second messenger could not be sent. I tried not to think of what a delay of four or five days might mean to Mr. Reevers and the other agents, for dwelling on it solved nothing, and did me no good at all. Yet, no matter how hard I tried, I could not get it out of my mind.

Over dinner the conversation revolved around Mr. Hamerton, his house, his Will, the hope that Leatherbarrow had already reached London, and of course, the forthcoming grandchild. When the gentlemen rejoined us after dinner, my aunt immediately set up a game of whist with Jago, Louis and Gisele. Unfortunately that made it difficult for me to speak to Jago without making a fuss, and I did not want to worry my aunt and uncle by telling them about Mr. Fenton. They were unaware he'd ever been at Westfleet, as they had gone to bed before he arrived and had not come down to breakfast until after he'd left.

Once Aunt Thirza had organised her own evening to her satisfaction, she announced that my uncle and I ought to check that everything was ready for our journey tomorrow. Thus dismissed we exchanged amused smiles and did as we were told.

When my aunt and uncle retired for the night at ten, as usual, I was finally able to convey the terrible news to Jago and the Gauvans. The gentlemen were greatly shaken, and Gisele was in tears. 'Poor Mr. Fenton. He was such a nice gentleman. Why would anyone want to kill him?'

'It must have been a chance attack,' Louis said. 'Smugglers, probably. I mean, it must be that,' he reiterated, as if trying to convince himself as well as us. 'After all, no-one outside this room knew where he was going, or why.'

'Not unless someone spoke of it,' Jago muttered, pursing his lips primly. And he demanded, 'Did you mention it to anyone, Drusilla?'

The righteous condemnation in his voice had me choking with rage, for clearly he thought that I, being a woman, must have been the one to speak of it. Taking a long deep breath, I looked him straight in the eye. In fact I had told Mudd, but that was several hours after Mr. Fenton had left Westfleet, and long after the poor man had died. Besides, no-one was more trustworthy than Mudd. 'No,' I said, 'I did not. Did you?'

'Me?' he retorted, aghast. 'Of course not. I'm accustomed to keeping secrets.'

'Would Mr. Pitt employ me if I couldn't do so too?' He didn't answer at once and I said, 'Or are you of the opinion that all women are incapable of........'

'I didn't mean.......' He ran a hand distractedly through his hair. 'Forgive me, ma'am. I just don't understand how this has happened.'

Still angry, I said, 'Well, it seems plain enough to me. Mr. Fenton was killed by someone who knew, or had been told, how and why he was going to Paris.'

Once we had all calmed down enough to talk it over sensibly, Jago and Louis agreed that, as only the money and a watch had been stolen, and not the letters, smugglers must have been responsible. For, as Louis said, 'How could it be otherwise, when no-one except ourselves knew he was on the Island?'

I understood why he'd said that, yet I was far from convinced he was right, although Jago pointed out to me, 'You know Drusilla, smugglers do commit murder on occasion. And Fenton was carrying a large sum of money.'

'Yes,' I said, 'but smugglers would never bother to drag a body fifty yards off the bridleway, or cover it up with such great care. Nor would they take his horse back to the inn at Yarmouth. Yet someone did, because Roche collected it from the Dog and Duck and took it back to Cowes that same morning. If you remember, Jago.'

'Of course, I remember.'

'If smugglers only wanted the money and the watch, why would they kill him? It doesn't make sense. I believe the murderer returned the horse to the inn to make it look as if Mr. Fenton had sailed to France, as planned. And no doubt he hoped the body wouldn't be found until it was too late to warn Mr. Reevers.'

They both stared at me in a blank way as if that thought had not crossed their minds, but Louis spoke first. 'I do see what you mean, Drusilla. So we'll look into it thoroughly while you are away.' That made me feel a little happier and I thanked him, silently praying they would get to the truth while I was in London.

34

Jago asked, 'You'd better tell me exactly where the body is, Drusilla.'

I gave him clear directions and added, 'Mudd carved a large arrow on a nearby tree. I'm sure you'll find it.'

'Right. I'll see to it first thing in the morning.'

I agreed that would be best and asked, 'What will you do about the letter to Mr. Reevers?'

'Well, my schooner should be back tomorrow or the next day, and I'll send another messenger straightaway. I will personally escort him to Yarmouth and wait until I've seen him leave for France.' But we all knew that, by then, it would almost certainly be too late. If it wasn't already.

Those thoughts preyed heavily on my mind when we left for London early the following morning. Yet, still I found myself hoping Mr. Reevers would be safe, even though the odds weighed so heavily against it.

Our journey began well with a comfortable sea crossing, and we put up at the George Inn in Portsmouth that night. But when I awoke the following morning I could hear rain lashing against the window, and if anything it was rather worse by the time we set off for the capital in a hired carriage. Mudd drove us, of course, but he knew how to protect himself in all conditions, and as it was summer at least it wasn't cold. In fact, the weather did not let up all day, and the continuous steady rain and extremely muddy roads made it a tedious and difficult journey.

We were about half way to London when my uncle fell asleep. The movement of the coach caused him to slump into the corner of the carriage and he soon began to snore. I watched in amusement as each snore caused his bottom lip to judder, and I couldn't help wondering if my aunt found that side of him amusing too. But, frankly, I doubted it. She was far more likely to wake him up. But what if her bottom lip juddered when she dozed off? That made me giggle, for she had her own standards in life and I was quite sure she would never allow herself to behave in such a manner. Not even when she was asleep.

I turned to look out of the carriage window, which was splattered with mud, as was every other carriage we passed. The streets in the towns we travelled through were fairly empty, suggesting that most people had sensibly stayed at home. In such weather it was hard to believe it was still summer.

As time went on I found myself thinking about Toby East, the English agent who went over to the French. He had been such a likeable, cheerful, pleasant man, and none of us had suspected he was working for France. Not until he slipped up in conversation, about two seemingly unimportant details. But they were facts that only a traitor could know.

The day Toby was recruited by the turncoat to assassinate the King, he had just learnt what had happened to the woman he'd loved. When he told me all about her, I saw how utterly devastated he was. He also said that the turncoat was a Frenchman supposedly working for us. But now Mr. Wickham had good reason to believe the turncoat was English. And that doubled the possibilities. Yet, whatever his nationality, it seemed likely he was still in Paris now. Consequently that's where Mr. Reevers had been sent to search for him. It was of the utmost importance that he identified this man. And that mattered more to the secret service than anything else at this moment.

When Mr. Pitt learned that such a highly trusted agent as Toby East had gone over to the French, he was greatly shocked. As a consequence, he had decreed that every agent who had been in Paris at the same time as Toby, was also to be kept under surveillance. No matter how high up they were in the secret service.

Toby's defection was so recent that every agent in Paris now had also been there at the same time as Toby. And that included Jago, Louis and Mr. Reevers. The turncoat had to be one of them. Of course, it could not be Mr. Reevers. We all knew that. But Mr. Pitt had given me the unenviable task of checking on Jago and Louis.

At the time I'd asked him if he seriously thought it could be Lord Elvington, but he responded with a firm, 'No, and I'm even more certain it isn't Louis. But after what happened with East, no-one who was in Paris at that time can be considered above suspicion. We cannot be too careful.'

He was quite right. Therefore it was vital for me to keep an open mind. Leaning back, I went through everything that had happened from the time Mr. Fenton arrived with Mr. Wickham's letter, until I saw him leave for Yarmouth the following morning.

Jago and Louis were the only agents who knew Mr. Fenton had spent that night at Westfleet. Could either of them have killed him? Jago hadn't left the house at all that morning, so it couldn't be him. But Louis had ridden off to Cowes to see Mr. Arnold half an hour before

Mr. Fenton left Westfleet. That did give him the opportunity. Louis was French-born, yet he was very English in manner and outlook.

While my uncle slept I began to think about the stable arrangements Louis had set up at the Dog and Duck Inn at Yarmouth. Most agents and messengers arriving on the Island did so at Cowes, where they were easily able to hire a horse. If they later sailed to France on Elvington's yacht, they could safely leave their hired horses at that particular Yarmouth inn. I did wonder if Roche had noticed anything out of the ordinary when he collected Mr. Fenton's hired horse from the Dog and Duck. Something he might not have considered worth mentioning to Louis or Jago, but had told the other grooms. If he had, Mudd would almost certainly know about it. Thus, when we stopped at an inn for some refreshments and to change horses, I asked Mudd if Roche had said anything.

'No, my lady. He doesn't speak to any of us unless he has to.'

'Doesn't he talk about the horses?' Most grooms liked to do that.

'No, my lady. He seems to prefer his own company.'

As I'd not spoken to Mudd about Mr. Fenton, since we found his body, I told him now that Lord Elvington and Mr. Gauvan were the only agents who were aware Mr. Fenton was at Westfleet that night. And only Mr. Gauvan was out at the time of the murder. 'He set off for Cowes half an hour before Mr. Fenton left for Yarmouth. But I find it hard to believe he's involved.'

Mudd nodded in agreement. 'He is a very pleasant gentleman, my lady. He always thanks me for anything I do for him.'

'Does he thank Roche too?'

'Yes, my lady.'

'Does Roche appreciate that?'

Mudd half smiled. 'It's hard to tell what Roche thinks about anything, my lady. Except that he is devoted to Mrs. Gauvan.'

Due to the bad weather and terrible state of the roads it was almost nine that evening when we reached South Audley Street in Mayfair, where my godmother was staying. This fine town house belonged to an old friend of Marguerite's, who was spending the summer at her country manor in Devon. The butler ushered us into what I soon saw was a highly fashionable and most attractive drawing room, where Marguerite was reading a book. The soft lighting from the large number of candles in the room, made her look at least ten years younger than her forty-five years. There wasn't a single streak of grey in her blonde hair, and her features still bore a remarkable resemblance to the beautiful portrait at Ledstone, painted when she was twenty. When she saw me, her whole face lit up. 'Drusilla – at last. It's wonderful to see you again. I have missed you so much.'

She held out her hands and as I grasped them I bent down to kiss her cheek. 'And I have missed you. Life on the island is never the same without you.'

Her eyes glowed with pleasure and then she turned to greet my uncle, offering to send for refreshments. But he refused, explaining, 'We dined at an inn at seven, ma'am.'

'That's probably just as well. You both look utterly exhausted. Would you like to be shown to your bedchambers now?'

'I would be most grateful,' my uncle said.

Marguerite informed us that Lucie and Giles had already left for home on their yacht, and said to me, 'Do you feel able to stay up for a little while, Drusilla? I've already told my maid to unpack for you, so you don't need to worry about that.' Adding with an enticing giggle. 'I have *so* much to tell you.'

I agreed, of course, and as soon as a servant came to show my uncle to his room we began catching up on all our news. The first thing Marguerite said was, 'I suppose you've heard. I'm going to become a grandmother.'

Her voice was so heavily laden with doom I had to hurriedly stifle the laughter rising in my throat. 'Yes. It's wonderful news, isn't it,' I said.

'I'm pleased for them, of course, but ---- oh, Drusilla, --- becoming a grandmother will make everyone think me dreadfully old.'

I bit my lip very firmly. 'No-one could ever think that,' I assured her. 'Why, there are times when I have been asked if you are Giles' sister. And several gentlemen have expressed a wish to get to know you *very* much better.'

She gave a gurgle of sheer delight, and her mood changed in an instant. 'Well, actually I have enjoyed one rather exciting adventure while I've been in London.'

'Only one?' I teased, for Marguerite's adventures were never ordinary.

'I went to a ball with Lucie and Giles, although I had no intention of dancing. Only then, you see, I was introduced to this rather distinguished gentleman, who informed me that I'd turned down his offer of marriage twenty-seven years ago. He said it had broken his heart and the very least I could do, to make amends, was to dance with him. Well, how could I refuse?'

I laughed. 'I hope he didn't tread on your toes.'

'Oh no. He is the most divine dancer.'

'Did you remember him?' I asked, intrigued.

'To be honest, I didn't. Well, I turned down so many offers,' she admitted artlessly. 'But naturally I pretended to remember him.'

'Naturally,' I echoed, suppressing a smile. 'How many times did you dance with him?'

'Four.'

'Four?' I echoed, pretending to be shocked.

'I know it was wrong of me, but he is very handsome and I did so enjoy it.' Her beautiful violet blue eyes gleamed with mischief. 'It was very hot that night and when we went out on the terrace for some air, I accidentally tripped over a step in the dark. But he caught me in his arms and carried me back inside, as if I was as light as a feather.' And she gave a long sigh of remembered enchantment.

I couldn't help but smile, nor could I resist asking the obvious question. 'Is he married?'

'He was, but his wife died last year.' She instantly saw what my next question was and held up her hands. 'No, I am not going to marry him. He......'

'But, he sounds wonderful,' I declared in mock protest.

'Yes, but he lives in a draughty castle in the north of Scotland.' She shuddered at the very thought of it, and I start to laugh, for Marguerite liked her creature comforts. Her sitting room at Ledstone Place was always warm. 'I will see him at the Sherburn House Ball on Saturday but-----' She stopped in mid-sentence and said, 'By the way, Mr. and Mrs. Rufforth have invited you and Mr. Frère too. It seems they know your uncle very well, and are eager to meet him again.'

'Oh, I'm sure he will be very pleased.'

'Yes, I am too. But I won't see Alistair again after the ball.'

That did not surprise me, for I knew she would never marry anyone, no matter how much she liked him, not if it involved moving away from Giles. He meant more to her than anyone in the whole world, and had done since the moment of his birth. She had married Cuthbert Saxborough, not just because he clearly adored her, for many a man had claimed that, but Cuthbert was very wealthy, and had provided her with everything she had ever wanted. Fortunately, his adoration had never waned, and in return she had played her part as a loving wife to perfection. When he died, she had been dreadfully upset, but she appeared to be enjoying life again now.

When she finally showed me to my bedchamber, I expressed genuine delight at the room she'd given me. It was quite large and I thought the pretty floral wallpaper, and the matching curtains round the four poster bed, were absolutely charming. All my clothes had been put away in excellent order and I asked Marguerite to thank her maid for me. Once I was alone I undressed and climbed straight into bed. When I visited other houses, not every bed was as comfortable as my own, but this one was, and I fell asleep almost at once.

First thing in the morning I sent Mudd to Downing Street with a note for Mr. Pitt. I mentioned where I was staying, and asked if he could spare me a few minutes of his time. The butler then showed me into the breakfast parlour, where I enjoyed a leisurely meal on my own, as no-one else was up yet. I was still there, indulging in a third cup of coffee, when Mudd returned with the news that Mr. Pitt could see me at half past eleven that morning. I had not said anything in my note to suggest there was any urgency, relying on the hope that Mr. Pitt would realise I would not ask to see him without a very good reason.

I would need my uncle to escort me, of course, and when he joined me a few minutes later, I showed him Mr. Pitt's message.

'So much secrecy, Drusilla. Doesn't it bother you?'

Glancing at the clock, I saw it was well after nine and I declared jokingly, 'It will do if we're late.'

'Am I permitted to have a morsel of breakfast?'

I laughed. 'Of course. Mudd will have the carriage ready and waiting at eleven. As for it worrying me, it doesn't unduly. I'm only doing a very small part of the work that government agents do, and not many women get such a chance. Frankly I find it exhilarating to be asked to do something, however small, to help beat the French and win this awful war.'

'So you won't be doing the kind of dangerous things that Mr. Reevers does?'

'No. He's far more involved than I could ever be.'

My uncle looked up from his ham and eggs. 'Drusilla, I don't mean to pry, but whatever has happened between you two? I thought you were going to marry him.'

I hesitated for a brief moment, then decided to tell him the truth. 'The thing is,' I began, 'two years ago he offered for an heiress. She wanted to marry him, and believed he cared for her, but her father was sharp enough to realise her fortune was the real attraction, and he sent Mr. Reevers packing.'

My uncle pointed out, 'Rumours often become exaggerated in the......'

'This one wasn't. He admitted it was true.'

'Admitted it? To you?' Not trusting myself to speak, I merely nodded. Cutting into a thick slice of ham, my uncle remarked, 'And you think that proves he's only after your money?'

I swallowed the lump rising in my throat. 'He --- he said he wouldn't have offered for Sophie if she'd been penniless.'

Shaking his head from side to side, my uncle said, 'No fortune hunter would ever admit such a thing.'

'He knew I wouldn't have believed him if he'd lied,' I said painfully.

'Hmmm.' He leant back in his chair and looked at me. 'You know, Drusilla, it's my belief he truly loves you.'

I lifted my shoulders. 'But what if you're wrong? I could not bear to marry him and then find out he was only after my fortune.'

My uncle reached across the table, covered my hand with his, and murmured softly, 'You must love him a very great deal, my dear.'

The fact that he could see how I truly felt about Mr. Reevers shocked me. I thought I'd managed to hide my feelings. If my uncle knew, what chance did I have of keeping it from Mr. Reevers?

'I can't risk making a mistake,' I whispered, my voice breaking up.

'Well, it's your decision, Drusilla. But deciding not to marry him may be an even bigger mistake.'

'If he's still alive.' My uncle's eyebrows shot up and I added, 'Paris is a very dangerous place.'

CHAPTER SIX

Mudd drove us to Downing Street in our comfortable hired carriage, and on our arrival an official took us through to the garden where Mr. Pitt was enjoying the sunshine. As we approached him he rose to his feet and bowed. He was a rather tall and fairly thin gentleman, and although I did not consider him to be handsome, every time we met I was always immediately struck by his powerful presence.

'It is a pleasure to see you again, Lady Drusilla,' he beamed. Once the customary greetings were over, a servant brought out a tray of drinks and set it on the small table beside Mr. Pitt. I accepted a little wine, as did my uncle, while our host chose his favourite port. It seemed to me this garden was the perfect place for him to relax, when he had a few minutes to spare. Sitting here, he could enjoy watching the bees and the butterflies going about their business, and listen to the birds singing.

My uncle spent a few minutes reminiscing about the years he'd lived in London, but aware Mr. Pitt was a very busy man, he soon pronounced, 'Sir, my niece tells me she wishes to speak to you alone, and as I prefer not to be burdened with secrets, may I be allowed to take a turn about your garden?'

His words brought a faint smile to Mr. Pitt's lips, as it probably made him recall the numerous secrets he had to keep. But his response was a polite, 'By all means, Mr. Frère.' A gardener was digging at the far end of the garden and my uncle wandered off in that direction, stopping to admire every rose bush he came across, the rose being his favourite flower.

Once he was out of earshot, Mr. Pitt invited me to tell him the reason for my visit. 'Have you discovered who the turncoat is?' he asked, with hope in his eyes.

'I'm afraid not, sir. I only wish we had. The reason I'm here concerns Mr. Hamerton.'

'Mr. Hamerton?' he repeated in surprise. 'The man whose patriotism was in question a few months ago?' I inclined my head and

42

he went on, 'It's only a short time since you assured me he was a truly loyal English gentleman. Salt of the earth, was the phrase I think you used.' I agreed that I had, and he asked, 'Are you saying you were wrong, ma'am?'

'No, sir. It's not that.' I took a deep breath. 'I wasn't wrong. But I'm afraid I have some very sad news. He died last week.'

'Died?' he echoed in a stunned voice. 'How did that come about?'

'Well sir, you may recall that his sister was married to one of Robespierre's closest confidantes.' He nodded slowly, and I went on, 'She smuggled a letter out to her brother, saying her husband had become as ruthless as Robespierre, and she was desperate to leave him and return to England.'

That swept the look of puzzlement off his face in an instant. 'And Mr. Hamerton went to fetch her?'

'Yes, sir.'

'I see,' he said, with a long sigh of understanding, and urged me to go on.

I drank a little wine and explained, 'Originally he planned to rescue her in August, when she made her annual visit to her husband's sister, who lives in Normandy. But she went early in July instead, and she must have managed to send a message to Mr. Hamerton informing him of her change of plan. He paid local fishermen to take him to France and---'

'Fishermen, Lady Drusilla?' he responded with a sceptical smile. 'Don't you mean smugglers?'

'That may be, sir,' I admitted. 'But who else would have agreed to take him?'

'No-one, I imagine,' he said in a resigned tone.

I went on to relate every detail Jackson had given me of the ill-fated venture that ended with him taking the badly wounded Mr. Hamerton ashore to a nearby inn. 'Mr. Hamerton sent his groom to fetch me and I only just got there in time, sir. He was very relieved to see me and he didn't waste a second.' And I repeated what he'd told me. '"Warn Mr. Pitt," he said. "The Frenchies mean to seize Pitt and take him to Paris. To the guillotine." Those were his exact words, sir. He tried to tell me how they planned to capture you, but I simply could not hear what he said, and a moment or two later I realised he'd stopped breathing.'

He nodded slowly, taking it all in. 'He was a brave man, Lady Drusilla.'

43

'Indeed he was, sir. The thing is, he was only on French soil for about an hour and met no-one except his sister. She must have told him of the plot. It's the only way he could have known. Whereas she can only have learnt of it through her husband. I'm convinced the reason she was so desperate to escape from France in July, was to warn you of Robespierre's unspeakable plot. That's why I truly believe it to be a serious threat, sir.'

He did not seem at all concerned, merely pouring himself another glass of port. 'I'm accustomed to threats, ma'am. The French blame me for everything that goes wrong in their country. When they run out of bread, or cows don't produce enough milk, or people commit treason and have to be guillotined, Robespierre insists it is entirely my fault.'

'Yes, I saw that in the newspapers. And that the people of Lyons guillotined your effigy, sir.'

'True,' he agreed in an indifferent manner. 'The fact is the French are always up to something. Earlier this year two would-be assassins were caught entering Holland on their way to England. They planned to kill the King as well as me. It's a risk anyone in my position has to accept.'

Horrified by his lack of concern, I pointed out rather forcibly, 'Sir, this won't be just another attempt on your life. If you were murdered in England, that would be mortifying enough. But if you were taken to Paris, put on trial and then paraded through streets of howling mobs to the guillotine for a highly public execution.......... well sir, think of the humiliation Britain would suffer. And the effect on our morale. It would be far worse than any assassination. Sir, I beg of you to take this seriously.'

Turning to me, he said, 'Lady Drusilla, I don't doubt what you say. But no Frenchman could possibly walk in on me unchallenged, no matter where I happen to be. And even if they did capture me, they still have to get me across the channel. The weather and the tides have to be right and........'

'Forgive me sir, but Mr. Hamerton knew how and where they meant to do this, and he would not have been so determined to tell me about their plan if he thought it would fail. He had excellent judgement and a great deal of common sense. I'm certain that he chose to tell me because he knew I would be able to speak to you personally. Then you would be ready for them, and could prevent it happening. He did not tell anyone else, despite his rapidly deteriorating health. Knowing him sir, as I did, I'm of the opinion he believed that, if this got out, the French would abandon the idea and think of another evil plot. And I'm sure you will agree that it is far better to know what they plan to do, rather than to be taken totally by surprise.'

He sat watching the haphazard flight of a small blue butterfly before commenting, 'You have given this considerable thought, haven't you, ma'am.'

'Well, the journey from the Island to London took two days, and there wasn't much else to do.'

He threw back his head and roared with laughter. Finishing off his glass of port, he poured himself another before saying, 'Very well, ma'am. I will do everything necessary to ensure this French plot does not succeed.' He spoke a little about the war, and then asked if the arrangement with Lord Elvington and Louis Gauvan using Westfleet Manor as a base for their activities had caused any difficulties.

'No, sir. That's no problem. Of course it helps that my aunt and uncle have known Louis almost all his life. His parents were their good friends when they all lived in London.'

'Yes, they were a delightful family,' he said in agreement.

I looked at him in surprise. 'You knew them, sir?'

'I was at Cambridge with their eldest son, Henry. Actually it was Henry who asked me if I could find Louis a position in one of the government offices. I'm told Louis is very well thought of, and he has been extremely helpful in raising the money needed for the Cinque Ports Fencibles. The companies of horse and foot, who will be part of our defences in the event of a French invasion. He did an excellent job and continues to take a great interest in them. In fact he and Gisele are joining me at Walmer Castle in a few weeks, when I'll be reviewing the Volunteers.'

I drank a little more wine and said, 'He'll enjoy that, sir. He also visits the Volunteers at Sandham Castle on the Island.'

'You approve of him then, Lady Drusilla?'

'I do. He treats my aunt and uncle with great kindness. I find him a most likeable and industrious young man, who is extremely thorough in fulfilling his duties.'

He smiled. 'I trust you find Lord Elvington just as industrious.'

I hesitated, and searching for something positive I could say about him I acknowledged that he was equally conscientious. 'He gets on well

45

with my aunt too, treating her with so much concern for her welfare and safety she does nothing but sing his praises.'

He laughed and asked, with a twinkle in his eyes, 'Does he treat you in that way too, ma'am?'

I sighed. 'Indeed he does, sir. He feels women should be protected from every kind of danger in life.'

'A chivalrous man.'

'He is, sir. But, one consequence of that is he strongly disapproves of my being involved in anything of a perilous nature.'

He gave an understanding chuckle. 'Something tells me that his disapproval won't stop you doing what you want.'

I laughed and agreed that it wouldn't. Changing the subject I asked, 'Have you heard about Mr. Fenton?'

'Yes and I've read Elvington's report. Murdered by smugglers, he says. But he doesn't say if he's sent another agent to Paris.'

'I'm afraid he had to wait for his yacht to return from France.'

His brow furrowed into a deep frown. 'All our agents could be dead by then.'

'Yes,' I agreed, tight-lipped, trying not to think of Mr. Reevers. 'I'm sure he will have sent someone by now, sir.'

'I pray that he has, Lady Drusilla.' And he said earnestly, 'We must catch this turncoat, ma'am. Any man capable of persuading Toby East to set up the Fat Badger Society on the Isle of Wight in order to assassinate the King and start a French-style revolution in England, is not likely to give up easily. If you hadn't stopped East, I dread to think what would have happened.'

'It wasn't just me, sir,' I pointed out truthfully. 'Mr. Reevers was very much involved, and I also owe a great deal to my groom, Mudd. And to Richard Tanfield, who saved my life, and that of my uncle.'

'Yes, I heard about that. But the King would be dead now if it hadn't been for you. The country owes you a huge debt, Lady Drusilla.'

'I happened to be in the right place at the right time, sir. Anyone else would have done the same.'

'Well, it's essential that this turncoat is put out of action before he tries a second time to start a revolution here.' And he added, 'I'm told he may be English, not French, as we thought.'

'So I understand, sir.'

He drank a little more port before saying, 'By the way, I am most grateful to you for allowing your home to be used as a base in the search for this traitor.'

'I'm happy to be able to help, sir.' I explained that none of our friends or acquaintances thought it odd that Jago and Louis were staying with us while on Alien Office business. 'In fact everyone was very pleased that Mr. Arnold now has some assistance in dealing with the émigrés.' This was their official reason for coming to the Island. 'My aunt and uncle also made it known that they were delighted to see Louis again, for he had been like a son to them when he was a child.'

We talked a little more about the situation before Mr. Pitt ended my visit by saying, 'Mr. Wickham would be obliged if you would call on him at the Alien Office later today, ma'am.'

I promised to do so and added with a smile, 'I look forward to meeting him.' Mr. Wickham had only recently become head of the Alien Office, but I had already been impressed by the letters he'd written to Lord Elvington.

On leaving Mr. Pitt I felt a great sense of relief at having finally passed on Mr. Hamerton's warning. I'd known about it for almost a week now and I hadn't realised quite how much it had preyed on my mind.

After an enjoyable mid-day nuncheon with Marguerite, my uncle accompanied me to the Alien Office in Whitehall. Mudd drove us there, of course, and we were ushered into Mr. Wickham's office straightaway. He had a most pleasing countenance, and spoke in such a friendly encouraging way that I took to him at once. There was another gentleman with him who caught my interest, for he had an American accent. Although I was acquainted with one or two people who'd visited America, I had never met a real live American before. And I was immediately struck by his extremely neat appearance. For, he was impeccably dressed, with not a hair out of place. In other ways he was quite unremarkable, being of medium height and build, with commonplace features, and dark brown eyes and hair.

Mr. Wickham introduced him to us, remarking that Tom Morel was a highly thought of colleague. I'd never heard of an American working for the Alien Office, and that made me even more curious. At that point, however, Mr. Wickham asked Mr. Morel to show my uncle round the offices, while he and I talked business. Once they had left the room, I sat on the opposite side of the desk to Mr. Wickham, and having arranged the folds of my gown neatly, I casually asked him if there were many foreigners employed here.

'A fair number. Those who speak both English and French fluently are like gold dust. Such people usually have one French parent and one English. They not only speak both languages, they also understand how the French think. That makes them ideal for flushing out spies when interviewing French émigrés. Younger sons in the aristocracy also make good spies, as they invariably speak excellent French from having travelled on the Continent. Usually they have no family connections with France, which makes them less of a risk.'

'Which category is Mr. Morel in?'

'He was born in France.'

'Oh, so he's not a true American,' I remarked, a little disappointed.

'No. He was ten when he sailed to America with his uncle.'

'Does he still speak French?'

'Fluently. Apparently he and his uncle always spoke French at home.' He picked up a letter opener and began toying with it, absently testing its edge for sharpness, as he informed me, 'Morel's job when he started working here was to interview French émigrés, and smoke out any spies. But he soon went on to become one of our secret agents in Paris and he has been most successful at that. Kindly keep this to yourself, Lady Drusilla, but it was Morel who warned me that the turncoat Mr. Reevers is searching for had betrayed all our agents to the French.'

'Really?' I responded in surprise, and recalling what was in the letter Mr. Fenton had brought to the Island, I asked, 'Is Mr. Morel the agent who is friendly with a member of the Committee of Public Safety in Paris?'

'Yes, and that contact had the list of names of our agents and where they were lodging. Details that were given to the Committee by the turncoat. Morel only caught a quick glimpse of the list, but when he saw his own name written at the top, he quite rightly decided it was time to leave Paris. Morel isn't the name he was born with, but like some of our other agents, he prefers to use a pseudonym for spying purposes. His contact, who was actually a close childhood friend, only knows him by his real name.'

'That was fortunate,' I said in relief.

'Indeed it was, ma'am. Or he would never have got out of France alive. Wisely he ensured they always met in a public place in Paris, and during their conversations he acquired some very useful information from this contact. Mind you, Morel was extremely distressed at not being able to warn our agents that they had all been betrayed to the French, but that was out of the question as he didn't know which one was the turncoat. Sensibly he decided to hurry back to London to inform us of the situation, so that we could deal with it. And that ma'am, brings me on to the sad demise of Mr. Fenton. Lord Elvington said in his report that he believed smugglers murdered Fenton for the money and the watch he carried. But I'd like your opinion, Lady Drusilla. You know the Isle of Wight far better than anyone here. So, please tell me ---do you agree with Elvington?'

I hesitated for a moment, thinking that if I mentioned my reservations about what had happened to Mr. Fenton's horse, he might easily dismiss that as being utterly trivial. As indeed it might yet prove to be. In the end I prevaricated. 'To be honest, Mr. Wickham, I don't know. We found the body late on Monday, and first thing Tuesday morning my uncle and I left for London. I had no time to look into things. On the face of it the murder does appear to be a chance encounter. The money and watch had gone, but the letters Lord Elvington wrote to the captain of the schooner and to Mr. Reevers, were still there.'

'I see,' he said, throwing the letter opener back onto the desk. 'Nevertheless, ma'am, the tone of your voice suggests you don't believe it was a chance encounter.'

I looked at him in some surprise, as I hadn't thought I'd given anything away in my voice, but I quickly realised that, in his job, he must be accustomed to listening to the manner in which people speak. 'No, I don't think it was. Yet I cannot offer you any sensible reason to support that feeling.'

'Just your own instinct?'

'Well----'

'Your hesitation ma'am, suggests there is something that bothers you.'

That's when I decided that if Mr. Wickham wanted my opinion, I should be totally honest with him. 'It concerns the horse Mr. Fenton hired in Cowes.' I explained Louis' system for returning horses hired by messengers, and that when Lord Elvington sent Mr. Fenton to France to warn Mr. Reevers of the betrayal, he was told to leave his horse at the Yarmouth inn. 'Well sir, the odd thing is, that although Mr. Fenton was clearly murdered on his way to Yarmouth, the horse was still left at the inn, as we would have expected. But we don't know who left it there.'

'Presumably it was the murderer. Or an accomplice.'

'Yes. Lord Elvington thinks smugglers were the murderers, but no smuggler would bother to return the horse to the inn. They'd just run off with the stolen goods.'

He looked at me thoughtfully. 'I see what you mean, ma'am.'

'Mr. Gauvan promised to look into it thoroughly while I was away, and he may have discovered the truth by now.'

'I certainly hope so,' he said, tidying the papers on his desk. 'We must get to the bottom of this business quickly. If the French do arrest all our agents, our secret service will be at a standstill in Paris. We will no longer know what is happening there. Nor can we send any more fine young men to that city until this turncoat has been caught. And it will be a while before we know who has been executed, for the lists are about two weeks old when we get them.'

The very thought that Mr. Reevers might already be dead, or that he might, at this very moment, be in prison awaiting his turn to climb the steps to the guillotine, set my bottom lip trembling so much, I had to bite it extremely firmly. Thankfully Mr Wickham did not appear to notice, and went on to say. 'Of course, if one of our Paris agents is not on that list, we will know who the turncoat is. But we will still have to capture him.'

CHAPTER SEVEN

Forcibly tearing my mind away from Mr. Reevers, I asked Mr. Wickham if he would show me how the Alien Office dealt with émigrés. 'Nothing would give me greater pleasure, ma'am, but unfortunately I have to attend a meeting in a few minutes.' He stood up and as he walked round to me, he said, 'I'll ask Morel to explain everything that goes on here, if that would be agreeable to you.'

'By all means,' I said, as I rose to my feet.

He opened the door of his office and waited for me to pass through, and as he shut the door behind us, he said, 'Morel had been here every day since he returned from France, desperate to hear if we have been able to save our Paris agents. Frankly I fear we have little chance of that.'

We went in search of Mr. Morel and found him showing my uncle where the records were kept. Mr. Wickham soon bid us farewell and as he hurried off to his meeting, Mr. Morel explained how the recent Alien Act had established the manner in which they were to deal with the émigrés. He opened an Aliens' entry book, in which the personal details of every émigré entering the country had been noted. Most were from France, of course. When he'd finished showing us around, I asked him how he had come to work for the Alien Office. 'Had you heard of it in America?'

'No, ma'am, I hadn't.' And he told me a little about his early life. 'I was the eldest of six children, and when my uncle decided to go to America, he offered to take me with him. My parents thought it a great opportunity for me and jumped at the chance. I was very excited and when we reached America my uncle got a job with a timber merchant, and was such a good worker that, within five years, he was running the place. Eventually he bought out the owner and was soon able to open more branches. Later he invested some of the profits in property, and became a very wealthy man. Sadly he died two years ago.'

My uncle and I said all that was appropriate and I asked, 'Was he married?'

'Yes, but they did not have any children. I worked for my uncle for many years. The hours were long and the work was hard, but my uncle promised to leave everything he possessed to me. I was very grateful, but I did not learn the full extent of his wealth until after he died. Only then did I realise that if I sold up everything, I would never need to work again and could live the rest of my life as a gentleman. That's when I decided to go back to France for the first time in twenty years. My parents couldn't read or write, and I didn't know if they were still alive. I wanted to bring them back to America but, unfortunately, they had both died.'

'I am sorry, Mr. Morel,' I said, and my uncle instantly added his condolences.

'You are most kind,' he said. I asked where they had lived in France and he said, 'In the south.'

My uncle inquired after his brothers and sisters, and was told, 'I had two brothers and three sisters, but they were dead too.'

I gasped. 'What --- all of them?'

'Yes, ma'am. Many people in their village died at that time.' I understood then. Epidemics were, unfortunately, all too common. And he went on, 'I stayed in France for a few weeks, but to my mind the revolutionaries were going too far. Then I met an Englishman travelling in France. This was in '92, before the war, of course. We got on really well and he invited me to spend some time at his home in London. I accepted, as I wanted to see London before I returned to America.'

'Do you like London?' I asked.

'Very much, and I soon made friends. One of them worked for the Alien Office, and well, one thing led to another, and I was offered a temporary position to help them cope with the émigrés. But, to me, that wasn't work. The fact is, I felt sorry for the émigrés, as I knew exactly what it was like to make a new life in another country, without being able to speak the language. It was too late to help my own family, but at least I could assist some of the countrymen of my birth. I only meant to do it for the summer, but as time went on I found I was really enjoying myself. Most émigrés were genuine, but a couple of times I came across someone who wasn't. I must say that rooting out spies was really exciting!'

Obviously he couldn't mention that he'd gone on to become a British secret agent. Nevertheless, my uncle was most appreciative that he had willingly helped England in their fight against the country of his birth. Mr. Morel protested jovially, 'Mr. Frère, may I remind you that I am an American citizen now.'

My uncle smiled. 'Well, I understand that. I'm French born too, but I've lived in England most of my life.' And he went on to explain how he'd been left a small estate in France in '88, but had lost it in the revolution.

I added, 'My uncle looked after his workers as he should, but it made no difference.'

'You must have regretted going back,' Mr. Morel said to my uncle.

'Well, yes, I do now. But it seemed the right thing to do at the time. It wasn't until we actually lived there that I saw how some members of the aristocracy treated their workers. There was nothing I could do about that. The attitude of those powerful men towards the people who worked for them filled me with such repugnance that, eventually, I decided to sell up and move back to England. But, by then, as I very soon found out, it was too late.'

'You lost everything, sir?'

'Not everything, no. I had all that mattered. My wife, my daughter, and my life.'

We thanked Mr. Morel for showing us round, and my uncle, observing that it had come on to rain heavily, said to me, 'You wait here. I'll find Mudd and have him bring the carriage up to the door.'

Once he'd gone, I told Mr. Morel there was something I wanted to ask him. First I reminded him the operation to find the turncoat was being run from my home, and I knew everything that was happening, and I said, 'Mr. Wickham told me in confidence that it was you who brought the news of the turncoat's betrayal of all our Paris agents.' His eyebrows shot up, but I carried on, 'He said you saw a list of our agents, with your name at the top.' He nodded slowly, and I said, 'Seeing your name on that list must have been a terrible shock for you.'

'It was, ma'am,' he agreed, with a shudder. He repeated what Mr. Wickham had said about Morel being a pseudonym and that, fortunately, his contact only knew him by his real name. 'What did you wish to ask me, ma'am?'

'Whether Mr Reevers was on that list?'

Again he showed surprise. 'Mr. Reevers, ma'am? You know him?'

'We both live on the Isle of Wight.'

'Oh, I see.' When I mentioned Giles lived there too, he exclaimed, 'Of course. I'd forgotten. That explains why they are great friends.'

'Yes, indeed.' I took a deep breath. 'Mr. Morel, you must know Mr. Reevers isn't the turncoat.'

He inclined his head in agreement. 'Yes, of course.'

'In that case, were you able to warn him of the betrayal?'

'Believe me I wish I could have done,' he said with a sigh. 'But I had been out of Paris for nearly three weeks, and only returned on the evening I'd arranged to meet my contact from the Committee of Public Safety. At the time I believed Radleigh was still in London. It wasn't until I arrived back here that I learnt he had returned to Paris. I am so sorry, Lady Drusilla.'

He could not hide the distress in his eyes and I thanked him for his concern, and asked, 'What did you do then?'

'Well, I wanted to warn the other agents, but that was impossible because I didn't know which one was the traitor. I reckoned I should inform Mr. Wickham of the turncoat's treachery, and let him decide what was the best thing to do. I left Paris within the hour.'

'At least you got out of France safely,' I murmured.

'True,' he said, smoothing out a slight wrinkle from a sleeve.

'Will you go back when things have calmed down?'

He shook his head. 'No. I'm thirty-two now and it's time for me to go home, find a wife and settle down. In fact, today is my last day at the Alien Office. I shall travel around this beautiful country for a few weeks, then leave for America before the winter sets in.'

'That sounds an excellent idea, Mr. Morel.' I could quite understand why he didn't want to return to France. After all, he'd done his duty and deserved to live the rest of his life in peace. I wished him luck, but before he escorted me outside, I asked him what the chances were of Mr. Reevers escaping from Paris. He hesitated, and I urged him to be truthful. 'In that case, ma'am, I'm afraid it's most unlikely he would have got away. I was told the arrests would all take place at daybreak on the same day, and that it would happen very soon.'

I swallowed hard, and managed to thank him for his honesty. Tears blinded me as he escorted me outside to where my carriage was waiting. Luckily they mingled with the heavy rain and my uncle did not notice. I did my best to hide my feelings and carry on as usual. It was the only thing I could do. But, stubborn to the last, I refused to give up hope entirely.

When we reached South Audley Street, my uncle excused himself from joining Marguerite on account of feeling rather tired, informing me that now he was an old man he needed an afternoon nap. I went into the drawing room, hoping to find my godmother alone, but she had a gentleman with her. Who, as I soon discovered, was her elderly admirer, Sir Alistair North. His daughter, who I judged to be about thirty-five, was with him. I assumed she had come to see if Marguerite would be acceptable to her as a step-mother.

Marguerite invited me to join them, which I did willingly; thankful to do anything that would take my mind off Mr. Reevers. Sir Alistair was a most charming man, all consideration and politeness, and obviously very taken with my godmother. He possessed a natural elegance, and was still handsome, although he had to be about sixty. He wasn't at all like Cuthbert Saxborough, whose only saving grace was that he'd adored Marguerite and always treated her as he should. Regrettably that did not apply to his servants, or to other women, including myself. For, he considered a woman's opinion to be utterly worthless.

Sir Alistair urged her to remain in London, tempting her with promises of all the things she liked most, such as parties, outings and visits to the theatre. She put a hand lightly on his arm. 'Alistair, I have been away for three months already, and I must go home. Drusilla and her uncle have come to London especially to escort me back.'

He took her hand in his. 'If you stay, I will escort you home – in good time for Christmas!'

She gave a tiny giggle, for she was thoroughly enjoying herself. 'You are most kind, but it cannot be. I will go to the Sherburn House Ball on Saturday night, and I shall leave London on Monday. Besides, you'll want to get back to Scotland for the grouse shooting.'

'I'll forego that for a few extra months with you,' he said, casting caution to the winds, and uncaring of his daughter's presence, or my own.

That brought the colour into Marguerite's cheeks, but she got to her feet and said, 'I will see you out myself, Alistair, but you must stop talking such nonsense. I could never leave my home on the Isle of Wight, and you would never leave your Scottish castle.'

They went out together, and his daughter, who had sat as silent as myself, rose to her feet and announced in disgust, 'There's no fool like an old fool, Lady Drusilla.' And with that, she swept out of the room.

I spent the night tossing and turning, praying that, somehow, Mr. Reevers had escaped arrest. I saw how unlikely that was, yet, foolishly, I still hoped. Knowing I had to keep busy until news came from Paris, I went shopping with my godmother the following morning, while my uncle visited old friends he'd made when he and my aunt had lived in London.

Marguerite adored shopping, and while I did enjoy buying hats and other accessories, my height made the purchasing of gowns much more difficult. I found the process of having my measurements taken and being told of the problems my height caused, decidedly boring, and had to force myself to be polite. Marguerite, however, liked to be in the fashion of the day, avidly reading every available magazine on that subject. She had unerring taste when it came to clothes, and I knew that if she said a style, material or colour, would suit me, she would be right.

But first I bought my aunt a present; an elegant and expensive pair of long gloves in her favourite dove grey. After that, with Marguerite's approval, I settled on several day dresses and two new evening gowns. They would all be dispatched to me when finished, brought by one of their best seamstresses, who would make any necessary alterations. I also purchased a pale green walking dress which actually fitted me, and which I liked very much. In fact I wore it that afternoon when we accompanied my uncle on a walk in Hyde Park. Many other people were taking the air too, for the sun had finally come out and swept away all the rain clouds.

Fears for Mr. Reevers were always in my mind, yet it was impossible to be sad when I was with my godmother, and her amusing observations concerning the attire of some of the other people parading in the park had me laughing out loud. They made my uncle chuckle too, and he had just started to make a comment of his own, when he stopped in mid-sentence and exclaimed, 'Good heavens. You'll never guess who is coming this way.'

CHAPTER EIGHT

I looked up, expecting to see one of my uncle's old friends. But the tall gentleman eagerly striding towards us was young and extremely well known to me. A gentleman I had feared I would never see again, and I was still fighting back the rush of joyful tears when he reached us. He bowed to Marguerite, shook my uncle's hand, and held out his hand to me. I took it, aware I was trembling. Neither of us spoke, and I feared my face had already given away my feelings, but I couldn't help it.

My uncle sized up the situation at a glance and turned to Marguerite. 'Ma'am, I don't know about you, but I could do with a rest, and there's an empty seat a little way ahead of us. Allow me to conduct you there before someone beats us to it.' He held out his arm for her to take, and as she did so, she raised her eyebrows at me a trifle, clearly horrified by the effect Mr. Reevers was having on me. She had never liked him, which I'd always put down partly to his height, some three or four inches over six foot, and to the fact that his bushy eyebrows, when drawn together, tended to give him a slightly intimidating appearance, especially to someone who had to look a long way up at him, as she did.

As they strolled off, Mr. Reevers suggested, 'Shall we walk a little?' I nodded, and he asked, 'Will you take my arm?' I did so, but to find he was alive, when I feared he might well be dead, combined with this sudden close physical contact, played such havoc with my senses that I found it impossible to speak. Which was as well, for if I had said what was in my heart at that moment, it would have led to our immediate betrothal. While I struggled desperately to keep a grip on my emotions, he said, 'When invited to walk with a gentleman it is customary to engage in polite conversation. Unless, of course, you have lost your voice.'

I couldn't help but laugh and it broke the spell, and I finally managed to say, rather inadequately, 'I was surprised to see you. I thought --- ' I took a deep breath as tears threatened to well up again with sheer joy that he was actually alive and safe. 'I thought you might be in a French prison.'

He stopped and stared at me. 'In prison? What made you think that?'

I looked up at him and somehow forced myself to speak sensibly, and at the same time I tried to ignore my overwhelming desire to be held in his arms. I explained how Mr. Wickham had learnt that the turncoat had betrayed all our Paris agents to the Committee of Public Safety, and that the French planned to arrest them all at daybreak on the same day. Gradually gaining a little more control of my feelings I went on, 'Mr. Fenton brought this terrible news to Westfleet the following day, arriving just before midnight, when I was playing Lottery Tickets with Jago, Gisele and Louis.'

'Lottery tickets?' he echoed in amused disbelief. '*You* were playing lottery tickets?'

'It was Gisele's choice, and I do try to please my guests.' And I carried on, 'Early the following morning we sent Mr. Fenton to warn you of the betrayal. But the poor man was murdered in Ledstone Woods.'

'Murdered?' he repeated in horror.

'Yes, he was stabbed. Mudd and I found his body a few days later.' As we began to walk on again I told him everything in detail, ending by saying, 'Jago thinks smugglers were responsible.'

'Really?' I heard the doubt in his voice, and he asked, 'Is that what you think?'

I shook my head. 'Smugglers would never bother to carry the body fifty yards off the path and cover it up. On the other hand, that is exactly what the turncoat would do to make us believe Mr. Fenton had reached Yarmouth safely and gone on to France.'

'I'm sure you're right, Drusilla.' And he sighed. 'Fenton was a good man. So, who knew where he was going?'

'Only Jago and the Gauvans. My aunt and uncle had already retired for the night and I had sent the servants to bed.'

Mr. Reevers was silent for a moment or two and then he asked, 'Do you think Jago or Louis could have killed him?'

'Jago couldn't have. He was in the house all morning, but half an hour before Mr. Fenton left for Yarmouth, Louis rode off to Cowes to see Mr. Arnold.'

He drew a long deep breath. 'So it could be Louis.'

'I pray that it isn't,' I said. 'Everybody likes Louis.'

'Everyone liked and trusted Toby East, yet he betrayed us all. That's why Mr. Pitt insisted that every agent who was in Paris when Toby went over to the French should be kept under surveillance. No matter how high their position. But while I was in Paris I did not see any of our agents acting suspiciously.'

'Well, there were concerns about security at the Alien Office. Perhaps someone there knew where Mr. Fenton was going. And why.'

'That's possible.' Mr. Reevers rubbed a hand around his chin and admitted, 'The truth is we have no idea who the turncoat is, or whether he is in Paris, or London, or on the Isle of Wight. Nor do we know if he is working alone, or has an accomplice. The fact is we desperately need him to make a mistake.'

'He hasn't yet.'

'True. But no-one is perfect, Drusilla.'

As I was feeling much calmer now, I asked him the one thing I really wanted to know. 'How did you manage to escape arrest?'

'I was lucky,' he said with a grin. 'Very lucky. On any other day.....' And he gave a wry grimace, only too aware how fortunate he had been. 'I happened to wake early that morning and my failure to identify the turncoat came straight into my mind. I had to find a solution and I decided to go for a walk, as that always helps me to think more clearly. It was just beginning to get light, and raining heavily, but I don't mind rain. After a while I turned into the street where one of our agents lodged, and I saw him being taken out and put into a carriage, obviously under arrest. Another agent lived close by, and when I walked on in that direction I saw him being driven away too. I didn't bother checking anyone else, and I knew there would be a carriage waiting near my lodging too.'

The picture that brought into my mind was terrifying, but it did not seem to affect him, and he went on to say, 'Fortunately, whenever I went out I always took my money, papers, and the passes needed to get out of the city gates, in case I ever had to leave in a hurry. I realised guards at the gates would be on the lookout for any agent not caught at his lodging, so I bought some old clothes, a moth-eaten hat, a spade, and an ancient horse and cart. Then I shovelled some ghastly rotting rubbish from the riverbank onto the cart and headed for a gate to the south.'

59

'To the south?' I queried and then smiled up at him as I realised why he'd gone in that direction. 'Of course -- escaping agents would be expected to head north.'

'Exactly.'

'And it worked?'

He grinned. 'The stink from the rubbish was so awful, they couldn't wait to get rid of me. Once I was well out of Paris I sold the horse and cart, bought a decent horse, and headed for the north coast, travelling at night.'

'Did you use the safe houses?'

He shook his head. 'I thought they might no longer be safe. Instead I made for a village near Calais, frequented by our smugglers, and paid them to bring me back to Kent.'

'I am thankful you're safely home,' I admitted.

'Yes, so I observed.'

I felt my cheeks flush. 'You took me by surprise.'

'I noticed that too,' he murmured in a caressing voice. He began to carry on in the same intimate manner, when something suddenly stopped him and caused him to mutter, admittedly under his breath, what sounded remarkably like an oath. I raised my eyebrows at him in mild amusement and he begged my forgiveness, before informing me, 'Your uncle and Mrs. Saxborough are heading this way.' I turned and saw they were about thirty yards away, and Mr. Reevers asked me, 'Tell me, when will you leave for London?'

'On Monday,' I said. 'We're escorting my godmother home.' And I explained, 'Giles and Lucie left for the island on their yacht a few days ago. Marguerite loathes sailing, but Lucie enjoys it, so they are returning by sea, as she wasn't feeling at all well.'

He asked in concern, 'Nothing serious I hope?'

'Not at all. Their first child is expected in January.'

His expression relaxed again. 'That is good news.'

'I think so, but Marguerite hates the thought of becoming a grandmother.'

'That doesn't surprise me,' he said with a grin.

'She says grandmothers are always perceived to be old, and she's not ready to become one yet. Fortunately a flirtation with a gentleman she refers to as her elderly admirer has made her feel young again.'

He gave an understanding chuckle. 'Is it serious?'

'He lives in a draughty castle in the north of Scotland.'

'The poor man. He doesn't stand a chance.'

'No, you're right. She would never leave Giles.'

Once Marguerite and my uncle joined us, Mr. Reevers soon went on his way, and it took me the rest of the day to completely regain my composure. I could not be sure of what he'd intended to say at the moment my uncle and Marguerite came into view, but I suspected he was going to ask me to marry him. And, in that moment, I was so overwhelmed with happiness to find he was alive I could easily have fallen into the trap I had been absolutely determined to avoid.

In truth I could think of nothing more wonderful than to become his wife, provided he truly loved me. But I still feared he was only interested in my fortune, and by the following morning I had made up my mind to distance myself from him again. For, if I didn't, I might end up making the biggest mistake of my life. And that was one risk I was not prepared to take.

After breakfast when I was busy ensuring all would be ready for our departure on Monday, he called at South Audley Street. It was a lovely sunny morning and was already becoming rather hot. He was surprised to find me alone, but as I explained, 'Well, my godmother is doing some last minute shopping, and my uncle has gone to see some old friends.'

'Good. That means you are free to come for a drive.' He indicated a fine looking open carriage waiting outside with a groom in the driving seat. 'Mr. Pitt wishes to see you again before you leave London.'

From the man running the country that wasn't a request but a command. 'Very well. I'll go and put a hat on.'

In fact I quickly changed into a cool looking apple green gown, put on a wide-brimmed white hat to keep out the sun, and was back with him in fifteen minutes. He laid aside the newspaper he had been reading and congratulated me on changing so quickly. 'I thought you might take an hour,' he teased.

I laughed and assured him I would never keep Mr. Pitt waiting that long. As we walked into the hall, realising Marguerite or my uncle might well return while I was out, I left a message with the butler that Mr. Reevers was taking me for a drive. In the short time it took to reach Downing Street Mr. Reevers talked of trivial matters, and on our arrival we were immediately taken out into the garden, where Mr Pitt was sensibly sitting in the shade. We had barely exchanged greetings when a servant arrived with some welcome refreshment, and I eagerly accepted a glass of lemonade to quench my thirst in this unusual heat.

Mr. Pitt thanked me for answering his summons so quickly and said, 'I've spoken to Mr. Wickham about the letter he wrote to Lord Elvington concerning the double agent's betrayal of our Paris agents. He said he wrote it when alone, and handed it personally to Fenton to deliver with all possible speed. Therefore no-one at the Alien Office can be involved in the murder, but I don't need to tell you how vital it is that we discover who killed Fenton. If it was smugglers, then it was a chance encounter. But if the turncoat was responsible, that is a very different kettle of fish. And if the French have arrested all our Paris agents, information from that city will dry up instantly, and we won't know what monstrous schemes Robespierre and his revolutionary government are planning. Nor can we send new agents there until the traitor has been caught. Now, you know what has happened on the Isle of Wight ma'am, and Mr. Reevers knows what has gone on in Paris. So it would make good sense for you both to work together on the Island to.....'

'Together?' I gasped.

He raised his brows in surprise. 'Yes. You are two of the most intelligent and capable people I know, and I believe that by working together you will catch the traitor.'

I had not expected this and, frankly, the thought of working closely with Mr. Reevers both thrilled and dismayed me. For how was I to distance myself from him now? But I soon realised I must set aside my personal wishes for the time being, and put the interests of the country first. His statement concerning the possible arrests made me ask, 'If Lord Elvington and Louis Gauvan no longer have agents in Paris to supervise, are they to remain at Westfleet?'

'Are you willing for them to stay, ma'am?'

'Of course, sir.'

'I'm much obliged to you, ma'am.' He sipped his own drink and put the glass down again. 'It will enable them to help the Customs officer at Cowes, who I'm told is in great need of assistance at present with interviewing the French émigrés.'

'That is true, sir.' And I took the opportunity to ask if he'd thought about the information I'd passed on from Mr. Hamerton.

'Have you told Mr. Reevers about this?' he asked.

'I haven't told anyone, except you, sir.'

'If you are to work together, I think you should do so, don't you?' he urged with a smile.

Mr. Reevers listened to my account of what had happened to Mr. Hamerton and expressed genuine sadness for the man he too had grown to like. I repeated the exact words Mr. Hamerton had used concerning the French conspiracy, and asked if he'd heard anything in Paris about this threat to Mr. Pitt.

He shook his head. 'No, not a whisper.' Turning to Mr. Pitt, he said, 'But it doesn't surprise me, sir. Robespierre will have offered someone a fortune to bring you back to Paris. If they succeed, you will be put on trial in public and you will be forced to endure an even more public execution. Robespierre probably believes that will make us sue for peace and it will also ensure no-one will topple him from power.'

Mr. Pitt had his own views on that. 'Well, he's wrong. My successor would carry on where I left off.'

'Nevertheless sir, we can't let such a terrible thing happen.'

Mr. Pitt smiled rather grimly. 'I can't say as I'm too keen on the idea myself.' And he promised to take sensible precautions.

His parting words, however, were concerned with the task he had given us, and they became engraved in my mind. 'No-one outside this room will know of our arrangement. But it is absolutely vital that you find this turncoat quickly.'

CHAPTER NINE

When we left Downing Street, the presence of the groom in the carriage made it impossible to talk about what Mr. Pitt wanted us to do. I'd hoped to discuss it when we reached South Audley Street, but Marguerite and my uncle were in the drawing room.

Marguerite eyed Mr. Reevers warily, as was her habit, but once we were seated, he did his best to please her by saying he was returning to the Island himself on Monday, and offered to be an extra escort, if that would be of use to her. Her attitude towards him instantly changed. She clapped her hands together and said, 'I would be most grateful, Mr. Reevers. One hears so many tales of highwaymen.' Instinctively she touched the necklace she was wearing. 'I couldn't bear to lose this. Cuthbert gave it to me on our wedding day.'

'Don't worry, ma'am,' he said. 'No highwayman will trouble you when they see you have two armed escorts.'

Marguerite was so pleased to have this worry removed that she rewarded him with a little polite conversation, asking him, 'Will you be making a long stay at Norton House this time?'

'I can't say, ma'am. My plans are a trifle uncertain at present.'

'Well, I trust you will be on the Island long enough to dine with us one evening.'

He inclined his head. 'I would be delighted, ma'am.'

'I expect you are looking forward to being at home again.'

'I am, ma'am,' he assured her. Norton House, some five or six miles from Westfleet, had been given to him by Giles Saxborough, his cousin. A generous gesture made after Mr. Reevers had been forced to sell his ancestral home to pay his deceased father's debts. Not that Giles considered it generous for, as he rightly pointed out, Mr. Reevers was his heir at present.

I believed the only income Mr. Reevers had now came from his work as a secret agent. That was why I still feared the only reason he wished to marry me was because I was wealthy. For, if we married, everything I possessed, my fortune, Westfleet manor and my estates, would become his. That was the law. If he truly loved me, then it would

64

not matter. But I could not bear the thought of marrying him only to find that all he cared about was my fortune. He could spend it entirely as he wished, for I would have nothing of my own and would be totally reliant on him for every single thing I needed.

From the age of twelve I had run the house and helped my father look after the estates. Westfleet Manor wasn't his main residence, but it was the only one he truly loved. Since his death, some eighteen months ago, I had looked after everything by myself, and enjoyed doing so. Frankly, I did not want to give that up.

My father, Robert Davanish, Earl of Angmere, had never liked the miles of flat marshes that surrounded his ancestral home on the mainland. As a young man he'd fallen in love with the Isle of Wight, seen this beautiful old manor house nestling at the foot of the Downs, and within sight of the sea. He bought it right away and lived there happily for the rest of his life.

He inherited his title several years after my mother died, and having reached an age where he was certain he would never marry again, he persuaded his heir, a cousin with five sons, to take up residence in the ancestral home and run the estates, as if it was his own. Which, of course, it was now.

Meanwhile, father had spent many years working on his 'History of the Isle of Wight.' The book included the historical details of the most famous Island families, involving far more research than I could ever have imagined. I'd helped him by writing the known facts on large sheets of paper, which we fixed to the wall in father's workroom. A method that had helped me solve the Saxborough murders and later, to find who was running the traitorous Fat Badger Society. And now I hoped it would help me to find the turncoat who had given Toby East that particular task.

It was enormously helpful to be able to see the facts at a glance, for it was all too easy to forget minor incidents if they weren't written down. I had already learnt that a seemingly trivial detail could help me to identify a killer, but so far that had not happened with Mr. Fenton's death. In truth, I wished with all my heart that smugglers had been responsible, but every instinct I possessed told me it wasn't so. If I was right, the traitor had to be one of the very few people who had known Mr. Fenton was on the Island. Facing up to that fact wasn't easy.

Well, whoever he was he had to be stopped, no matter how much of a gentleman he was, or how much I liked him. For, he had recruited

Toby East, and now that his attempt to start a revolution in England had failed, I was convinced he was the person who planned to seize Mr. Pitt, to help France win the war. The very thought of Mr. Pitt being taken to Paris, where he would be forced to climb the steps to the guillotine in front of a screaming, howling mob of sans-culottes, filled me with such anger that I would happily have shot the turncoat on sight.

That evening my uncle and I accompanied Marguerite to the ball at Sherburn House, where my uncle was greeted with great pleasure by our hosts, Mr. and Mrs. James Rufforth, who were old friends of his. In truth I was thankful for a little light relief, as I have always enjoyed dancing. When we arrived the ball had already begun and I was surprised to see Mr. Reevers there. The lady he was dancing with was very beautiful, and when I asked Marguerite who she was, she said casually, 'Oh, that's Eleanor Pound. A wealthy widow, but he won't get anywhere with her.' She put her hand on my arm and said in sympathetic understanding, 'You know Drusilla, I did warn you what kind of man he was.'

One of Marguerite's acquaintances came up to her then and saved me from having to answer her. I could not help but observe that Mr. Reevers and his partner danced the minuet extremely well, and continued with a country dance afterwards. I was never short of partners, but when the musicians left the room for a short break, Marguerite moved a few seats away to talk to a friend. My uncle was already chatting to a couple he'd known in London, and Mr. Reevers, observing I was alone, walked over to me. He asked my permission to join me, which I gave and I immediately commented that I hadn't known he would be here tonight.

'Ah well, you see I was at school with our hosts' eldest son, and I happened to bump into him this morning, and he kindly invited me.'

'That was good of him.' And I commented casually, 'You seem to be getting on rather well with Mrs. Pound.'

His lips twitched slightly. 'She's an excellent dancer.'

'She's very beautiful too.' Despite the constriction in my throat, I went on, 'And rather wealthy, I believe.'

He looked at me, deep understanding in his eyes. 'Do you expect me to cultivate her company?'

'How should I know what you want to do?' I muttered huffily.

'You know very well what I want, Drusilla.'

66

One of his friends interrupted us briefly at that moment, and once we were alone again, I told Mr. Reevers, 'I wish Mr. Pitt had not insisted on us working together.'

'You are not the only who is suffering.'

'You would rather be back in France, I suppose.'

'No. I could not wish to be away from you. Only that we were together under happier circumstances.'

'I'm sure you do. But, may I remind you that if Sophie's father had not realised what you were about, you would be married to her now.'

'No doubt. I am most grateful to him, believe me. It must be the worst kind of hell to be married to someone you like and admire and would not want to hurt, but to love someone else. As I do.' I didn't trust myself to speak, for fear of letting him see how much he truly meant to me. But, at that moment, the musicians began to return, and he asked politely, 'May I have the honour of the next dance?'

I accepted, equally politely, and casually asked, 'Do you enjoy dancing?'

'It depends on who I am dancing with,' he said as the musicians began to tune their instruments again. 'Actually I am rather fond of the music.'

I looked at him in surprise, as I hadn't expected that, and I said, 'So am I.'

'I'm glad we agree on something,' he murmured, as we made up our set for the cotillion. The steps soon took us away from each other, and the dance gave us little chance to say more than a brief word or two when it brought us together again. When it came to an end, he thanked me, bowed and walked away. As he did so, Marguerite introduced me to another man of her acquaintance, who immediately asked me to dance. I did not speak to Mr. Reevers again that evening, but I did my best to enjoy the ball.

At one point when Marguerite and I were taking a rest from dancing, she told me that, half an hour earlier, she had felt so hot that Sir Alistair had escorted her to a cool ante room. 'Once I was seated, he got down on one knee and begged me to marry him,' she declared, revelling in her triumph. 'I could have prevaricated, but I thought I ought to refuse him at once. You see, I could hear his knee creaking, and I thought if I kept him in doubt for more than a minute, he might not be able to get up again.'

I could not help but laugh. Discreetly, of course, behind the beautiful fan I had bought in Paris before the war, when travelling with my father.

We left London early on Monday as planned. It was another blisteringly hot day, which made for a rather uncomfortable and tedious journey. On the way to London the weather had been atrocious, with steady rain all the way. But since then, several days of hot sun had turned the muddy roads into dust, and I couldn't decide which was worst, the rain or the dust. When we stopped to change horses, most people were complaining about the heat, mopping their brows, and ordering drinks. Nevertheless we arrived in Portsmouth in time for a late dinner at the George Inn, and the heat had made us all so tired that, after dinner, it seemed eminently sensible to simply retire for the night.

In the morning we were greeted by more glorious blue skies, hot sunshine, and such calm seas that Marguerite was easily persuaded this was the perfect time to cross the Solent. I did not tell her that both Mudd and Mr. Reevers had predicted it might not stay calm for long.

Unfortunately they were right, for in the final hour of the crossing it became rather choppy, and I felt a trifle guilty when Marguerite succumbed to seasickness. But she put a brave face on it, for she was eager to get back home again. Her desire to be reunited with Giles always overcame any other difficulty.

Once we reached Cowes I was itching to get back to Westfleet, but Marguerite was too exhausted to go any further, so we spent the night at the "Rose and Crown." As Mr. Reevers did not need to stay, he soon left for Norton House, promising to call at Ledstone Place on the way, to ask Giles to collect Marguerite in the morning. I sent Mudd home with instructions to inform my aunt that we hoped to be back before nuncheon tomorrow, and for him to return to the inn with our own horses by nine in the morning.

While Marguerite rested on her bed before dinner, my uncle and I went for a walk by the sea, where the waves were now crashing majestically onto the shore. 'It's good to be back on the Island,' I said contentedly.

'It's certainly much quieter than London.'

Knowing he'd enjoyed the many years he spent in London, I asked, 'Do you miss living there?'

'Not really. The older I get, the less I miss the bustle of the place, and the more I enjoy being here on this beautiful island.'

We strolled along happily, my arm tucked through his, talking about his forthcoming grandchild and the joy of seeing Lucie tomorrow. I thanked him for being so kind as to escort me to London, and as we began to head back to the inn I saw Mr. Arnold coming towards us. William Arnold, the Cowes customs officer and Island postmaster, was an old friend, and a much respected public servant.

He didn't notice us at first, as he was striding along, looking rather harassed. It was his job to prevent local smugglers bringing illegal goods ashore, which wasn't easy on an Island with so many landing places, for it was impossible to keep watch on them all. And since the revolution in France, he'd also had to deal with émigrés landing on the island. Which, as he said, when he eventually saw us, was the cause of his furrowed brow.

'Ever since that devil, Robespierre, called for Terror to be the Order of the Day, we've had a huge increase in Frenchies to deal with. It's true that they are our enemies now, but I can't help feeling sorry for them. Especially the women and children. Most have been forced to leave their worldly goods behind and are thankful to have escaped with their lives. Not many speak English, of course, and regrettably not all are what they appear to be. Frankly, I don't know how I would have managed without Mr. Gauvan's assistance. He's been a tower of strength. I see to it that they are registered and he interviews them to check if they are genuine émigrés. And, this morning, he caught two spies.'

'Did he, indeed? That is wonderful. Where are they now?'

'Locked up, I'm thankful to say. Protesting their innocence, of course, but Mr. Gauvan heard them gabbing away in French and knew what they were up to. They thought he wouldn't understand because they spoke so fast.'

'That must have been a good moment,' my uncle said.

'It was, Mr. Frère, I don't mind admitting.'

We soon went on our way, and my uncle said how pleased he was that Louis was making himself useful. 'Your aunt and I have always been very fond of him. It's a pity about his accident, but at least he won't need to risk his life again in Paris.' As I knew, Louis had been a secret agent for two or three years until he fell off his horse and damaged his knee so badly he could no longer run. A handicap for a spy. 'Although I gather he first met Lord Elvington in Paris.'

'Yes, but Jago won't be returning to France either.'

'So Louis told me. Do you know why, Drusilla?'

'It's because he is heir to his father's title now.'

'Jago is? I hadn't realised. He's never spoken of it to me. I thought he had two older brothers.'

'He did. But the eldest died two years ago of some disease that baffled all the doctors. The second was killed at sea in Lord Howe's great defeat of the French on the first of June. That's when Jago's father begged him to give up spying abroad. And to get himself a wife."

'Ah, I see. That's perfectly understandable in those circumstances. Does Jago have a wife in mind?'

'Not that I know of, but he rarely talks about his private life. The only thing he told me was that he'd never yet met anyone with whom he wanted to spend the rest of his life.'

'A pity. He seems a decent fellow.'

That evening I walked down to the stables, at the back of the inn, where the head groom greeted me politely. I mentioned that Mudd would be bringing our horses tomorrow morning, and he assured me he could easily accommodate them until we were ready to leave. Looking around at the horses in the stables, I casually asked him which one Mr. Fenton had hired.

'That was Tarquin, my lady. He's just along here.' I followed him, made a fuss of Tarquin and said that he looked to be a good-tempered animal. 'He is, my lady. He's ideal for hiring out.'

'I trust he was returned to you in good time,' I said pleasantly, as if making conversation.

'Oh yes, my lady. Mr. Gauvan's groom, Roche, is always most prompt about bringing the horses back. Tarquin was here by noon the day after Mr. Fenton hired him. He's the horse we usually hire out to Mr. Gauvan's messengers, as he's fast, reliable and good-natured.'

'Well, I'm glad the system is working well,' I said, as he saw me out of the stables. To him everything appeared to be perfectly normal. Tarquin had been left at the Yarmouth stables, as was expected, and Roche had returned him to Cowes. Therefore, if I hadn't found Mr. Fenton's body, we would have believed he had sailed to France as arranged. Whereas a missing horse would have had us setting up a search for Mr. Fenton. Would smugglers have gone to such lengths? I was absolutely certain they would not. And I was equally certain it was the murderer who had returned Tarquin to the Dog and Duck at Yarmouth.

Giles arrived at the inn shortly after eight the following morning and I went outside to greet him. I was delighted to see him, for we had always been the greatest of friends, and as children we had occasionally sneaked out at night to watch the local smugglers at work. He had inherited his mother's angelic looks and blond hair, but that's where the resemblance between them ended. He had clear blue eyes, but was so slight in stature that he looked as if a strong gust of wind would bowl him over. Yet, he was the most determined person I knew, who invariably found ways to do what he wanted, albeit in a subtle and unselfish manner.

I said at once that I was delighted to hear that he would soon become a father. 'It's wonderful news. You must be very pleased.'

'I am,' he said, thanking me with a grin. And he asked, 'Do tell me how you persuaded my mother to cross the Solent so quickly? What did you do? Twist her arm?'

Laughing, I assured him it had been easy to convince her. 'But I'm afraid she was a little seasick as we neared Cowes.'

'Yes, so Radleigh told me. But being back at Ledstone again will make her very happy. It was most kind of you and Mr. Frère to go to so much trouble to escort her home.'

'Not at all. I desperately needed some new clothes and that gave me the perfect excuse.'

'Was that the only reason?'

'Of course,' I said.

He looked me straight in the eye and laughed. 'You know Drusilla, I really will have to teach you how to lie convincingly. You've never been any good at it.'

'I know,' I admitted sorrowfully. And I went on, 'Do you miss being in the secret service?'

He shook his head. 'I'm far too busy looking after my estate. As you know Drusilla, my father did very little for our tenants, and would never listen to the suggestions I made for renovating their homes. But it is being done now.'

71

Before I could answer, Marguerite came out of the inn and threw her arms around her son's neck, as if they had been parted for months, rather than a few days. I left them together and went inside to see if my uncle was up yet. I found him having his breakfast, and it wasn't long before Mudd arrived with our horses.

We watched Marguerite and Giles set off for Ledstone, and with no more ado we also left for home. Cloud began to engulf the island as we headed south, but I didn't mind. To me Westfleet Manor looked magnificent whatever the weather, and I gave a sigh of joy when the house came into view. The original building had stood in that same peaceful setting for a little over two hundred years and the additions my father had made to the house had added to its beauty and tranquillity. The gardens were as immaculate as ever and as we rode up to the house Luffe came out to greet us. My uncle and I dismounted and handed our horses over to Mudd, who took the sweating animals off to the stables to be looked after.

As we entered the hall, Luffe reassured us that all was well and at the same time, my aunt came out of the drawing room, her face wreathed in smiles at the sight of my uncle. Leaving them to enjoy their reunion alone, I went into the library, where Lord Elvington was most likely to be. He looked up from the papers he was studying and, after greeting me, asked if I had enjoyed my visit to London. I responded by telling him about the Ball we had gone to, and who we had met there. Only then did I ask, 'Have you found out who murdered Mr Fenton?'

CHAPTER TEN

J ago gave a slight shrug. 'I'm absolutely convinced it was smugglers.'

'What proof do you have?' I asked, as I sat down.

He threw his hands up in the air in a gesture of helplessness. 'None whatsoever. But smugglers are very good at hiding what they do. In any case, Drusilla, who else could it have been? Apart from you, me and Louis, no-one knew Fenton was here. It must have been a chance encounter.'

'Did you find out who took Mr. Fenton's horse back to the inn at Yarmouth?'

'I'm afraid not. Louis made inquiries at the Dog and Duck, but none of the grooms saw it being brought in.' I groaned inwardly, for I had so hoped someone had witnessed the horse coming back in. 'I can see you are disappointed Drusilla but, as you know, messengers who sail to France on an early tide often leave their horses at the stables before anyone is about. But the grooms did see Roche collect the horse and head off for Cowes.'

'Well, that is something I suppose.' And I asked, 'Did you send another messenger to Paris?'

'Yes, on the day after you left for London. But, as I found out this morning, when Mr. Reevers called on me, it was a wasted journey.' And he added in considerable anguish, 'From what Mr. Reevers said about the arrests he saw taking place, we've almost certainly lost all our Paris agents. Those poor young men guillotined. If I ever get my hands on that turncoat I'll------' he stopped suddenly and looked up at me. 'Forgive me, Drusilla. I should not say such things to you.'

'Why not? I feel the same as you do. I want him arrested, but if that isn't possible I would willingly shoot him myself.'

He stared at me, so shocked he could hardly speak. 'In cold blood?' he whispered.

'Isn't that what you would do, if you had to?'

'Well, yes. But, really Drusilla,' he protested, distress clearly etched on his face. 'To think that you – a woman - should say such a thing.'

Despite the seriousness of our conversation I was rather amused by his belief that women were totally incapable of facing dangerous or difficult situations. 'Women are much stronger than you think.'

His lips twisted into a self-derisive smile. 'So it would appear.'

Indicating the mass of papers on the desk, I remarked casually, 'You seem to be very busy.'

'Well, until we learn which of our Paris agents were guillotined, there's nothing we can do except catch up on paperwork.' British newspapers printed lists of those executed, often with their ages and occupations. 'We'll know who the turncoat is when we see who is missing from the list. The traitor's name won't be there, and then we can go after him.' I did not expect it to be that simple, but I said nothing, and he went on, 'So for the moment our orders are to concentrate on assisting Mr. Arnold with the émigrés arriving on the Island, which we've had very little time for until now. Louis is in Yarmouth at present interviewing yesterday's arrivals, and Mr. Arnold sent a messenger earlier to say another French boat had arrived in Cowes first thing this morning. I'm going along to help shortly.'

'I'd better leave you to finish whatever you are doing then,' I said, and as I got to my feet, I asked, 'Has Gisele gone with Louis?'

'No. She's out riding. Roche is with her, of course.'

I left him and went down to the stables to see the horses. I always missed them when I was away, and I spent some time making a fuss of them. Although I had only been away about a week, it seemed very much longer to me. I was watching Mudd training a horse in the paddock when I saw Jago ride off to Cowes.

A few minutes later Gisele came back from her outing. She looked the picture of health, which did not surprise me for she loved riding as much as I did. Once she'd handed over her horse to Roche, she came to join me. She inquired politely if I'd enjoyed my trip to London and I repeated much of what I'd told Jago. Remembering she and Louis normally lived in London, I asked if she missed her home. 'Not in the least,' she said. 'I love the countryside best of all. Your house is so beautiful. It reminds me of my life when I was a child.'

'You grew up in Kent, didn't you?' I said, recalling something Louis had mentioned.

Her face lit up at once. 'That's right. It was wonderful there. My grandparents had a magnificent mansion, where I could ride for miles in the grounds.'

74

'You lived with your grandparents?' I declared in surprise, not having been aware of that.

She nodded. 'They were my mother's parents. My mother was widowed when I was three, and after that we spent all our summers with them. When I was fourteen my mother died, and then I lived with them permanently.'

'Are your grandparents still alive?' She shook her head and seeing her eyes fill with tears, I said, 'I am sorry, Gisele. I didn't mean to upset you. Do you still visit the house?'

'Not any more,' she mumbled, and excused herself saying, 'I must go and change. I've been invited to nuncheon at the parsonage.'

Watching her walk off, I thought how young and vulnerable she looked; much younger than her twenty-three years. She and Louis had been married almost a year and seemed happy, which I hoped would help her forget the sorrows of losing her family. I was sure children would bring her great joy too and give her the purpose she needed in life.

Over our rather leisurely mid-day meal, my aunt went into great detail about her exciting reunion with Lucie, which naturally had made her very happy. Then she asked lots of questions about our stay in London. Uncle Charles answered most of them, while I did my best to describe the latest fashions. I had almost finished my meal when I inquired if anything else of interest had happened while we were away.

'Well,' she said, 'Julia's sister, Lizzie, arrived the day after you left. She's a very sweet child. Just nineteen and very pretty, if a trifle shy.'

'Is she like Julia?'

'Not in looks. She's petite and dark-haired. Julia says Lizzie takes after their mother. I gather Julia gets her height and red hair from her father.' My uncle then began to talk about a book he was reading and this kept us entertained until our meal was over.

Afterwards I went in search of Granger, my head gardener, who liked to bring me up-to-date on the state of the gardens, after I had been away from home. He was the best head gardener on the Island and I made sure he knew I appreciated his efforts. We walked around the gardens for half an hour and I expressed my genuine delight with the way everything looked. The roses, in particular, were at their best, and I was enjoying the lovely fragrance of a white rose when I saw Mr. Reevers walking towards me.

75

Determined not to show how pleased I was to see him I carried on talking to Granger, only turning to greet him when Granger went off to carry on with his duties. Mr. Reevers bowed and said, with a smile, 'Luffe said you were out here. I hope I haven't interrupted your business with Granger.'

'Not at all.' We took a stroll round the grounds, and he appeared to be deliberately keeping some distance between us. Seemingly acting in accordance with my telling him that nothing had changed. Or perhaps he was putting the need to find Mr. Fenton's killer above everything else. Whatever the reason for his correct behaviour I knew I should be grateful. For having made my decision not to marry him, I meant to stick to it. I just wished it didn't make me feel so miserable.

'I saw Jago this morning,' he said.

'Yes, so he told me.'

'He still thinks smugglers murdered Fenton.'

'So does the local constable, but I don't agree. Have you seen where Mr. Fenton's body was hidden?'

He nodded. 'Jago took me out there.'

'He didn't tell me *that.*'

Mr. Reevers lifted his shoulders. 'He probably didn't think it important.'

I thought of the many things Jago didn't think important enough to tell me, things that caused me a great deal of frustration, but this was a problem I had to sort out myself. Instead I told him what I'd learnt about Tarquin, the horse Mr. Fenton hired in Cowes, and his eyes darkened when I explained that Louis had made inquiries at the inn, hoping to learn who had brought Tarquin in after the murder. 'Only he was told no-one had seen who returned the horse.'

'That is a pity.'

'Indeed. But Mudd did ask his father if he'd heard any rumours about who had killed Mr. Fenton.'

'And had he?' he murmured hopefully.

'No. He said local smugglers definitely weren't involved. They all think the Frenchies did it.' The murder had become public knowledge while I was in London, as naturally Jago had to inform the coroner of Mr. Fenton's death.

Mr. Reevers said, 'Well that old rascal would know if anyone does.'

'He's not a rascal,' I protested. 'He's a nice old man.'

'Try telling that to a Riding Officer,' he retorted with a chuckle. 'I've heard some amazing tales of how Mudd senior fooled the Customs service in the old days.'

I couldn't help but smile. 'No doubt, but he's respectable now. At least I think he is. I'll always be grateful to him for persuading my father to take John on when I was a small child. I believe he wanted to keep John out of the smuggling fraternity.'

'Probably the best thing the old scoundrel ever did,' he agreed cheerfully.

'He also taught his son how to keep a secret.'

'That doesn't surprise me. All smugglers know when to keep their mouths shut.'

'Well John certainly does, and that's been particularly useful since I've started working for Mr. Pitt.'

'Yes, in your situation, an assistant is vital.'

Turning a corner we encountered a pleasant sea breeze, which I would normally have enjoyed, but I was so downhearted by the lack of information in our search for the traitor that I barely noticed it. And I asked Mr. Reevers, 'Do you have *any* idea who the turncoat is?'

'I'm afraid not. None of our Paris agents showed any sign of devious or odd behaviour in the two weeks I was there. The fact that he has got away with it for a long time suggests he is a highly experienced agent. Someone who knows how to deceive people, while giving every appearance of being a true patriot.'

'Like Toby East,' I commented.

'Exactly. We all believed he was loyal,' he said with a sigh. 'I'll ask Giles if he had doubts about any of our agents when he was in Paris.' Giles Saxborough had been in the secret service for several years, only retiring when he married. He and Mr. Reevers were great friends as well as cousins and had often worked together in France. 'If I learn anything worthwhile I'll call back later.'

He was still keeping his distance, and talking in a sensible manner about the task Mr. Pitt has given us, but when he turned to take his leave, I looked up and caught my breath at the expression in his eyes. That had not changed, and after he'd gone I walked through the orchard and up onto the Downs, where I could be quite alone, and where I could curse out loud as much as I liked at being forced to work with Mr. Reevers. For, the more I saw of him, the harder I found it to keep him at arm's length. But I was determined to do so. If I didn't, I feared I might regret it for the rest of my life. When he offered for Sophie Wood it was her fortune he'd wanted. And I had absolutely no intention of letting myself fall into the same trap.

He didn't return that day, however, which told me Giles could not help him. Later the weather took a turn for the worse, with the pleasant breeze rapidly increasing into a severe gale. As the temperature plummeted, doors that had been left open at Westfleet were now shut to keep out the cold air. Aunt Thirza, who was reading a book of her favourite poems in the drawing room, sent her maid for a shawl, which she pulled round her shoulders, informing me that, in her opinion, summer storms were worse than those in winter. 'This is going to be a bad one,' she added with an involuntary shiver. 'I can feel it in my bones.'

'Would you like the fire to be lit?' I asked.

'What – in August?' She was astounded. 'Of course not.'

I didn't argue, although I could never see the point of sitting shivering in front of an empty fireplace just because the month was a summer one. But my uncle walked into the drawing room at that moment, rubbed his hands together and declared with an involuntary shudder, 'It feels more like October. Shall we have the fire lit, Drusilla?'

My aunt invariably bowed to my uncle's decrees, in a way she would never submit to mine. Smiling to myself, I rang for Luffe and having given the necessary order, I went off to my workroom. It seemed unlikely there would be any more visitors on such a day, and it gave me the perfect opportunity to write down all the facts I had concerning Mr. Fenton's murder.

By the time I'd finished writing and had fixed the sheet of paper onto the long inside wall of the workroom, the wind had strengthened into ferocious gusts that sent fallen leaves swirling up into the air, caused branches to snap and bowl across the lawns at a terrific rate, and made the windows rattle alarmingly. It was one of the worst summer gales I could remember, and when I rejoined my aunt and uncle in the drawing room, they were trying to reassure Gisele, who was worried about Louis being out in this weather.

Louis and Jago were in Cowes assisting Mr. Arnold, and I understood her fears, for if anything happened to Louis, not only would she lose the man she loved, but she would be left with very little to live on. So I assured her, 'They won't ride home in this, Gisele.'

'That's just what we were saying,' agreed Aunt Thirza 'They'll put up at an inn.'

'Or,' my uncle said, 'they might stay with Mr. Arnold. He'll see they're looked after, never fear. Louis will be perfectly safe.' And I went off to tell cook we weren't expecting the gentlemen back tonight.

The following morning a groom brought a message for Gisele from Louis, and we learnt that Mr. Arnold had insisted they stayed at his house, where they had been royally entertained. They would be home later, he wrote, and in good time for dinner.

The gale has already lessened to a strong breeze, but the garden staff would be kept very busy trying to get everything back to normal. Nevertheless I wasn't expecting any other repercussions from the storm, for such events were not uncommon on the Island. Especially where we were, in the west. But one outcome of this storm was about to cause a far bigger uproar than I could ever have imagined.

CHAPTER ELEVEN

O nce I knew Jago and Louis were perfectly safe, I went into the workroom and studied all the facts I had noted down yesterday about Mr. Fenton's murder, hoping for inspiration to strike. Regrettably it did not and that afternoon I rode over to Breighton House to see Julia and Richard, feeling that a pleasant hour spent there would take my mind off things, and help to free my thoughts. Richard was out, but Julia was resting in her drawing room. She greeted me with obvious pleasure, and we immediately began to commiserate with each other on the damage yesterday's devastating storm had done to our gardens.

I went on to tell her that Jago and Louis had spent the night with the Arnolds in Cowes, and Julia smiled and nodded. 'I would expect nothing else. Our islanders are so kind, Drusilla. They always rally round when people are in-----' She stopped speaking as the door opened and Jago was ushered into the room.

The moment he saw me his face turned a trifle pink. 'I didn't know you were here,' he muttered awkwardly.

Before I could answer Julia greeted him with obvious pleasure and said, 'I gather you stayed with the Arnolds last night. '

'Yes, and very delightful it was too. But I thought I should call in on my way back to Westfleet – er - to reassure – er — you, that Louis and I were quite safe.'

'That is kind of you,' Julia said. 'Lizzie will be very relieved. She was rather worried about you. She's in the garden with Edward, if you would like to speak to her.'

'Well – yes, if I may. Only for a few minutes, of course.'

After he'd bowed and left the room I turned to Julia in wide-eyed astonishment. 'What was that all about?'

She giggled and said, 'Well, what do you think? Lizzie and Jago are totally smitten with each other.'

'Smitten?' I gasped. 'Jago? You can't be serious. Why, they only met about a week ago.'

She laughed. 'True, but he seems to be utterly besotted with her.'

I shook my head in disbelief. 'I never imagined he'd allow himself to become besotted with anyone. He always likes to be in total command of his feelings.'

'Well, he isn't now, Drusilla,' she said with a smile. 'He's behaving like most young men in love.'

'Good God! He must be human after all,' I murmured light-heartedly. And as the likely outcome of their love match sank in, I remarked, 'It looks like you'll have a duchess in the family one day.'

'Yes. Mama *will* be pleased,' she declared in amusement. 'I was a great disappointment to her marrying a mere naval officer. But she will like Lord Elvington. He treats Lizzie with every possible courtesy.'

'*That* doesn't surprise me, Julia. He's the perfect gentleman. Very prim and proper. Frankly he drives me mad at times, trying to protect me from things he believes will upset me.'

'Ah, but Lizzie likes being protected, so his manner will suit her very well.' And she confided, 'He's been here every day since she arrived, taking her out for a drive, or a walk, or a stroll round the gardens. All very proper. I have no fears about his behaviour.'

'No. He's a dead bore,' I said, laughing.

We talked about it for some time, occasionally catching a glimpse of Jago and Lizzie walking in the garden. Edward, I noticed, was now playing ring-a-ring-a-roses with his nursemaid, but she was young enough and short enough not to mind falling on the ground with him.

When Julia and I finally ran out of things to say about the new romance, she returned to the subject of yesterday's storm, and asked if I'd heard about the yacht that had capsized in Dittistone Bay.

I shook my head at her. 'Who was foolish enough to take a yacht out in that weather?'

'They weren't from the Island, Drusilla. They were French émigrés. Three aristocrats who had been living in Spain for the last year or two. They found that life there did not suit them as much as they had hoped, and decided London would offer the society and culture they were missing. Two of them left families in Spain, who would follow once suitable homes had been acquired. But by the time our Island came into sight the weather was deteriorating so rapidly they decided to put in at Dittistone Bay.'

'Very sensible,' I said.

'Indeed. But just as they reached the bay they were caught up in a sudden violent squall that broke the mast and swept the yacht onto the rocks.'

Such happenings were not uncommon on the back of the Island. Many ships had come to grief here over the years. In storms, or on the underwater ledge that ran along our part of the coast. As a result, graves of foreign seamen were to be found in several Island churchyards that were close to the coast. And I asked, 'Did the gentlemen manage to get ashore safely?'

'One did, by clinging to a piece of wood from the yacht. Sadly the others drowned.'

I gasped in dismay. They were unknown to us, but I couldn't help feeling sorry for them, and I said, 'Has anyone been able to inform their families?'

'The gentleman who survived, the Comte de Saint Martin, lost his family in the revolution, but he provided Richard with the names and addresses for the wives of his companions. Richard wrote the necessary letters and took them to Mr. Arnold, to ensure they were sent off with all possible speed.'

'That was good of him.'

'As he said, it was the least he could do.'

'Is the Comte badly hurt?' I asked.

'Well, he has a broken leg, but some fishermen got him to the inn.' There had been an inn close to the shore at Dittistone bay for at least a hundred years. 'Dr. Redding came at once and set the leg, but said it was a bad break and the Comte needed complete rest. Obviously he couldn't stay at the inn, or cross the Solent in that state. The poor gentleman is sixty years of age, so Richard suggested he used Mr. Hamerton's house until he felt well enough to leave the Island.'

'That's an excellent idea, Julia. I hope the Comte appreciates it.'

'I'm sure he does, although according to Richard, the poor man was too exhausted last night to say much, but when Richard called on him this morning he was feeling a little better. And it will give the servants something to do until we find a proper tenant.'

We were still talking about the Comte when the door burst open and Edward, her three year old son, raced across the room, beaming with excitement. 'Illa – Illa – I saw you through the window.' "Illa," was his first attempt at pronouncing my name, and somehow it had stuck. I got to my feet and when he reached me I scooped him up and gave him a big hug. He was my Godson and I adored him. The fact that he always seemed pleased to see me sent a warm glow through me.

Following him belatedly into the room was his nursemaid, who bobbed a curtsy to me and said to Julia, 'I'm sorry, ma'am. I only turned my back for a second and he was gone.'

Julia, understanding exactly what had happened, told the girl not to worry, and that she'd ring when she wanted Edward taken back to the nursery. As she left, I sat Edward on my lap, and asked him what he had done while I was in London.

He gave a delicious giggle. 'I bin naughty, Illa,' he confided in a whisper. 'I put a frog in cook's pocket.'

'Did you?' I said, trying not to smile. 'What did she do when she found it?'

'She screamed,' he announced, his eyes gleaming with gleeful satisfaction.

I bit my lip firmly, and Julia said, 'Yes, and cook told Papa. And what did Papa do?'

Edward hung his head and muttered, 'He smacked me, but it didn't hurt for long.' And with a total lack of guile, he asked me, 'Do you like frogs, Illa?'

'I love them,' I said, and chuckled at the disappointment on his face. But he soon thought of something else he liked to do, and urged me to play Pat-a-Cake, which he adored, hitting my hands in a highly enthusiastic manner at every appropriate moment. Looking across at Julia, who was expecting her second child in November, I murmured, 'Something tells me you are hoping for a quiet, well-behaved daughter this time.'

'Yes, I am,' she admitted, with a rueful smile. 'One boisterous child is more than enough.' She loved Edward to distraction, but there was no question that he was quite a handful.

I returned home in good time for nuncheon where, unsurprisingly, the Comte was the main topic of conversation. My uncle was so concerned by what he'd heard in the village that he decided to call on the Comte that afternoon to see if he could assist the gentleman in any way. Later, after he'd left, my aunt and I went into the drawing room, where she took up her embroidery, and I settled down to read. We were still there when he returned, and he assured us at once that Richard had done everything possible for the invalid's comfort.

'What kind of a man is he?' my aunt asked.

'He's most charming, has excellent manners, thinks just as he ought, and is very grateful to everyone who helped him. He left France about two years ago, after sans-culottes burned his chateau to the ground. His wife and only child, a son of twenty-five, died in the fire, and....'

'Oh, the poor man,' my aunt whispered. We had heard many similar tales since the revolution began in '89, but they still had the power to shock.

'How did he escape?' I asked.

'On the night of the fire he was staying at a friend's house.'

'That was lucky,' I said.

'Indeed. And he'd also had the good sense to hide a large sum of money and most of their jewellery under the floor of the gazebo in the garden. He dug that up in the middle of the night, went straight to his yacht and sailed off to Spain.'

As we well knew, most émigrés had not been so fortunate. The majority, forced to flee for their lives, had brought very little with them. I asked, 'Which part of France does he come from?'

'Saint Martin. The same as his name.'

That was a place name I had seen on the map in several different parts of the country during the summer of '88, when father and I travelled around France. 'Do you know which one?' I inquired, explaining there were quite a few.

'I did mean to ask him, but he talked at such length explaining how he got out of the country, that it went out of my mind.'

I thought back to that happy, carefree summer, when father and I had seen the best, and the worst, of France. The magnificence of the scenery was marred in my memory by the hovels some of the poor lived in, and the terrible poverty they endured. I could not have lived with myself if any child on my estate had suffered the kind of terrible hunger I saw in some places. It was a situation my uncle and I had discussed many times, so I did not refer to it again, but merely said, 'When we were there, no-one spoke a word of English, and father was reduced to miming what he wanted, as they didn't understand the little French he did know. It makes me smile whenever I think of it. I do remember it was very hot, so England will seem cold to the Comte.'

My uncle grinned. 'He said he thought our weather was most invigorating.'

I laughed. 'That's one way of putting it. But I suppose weather won't seem of much importance after what he's been through in

France, and in yesterday's storm.' A man who'd escaped a violent death twice in two years did indeed have much to be thankful for.

About an hour later, Mr. Reevers called and politely invited me to join him on a ride over the Downs, now that the weather had improved. I accepted equally politely, and hurried off to change into a riding dress, stopping briefly in the hall to tell Luffe to send a message to Mudd, to saddle Orlando and be ready to accompany me in fifteen minutes.

Working with Mr. Reevers, as Mr. Pitt wanted, gave me certain difficulties as an unmarried woman. For, the proprieties demanded that I must always be accompanied when I went riding with Mr. Reevers. If the weather was inclement, we could not talk about the investigation indoors at Westfleet, as we were never left alone. Although we could do so when walking in the garden. In the past my uncle had escorted me to Norton House, Mr. Reevers' home, retreating to the library while we talked. This did give us some freedom.

Nevertheless, in many ways, riding was best, as we could speak freely in front of Mudd. Up on the Downs there was usually a shepherd attending to the sheep but, otherwise, we rarely saw another soul, which again allowed us to stop and talk. Today, after enjoying a long fast gallop, we made our way to Hokewell Bay, where Mr. Reevers suggested a stroll along the cliff top. Dismounting, we left the horses in Mudd's care, and set off in the direction of Dittistone Bay. The wind had almost completely dropped now and it was most pleasant in the sunshine.

Mr. Reevers kept a distance between us again, which would have pleased my aunt, if she'd seen us. Once we'd admired the view with the sun sparkling on the sea, and watched the waves crashing onto the sandy beach below, we talked about who could possibly have killed Mr. Fenton. As I reminded him, 'Jago was at Westfleet at the time of the murder.'

'He didn't go out at all?'

'No. I woke early that morning and I happened to be standing at my bedchamber window when I saw Louis ride off towards Cowes. He'd arranged to have breakfast with Mr. Arnold, and was to spend the day with him, so that he could observe the difficulties the émigrés gave the Customs service. Half an hour later Mr. Fenton set off for Yarmouth. In fact I went down to the stables just in time to see him go. Jago was already there, giving him his last minute orders. Then Jago and I had breakfast together, and after that we spent most of the morning dealing with routine matters concerning the turncoat operation.'

'Mmmm. I see. So Louis left half an hour before Fenton?' he murmured.

'Yes,' I said.

Neither of us spoke for a moment or two, not wanting to believe that Louis could be the murderer. Eventually Mr. Reevers said, 'Well, it doesn't do to jump to conclusions.'

'I haven't.'

'No, I didn't think you would.'

'I cannot believe he's the turncoat. I mean, not only have my aunt and uncle known him virtually all his life, but Mr. Pitt knows Louis and his family too. He was at Cambridge with one of Louis' older brothers.'

He stopped walking and looked at me. 'That I didn't know.'

He stood for a moment staring out to sea, obviously thinking. Watching him, I noticed a black curl had found its way around his left ear, as it often did and, foolishly, my heart melted. If he turned round now I feared he would see how much I truly cared for him. Thankfully, he barely glanced at me when he spoke again. 'I'll send my messenger to Wickham first thing tomorrow. We need to see everything he knows about Louis and Jago. Their records, their background notes, what they worked on in France, and any problems they've had during their secret service career.'

'An excellent idea,' I agreed.

'I'm glad you approve.' And he smiled at me in a way that set my pulses racing. 'If the weather stays fine we should have all the necessary information within a few days. Meanwhile, I'll keep Louis under observation.'

I nodded, for it had to be done. 'What do you want me to do?'

For a second his eyes gleamed, but when he spoke, his voice was perfectly rational. 'You have an aptitude for spotting anything that seems odd or out of place. If I watch Louis when he's out and you do so at Westfleet, we should soon see if he's involved.'

That seemed eminently sensible and later that day I strolled round my garden thinking about Louis, praying he wasn't the murderer. Louis was cheerful and kind-hearted, and I liked him. But I had liked Toby East too. He had appeared to be every bit as loyal to Britain as Louis seemed to be now. And we had to learn from our mistakes.

The other thought that came into my mind was, if Louis really was the traitor, what would happen to Gisele? The poor girl had lost all her family and her childhood home. She would have their house in London, but how would she survive without an income? It was too awful to think about. As a widow of a traitor, a second marriage was highly unlikely. Yet we couldn't allow her situation to affect how we acted. The traitor had betrayed all our secret agents in Paris to the French government, and was probably involved in the plot to abduct Mr. Pitt.

It was true that Louis had the opportunity to murder Mr. Fenton, but that didn't mean he had done so. What we did know was, it couldn't possibly be Jago. Then another thought struck me. Louis and Jago had worked together in France. What if they were working together here? After all, no-one else had known Mr. Fenton was on the Island.

Yet I couldn't rid myself of the strangest feeling that there was something I had missed. It was a feeling that kept me awake half the night, all to no avail. For, if I had missed something, I did not have any idea what it was.

CHAPTER TWELVE

M r. Reevers sent his groom with a note informing me that his messenger had set off for the Alien Office in London first thing that morning. I did not see Mr. Reevers for the next three days, as he was busy keeping Louis under surveillance. It was useless to pretend I did not miss him, and that made me restless. I spent my time riding, visiting Julia and Richard, as well as everyone at Ledstone. Jago and Louis were out dealing with émigrés every day, and when they were at Westfleet neither of them gave me any cause to doubt their allegiance to King and Country.

I eventually saw Mr. Reevers at a dinner party given by Julia and Richard, where we managed to snatch a quiet moment together in the garden, when he told me Louis' behaviour away from Westfleet had been faultless. 'Who else can it be?' I murmured.

'Jago?' he queried without conviction.

'He conducts himself in far too correct a manner to be a traitor.'

Mr. Reevers grimaced. 'True. And he was the one who insisted on conducting the turncoat operation from a safe and secure base.'

Other guests came within earshot then and soon we all went in to dinner. Everyone from Westfleet and Ledstone Place came to the party, and it was a most convivial evening, with good conversation and a great deal of laughter.

Julia had seated Lizzie and Jago next to each other, and there was no mistaking the love in their eyes when they looked at each other. It made Jago seem so much more human.

Giles, Lucie and Marguerite talked of their three month trip to Yorkshire and London, my uncle and I spoke of our visit to the capital, and Mr. Reevers related how he'd chanced to bump into us by accident in Hyde Park. Inevitably the war with France crept into the discussion and Jago commented, 'I find it appalling that Robespierre blames Mr. Pitt for every catastrophe in France. He even said Pitt had turned good revolutionaries into traitors, and that had forced his government to guillotine them.'

Lucie asked, 'Will the people really believe that?'

'The uneducated will,' Jago replied.

'That kind of thing is meant to fire them up to fight even harder,' Giles observed.

Mr. Reevers nodded in agreement. 'The odd thing is that Robespierre even knows how to make the people laugh. Like the Modern French Feast that was mentioned in the newspapers recently. They printed the Bill of Fare he had concocted. It started with Kings' heads halved, garnished with Royal relatives. Followed by grilled Spaniards and a soup of Dutchmen, but it was the ending that was particularly outrageous. The British Cabinet were put in a large raised pie, with Mr. Pitt's head on top. That would have had them chortling all over France.'

'Oh, yes, I saw that,' exclaimed Gisele with a shudder. 'What they said about Mr. Pitt was sickening.'

Louis put his hand over hers. 'Don't let it upset you, my love.' I had read it too, of course. And to me that made Robespierre plans for Mr. Pitt all too clear.

But Louis sensibly changed the subject and began telling us about the Cinque Ports' Fencibles. 'Mr. Pitt believes these volunteer companies of horse and foot will be a vital part of our defences should the French invade.'

'He's right to encourage them,' Mr. Reevers declared. He was seated exactly opposite me, giving me far too many opportunities for him to set my heart racing. 'We'll need every man we can get if the French do invade.'

Marguerite asked in a fearful voice, 'Do you think they will?'

'I don't think there's a chance,' Giles pronounced at once, trying to allay his mother's worries. 'Transporting soldiers across the channel in large numbers is not easy. Anything could happen to them. Like a sudden squall or .....'

'You mean --- like the one that nearly killed the Comte,' Gisele put in quickly, looking a little relieved herself.

'Exactly,' Louis remarked, as he selected an apple from the dish of fruit. 'Even if the weather wasn't too bad many soldiers would still be seasick on the long crossing over the Channel, and end up too weak to fight.'

'Too weak, too wet and too cold,' Jago pointed out. 'Waves are bound to splash over the sides of their landing craft.'

The gentlemen, feeling they had assuaged the worries of the ladies, talked about the men who'd joined the Volunteers, and I said to Louis, 'Didn't you help to raise these companies?'

'Mr. Pitt asked me to assist,' he explained quietly. 'The local men were so determined to do everything they could to defend our country, it was a privilege to help them. Next month Mr. Pitt is to review the Volunteers, and he has kindly asked us to stay at Walmer so that we can accompany him.'

'Quite right too,' my aunt remarked, sipping her wine. 'After all the work you've put in.'

Marguerite joined in with her view of the situation. 'I do like to see soldiers marching. They make me feel so much safer.'

To which Gisele responded with a heartfelt, 'How I wish this awful war was over.'

Lizzie smiled at her. 'Yes, wouldn't it be wonderful if we could live out our lives in peace.'

At the very moment Lucie began to add to those wishes, the butler entered the room and informed Richard that Mr. Pink, the butler from Mr. Hamerton's house, wished to speak to him urgently.

Richard, looking slightly exasperated, declared, 'Oh, very well. Send him in, Wade.'

'In here, sir?' Wade inquired, a little surprised, but a swift affirmation sent him on his way.

'It won't be anything much,' Richard assured us. 'Pink is a fusspot. Good at his job, mind, but a bit of an old woman.'

Conversation started up again, but was quickly silenced when Pink entered the room. For he had a large bruise forming above his right eye, a sight that made Richard demand, 'Good God, Pink, what on earth have you been up to?'

The stately, middle-aged butler summoned up every particle of his dignity. 'Sir, *I* have not been up to anything. I regret to say that the Comte threw a bottle of claret at me.'

'A bottle ----?' Richard repeated in disbelief.

'Yes, sir. A full one.'

Richard stared at him in stunned silence, before spluttering, 'But ---- but --- why?'

'Well sir, I had, inadvertently, placed the salt cellar on the left of his dinner tray, when he had specified I was to put it on the right.' We all stared at him in stunned silence. How could a gentleman react in such an outrageous manner over any mistake, let alone something that trivial. Pink went on, 'Sir, none of the servants wish to be disobliging, but if the Comte stays, we will all be looking for another place. We were very happy working for Mr. Hamerton. He was a good, kind, Christian gentleman. But the Comte throws things at everyone. He shouts and complains about everything we do for him, and is always threatening to have us dismissed. He swears a great deal, even at the young maids, and he had cook in tears, insisting her roast dinner wasn't fit enough for pigs, and.......'

'But that's nonsense,' Julia broke in, indignantly. 'Richard and I dined at Mr. Hamerton's house several times, and the food was excellent.'

'That was our experience too,' said my uncle. Shaking his head in bewilderment he went on, 'When I called to see the Comte he was most charming and extremely polite.'

Richard nodded in agreement. 'He behaved like a perfect gentleman to me too.'

'Yes, sir,' Pink said. 'He's always like that with visitors, to people of his own class. But he treats us like slaves. We're not allowed to disturb him in the mornings until he rings for breakfast, which he might demand at six, or at ten. It's the same with other meals. Last night he wanted dinner at ten. Well, cook goes to bed at ten, as she has to be up at six. And he rings for the slightest thing.'

'Such as?' Richard inquired.

'Sometimes it's just to move his bedcovers back a few inches, or to pass him the glass of wine that I had already placed within close reach of his hand, or to straighten his night cap, and he bellows if I'm not there in ten seconds. Begging your pardon, sir, if I'm speaking too plainly, but if that's how the nobility carry on in France, I'm not surprised they've ended up on the guillotine.'

Pink was understandably overwrought, but Richard quickly calmed him down, promising to speak to the Comte. 'I'll come over straight after breakfast tomorrow. As you can see, it's not convenient now, but I will deal with it.'

'Thank you, sir,' Pink said, looking greatly relieved.

'I'm sure we can sort it out.'

'I hope so, sir. None of us wants to leave.'

When Pink had gone, we all looked at each other in silent astonishment, not quite knowing what to say about the Comte's outrageous behaviour. In the end it was my uncle who commented first. 'I wish I could assure you that the French nobility don't behave like that, but I regret to say that many did treat their servants like slaves. I saw it myself when we moved to France in '88. Not everyone did so, I'm thankful to say, but sadly some who did show proper consideration for their servants still went to the guillotine.'

'The good paying for the sins of the bad,' Giles said with a sigh.

We all agreed, however, that the behaviour Pink had spoken of, could not be tolerated, and Richard assured us, 'I will make that exceedingly clear to the Comte tomorrow. In fact, the sooner he's packed off to London the better it will be for everyone. I'll speak to Dr. Redding about arranging it.'

Later that evening, when everyone began to take their leave, Mr. Reevers quietly asked me if I'd like to go riding in the morning.

'Tomorrow is Sunday,' I pointed out.

'Yes. And I won't need to keep an eye on Louis while he's in church. Besides, my messenger arrived back just as I was leaving this evening.'

'Really?' I said in surprise. 'That was quick.'

'Knowing how urgent it was, he rode down from London overnight, to ensure he could cross the Solent today.'

'Very sensible.' For, of course, there were no passenger boats on a Sunday.

'Indeed. Well, will you come riding? I want to show you the information he brought back.'

I was very eager to see it, but as I said, 'My aunt will expect me to go to church.'

'Pretend you have a headache.'

'She wouldn't believe me. I never get headaches.'

'Really? I thought all women had headaches,' he said with a grin. I couldn't help smiling, for many women did use that as an excuse to avoid going somewhere that bored them. And he suggested, 'Just tell her you don't feel like going.'

'That wouldn't be a lie. I can't abide Mr. Upton's sermons. They're too long, too irritating and far too boring.'

His eyes filled with laughter. 'That's settled then. I'll call for you once they've set off for church.'

I did usually go to the service on Sunday mornings, it being expected of me in my position. As father used to say, it set a good example, and despite my dislike of Mr. Upton, I was in favour of people attending church. It was also a good meeting place. But, this Sunday, I did not go. In the end, I told my uncle that I needed to confer with Mr. Reevers on a matter of some urgency.

'Your aunt will want to know where, and how, you are meeting him.'

'We're going for a ride on the Downs,' I said. 'Mudd will be with us, of course.'

'Does Mudd know everything that's going on?'

'Yes,' I said. 'I need him to help me. In fact, I couldn't manage without him.'

Whatever my uncle told Aunt Thirza it certainly stopped her making a fuss about my absence from church that morning. Her only comment being, 'As long as you don't make a habit of it, Drusilla.'

I was ready and waiting when Mr. Reevers arrived, and within a few minutes we were riding along the lane that led from Westfleet to the Downs, with Mudd following at a suitable distance. The lane was full of puddles after such heavy overnight rain, but the sun was already hot enough to start drying the ground a little. First we enjoyed a good long race, and Orlando being a faster horse than Mr. Reevers' mount, I had no trouble winning, but he didn't seem to mind. This pleased me, as most men did not care to be beaten by a woman at anything.

We stopped to enjoy the view on what was a wonderfully clear day. Far below, the sun glistened on the sea, gulls screamed overhead, interrupted only by the occasional bleating of the large number of sheep on the Downs. It was hard to believe we could be at war on such a day, when everything was so peaceful here. Dismounting, we handed our rather mud-caked horses over to Mudd to look after, while we took a stroll, and as we walked off I asked Mr. Reevers what information his messenger had brought back about Jago and Louis.

'Well, in truth, there isn't anything unusual.'

'Oh, really,' I retorted in exasperation, for he'd instantly shattered all my hopes. 'You could have told me that yesterday.'

He grinned at me. 'Yes, but if I had, you would now be in church being bored rigid by Mr. Upton.'

'True,' I admitted, my annoyance turning to amusement. And I asked, 'Have you brought the documents with you?'

'Of course. I knew you would want to see them.' He removed them from his pocket, pointed to a nearby stony outcrop, already dried by the hot sun, and suggested we sat there, it being easier to study the documents sitting down. Thankfully there was only a slight breeze today, which did not ruffle the papers unduly as I read them.

They contained all the usual information about birth, parentage, schooling and background, followed by the details of their employment in the secret service. This showed that Jago and Louis had worked together in Paris for nearly two years, and that Louis had left France after damaging his knee in a riding accident. Shortly after that, Jago had also returned to work in England at his father's behest, when he became the only surviving son. Jago and Louis had excellent records, with no critical comments, except that Louis was a little inclined to act on impulse, and Jago was rather short on imagination at times. I smiled, thinking how true that was of both of them.

They had never been questioned by the French authorities, and both had supplied the Alien Office with much useful information during their service. They had not shared the same lodging, however. Jago had wanted to live alone, but Tom Morel had stayed with Louis when he first went to Paris.

Once I'd finished reading, I said, 'Well, that doesn't help us at all.' We could hear a rider cantering on the hillside above us, and just as Mr. Reevers started to answer me, the horse gave a long shrill terrified whinny. This was quickly followed by a man's explosive exclamation and sounds that suggested horse and rider had parted company. We both leapt to our feet and looked up at the rising hillside above us, where we could just see the rider scrambling to his feet. I stared at him in astonishment, having recognised him immediately. Mr. Reevers looked every bit as stunned as I was, but he found his voice first.

'Tom?' he called out, as if convinced he must be mistaken. 'Good God. I thought you were dead.'

CHAPTER THIRTEEN

M r. Morel stared down at us, utterly dumbstruck, and Mr. Reevers shouted, 'Stay where you are, Tom. We'll come up to you.' We both climbed up the hillside, but Mr. Reevers was ahead of me and reached him just as Mr. Morel managed to catch hold of his horse. Once he'd tethered the animal to a nearby isolated tree, he shook Mr. Reevers' hand heartily, assuring him he was unhurt. Grinning from ear to ear, he declared jovially, 'So, you thought *I* was dead, did you?' And he laughed out loud. 'Well, I thought *you* had lost your head on the guillotine. How did you manage to escape?'

I heard and saw much of what was happening as I took the last few steps up the hillside. But not wishing to interfere in their friendly reunion I went over to soothe Tom Morel's horse, which was so free of mud I assumed it must have been hired from a nearby inn. While I quietly fussed over the horse I listened to the breathtaking stories the gentlemen were exchanging, of how they had escaped from France. Making it sound like a game, as men do. It was only after they had congratulated each other on their good fortune that Mr. Morel became aware I was watching them. I smiled in understanding of his behaviour, and he bowed, clearly mortified at having totally ignored me.

'Lady Drusilla, please forgive me.' Spreading his arms wide, he declared, 'What can I say? I have no excuse for my bad manners, except that I feared Radleigh had been arrested with the other Paris agents. You cannot imagine how I feel to find him alive and well....'

I said, tongue-in-cheek, 'You may just have given me an inkling of your feelings.' He laughed, and Mr. Reevers asked where we had met. 'In London,' I said. 'At the Alien Office. It was Mr. Morel who showed me round.'

'You were fortunate, ma'am,' enthused Mr. Reevers. 'He knows the place inside out.'

His friend said with a grin. 'It has been great fun too, but that is all at an end now. I've just resigned from the service and I'm going.....'

Mr. Reevers' bushy eyebrows shot up. 'Resigned?'

'Well, I've had a few narrow squeaks in Paris, and this time I only got out of France by the skin of my teeth. I'm getting too old for this game Radleigh, and in any case it's time I went back to America. But, as I told Lady Drusilla in London, I wanted to see as much as I could of this lovely country before I leave.'

'I'm pleased you've included the Island in your travels,' I said.

'How could I not do so, ma'am, after you sang its praises so eloquently? I must say that the little I've seen of it so far has made me very glad that I came.'

Mr Reevers remarked in a bantering tone, 'Are you ever at a loss for words, Tom?'

'No Frenchman ever is.'

'I wouldn't say that too loudly around here.'

'Ah, but I'm an American citizen now.' When I listened very carefully, I could occasionally detect the faintest hint of a French accent. And his time in England had softened his American pronunciation.

'When did you arrive on the Island?' I asked.

'This morning,' he said.

'On a Sunday?' I remarked teasingly.

'Well, I actually left Hamble yesterday morning. A friend brought me over in his yacht, but we were caught in heavy rain. There was virtually no wind, so progress was dreadfully slow and we didn't reach Cowes until around eight this morning. The thing is ma'am, I wanted to say farewell to all my friends before I went back to America, and to see something of the Island too. So I hired a horse at an inn, had breakfast there and then rode straight down this way.'

'Really?' I murmured, and asked in some amusement, 'Do tell me how you managed to keep your horse clean after riding a dozen miles on such a muddy trail. I've never been able to do that and I would be grateful for your advice!'

He laughed out loud. 'Oh, it's quite simple really. I stopped at a village inn a mile or two back and we both left spotlessly clean. I don't like to call on friends when I'm covered in mud.'

Mr. Reevers grinned. 'Well, you do have a reputation to keep up, so you'll need another bath now. But what caused you to fall off your horse?'

'Two large birds suddenly swooped and dived right in front of us.' They laughed about that too and then Mr. Reevers asked where he was staying on the Island. 'Oh – I'll stop at an inn......'

'You'll do no such thing. Come and stay with me at Norton House. There's plenty of room.'

'Well, I --- er--' he began hesitantly. 'Wickham said you're trying to unmask the turncoat. I wouldn't want to hinder you.'

'You won't,' he affirmed pleasantly.

Reassured, Mr. Morel said, 'In that case, I accept.' And swept him a perfectly executed low bow. Looking up at the cloudless blue sky, he remarked, 'Does the sun always shine here?'

'Of course,' I said, smiling, and invited him to call at Westfleet whenever it suited him.

He bowed again. 'I would be honoured, ma'am.'

'I look forward to it.'

Tom walked back with us, leading his horse, to where Mudd was waiting. As we did so, I told Mr. Reevers there was no need for him to accompany me home. 'I'm sure you and Mr. Morel will have much to talk about.'

He agreed without hesitation, and watching the two gentlemen ride off without a backward glance, I couldn't help feeling slightly put out at the speed with which Mr. Reevers had abandoned me, even though I had given him permission to do so. I reminded myself that I had asked him to keep his distance, and he had complied. If he'd ignored my request, I thought, as Mudd and I headed for home, I would have been angry. I ought to be pleased he was behaving as I'd asked. Yet, I wasn't. Oh, this is ridiculous, I told myself. I was acting like the kind of woman I had no time for. One who could never make up her mind what she wanted. Of course I knew what I really wanted, but feared that would end in tears. My tears. And that was a risk I could not bear to take.

Once back at Westfleet, the conversation over our mid-day meal soon turned to this morning's church service, and my uncle informed me, 'I wish I'd come riding with you and Mr. Reevers. You missed the most boring sermon I'd ever heard.'

'How very true,' Louis agreed with a groan. 'Upton droned on for half an hour, lecturing us on humility.'

I had just popped a strawberry into my mouth, and as I swallowed it, his words made me choke. Fortunately a glass of water was to hand,

and when I could speak again, I burst out, 'Humility? Mr. Upton? He's the most pompous little man I've ever met.'

'You shouldn't make fun of his height, Drusilla,' my aunt scolded. 'He can't help being short.'

'True, but he has no right to tell us to be humble. He doesn't know the meaning of the word.'

'On the contrary,' my uncle assured me, his eyes dancing. 'He informed us of its meaning. He said, to be humble was, to have a low view of one's own importance.'

I started to laugh then, which set the others off, and soon we were all gasping for breath at the very idea that Mr. Upton would ever have a low view of his own importance. Even my aunt had to mop her eyes. When I was finally back in control, I said, 'I'm surprised the congregation didn't go off into hysterics too.'

Jago admitted, 'One or two gentlemen did give a snort.'

This set Gisele giggling again, and she confided, 'Roche says Mr. Upton likes telling everyone what to do when he's in church because, at home, he has to do what Mrs. Upton tells him.'

We all gazed at her in astonishment, and I asked, 'How does Roche know that?' For, none of us had ever heard that before.

'Roche is friendly with their groom, who's been with them since they married. He knows everything that goes on. She's polite to her husband in front of other people, but not when they're alone.'

This astonishing revelation remained the subject of conversation when we repaired to the drawing room for a short rest after our delicious meal, for not one of us knew that his wife ruled the roost behind closed doors. The fact that Roche was friendly with the Uptons' groom surprised me too, for Mudd had said Roche didn't mix with the grooms at Westfleet. But I had no chance to comment on that, for at that moment Luffe ushered Richard into the room, and the news he brought swept everything else right out of our heads.

After exchanging the usual greetings, I invited him to take a seat, and once he had done so, I asked how he'd got on this morning with the Comte, assuming he'd come to tell us the outcome of this visit. He looked rather pale, and I hoped the Comte had not responded by throwing things at him too. But I couldn't have been more wrong, and we soon learnt the reason for Richard's pale face.

'I arrived just before ten,' he began, 'and Pink told me the Comte hadn't yet rung for his breakfast. Well, not having any time to waste, I went up to his bedchamber and knocked on the door. There was no answer, and thinking he might be unwell, I went in.' He hesitated, as if uncertain how to go on, and in that moment, I realised what he was about to say.

'He's dead, isn't he,' I murmured quietly.

Aunt Thirza gasped, but before she could speak, Richard looked at me and said, 'Yes.'

When he didn't elaborate, my uncle asked, 'What was it? A seizure?'

'No. I'm afraid – well, there's no easy way to say this. I'm afraid he was murdered.'

'Murdered?' my aunt whispered in horror, and no doubt thinking of the problems the servants had endured with the Comte, she begged, 'Please tell me it wasn't Pink.'

'I doubt it. Pink fainted when he saw the Comte's body.'

For a moment we all remained silent, as we tried to take in this appalling news. It didn't seem possible that any man on our friendly Island could have been murdered in his bed. Eventually Jago asked, 'How was he killed?' .

'Stabbed. Many times. It was a ferocious attack. There was blood everywhere and------'

Louis broke in, 'Fenton was stabbed too. Perhaps it was the same man.'

Mr. Fenton's murder had become public knowledge while I was in London, as Jago had correctly informed the coroner and the local constable. And Mr. Upton too, of course, in order to enable a Christian burial to take place on the Island. Jago also thought the constable might find the smugglers who he believed were responsible. But that had not happened.

I asked if the knife had been found and Richard shook his head. 'I made a thorough search while I was waiting for Dr. Redding to arrive, but I couldn't find it. The constable intends to make his own search. I hope he has more luck than I did.' And he added, 'It may be that robbery was the motive. The murderer stole the four rings the Comte always wore. I'm told they were worth a great deal of money.'

'Did the doctor say what time he was killed?' I asked.

'He thought it would have been between one and five in the morning. The constable had started to interrogate the servants by the time I left. It seems everyone in Dittistone knew about the problems they were having with the Comte.' He stood up then. 'I must go,

Drusilla. I promised the servants I would be back within the hour. I pray with all my heart that the murderer is not one of them.' And a murmur of agreement ran around the room.

I did not believe they were responsible, for most of the servants were women and they must have been reassured by Richard's promise to speak to the Comte this morning. The stables weren't in use at present, and although a strong youth was employed to do heavy work and to carry messages, he lived in Dittistone, as did the gardeners. Pink was the only man who lived in the house itself.

The local constable called on me later to ask what Pink had said to us the previous day. I complied with his request, but commented in a firm voice, 'I really do not believe he is the murderer.'

'But, my lady, who else can it be? The Comte hadn't met anyone on the Island, except Mr. Tanfield, Mr. Frère and the doctor. Mr. Pink denies it, of course. But then, villains always do.'

I pointed out, 'You do know Pink fainted when he saw the body?'

He nodded. 'He could have done that to make himself look innocent. Murderers get up to all sorts of tricks when they're forced to face what they've done.'

'Yes, but did he have blood on his clothes?'

'No, my lady. I expect he got rid of them overnight.' And he went on, 'It must be Mr. Pink, my lady. There was no sign of an intruder breaking in.'

'Well, it was very humid last night, even during the heavy rain, and I expect the windows would have been left open. So an intruder could easily have got in.'

When I reminded him that Mr. Fenton had been stabbed too, he scratched his head, and said he didn't think Pink was responsible for that, as he couldn't have known the man was on the Island. 'I did check with the other servants, my lady, and they said Mr. Pink was in the house as usual that particular morning.'

'Do you think we have two murderers at large on the Island then?'

The constable shook his head from side to side, several times. 'It doesn't seem likely, does it, my lady. It's a rare puzzle this one.' That was true, nevertheless the one thing I was absolutely certain of, was that Pink had not killed the Comte.

Frankly, I did not expect the constable to solve either crime, but what right did I have to make a judgement on his ability, when so far, Mr. Reevers and I had failed to solve Mr. Fenton's murder. Louis was still under suspicion, having been out alone at the time it happened, but I hoped Mr. Arnold would be able to settle that for me. I knew exactly when Louis had left for Cowes that fateful morning, and roughly how long it would take him to reach Mr. Arnold's house, where he was to join them for breakfast. If he was the culprit, it must have delayed him by an hour or two. Probably nearer two, if he took Tarquin back to the Yarmouth inn. If Mr. Arnold could recall what time Louis arrived that morning, I would know if he was guilty or not.

Thus on Monday morning I set off for Cowes after breakfast, accompanied by Mudd, and called on Mr. Arnold at his office. But he could not help me. 'I'm very sorry ma'am, but that was the day our youngest child was ill with a fever. My wife looked after her all night,' he said, 'and I took over at six so she could get some sleep. I sent for the doctor first thing, and everything was at sixes and sevens. Mr. Gauvan did take breakfast with us, as arranged, but what time he arrived, I cannot recall. When I got home that evening our daughter was very much better. But that's children for you. Up one minute, down the next. Still, it was a great relief, I can tell you, ma'am.'

'I can well believe it.'

'I only wish I could be of more help.'

I told him not worry, and went on my way. I'd had such hopes that Mr. Arnold could make it clear whether or not Louis was innocent or guilty. Under normal circumstances he would have done, but worry about a child stopped parents thinking of anything else. I understood, and accepted that, although I found it immensely frustrating in this particular instance. But that was life.

My aunt and uncle were spending the day at Ledstone and I'd asked cook to leave me a cold meal, as I was uncertain what time I would be home. I was thankful I had made that arrangement, as I decided to call on Dr. Redding on the way back, as he was the only person who could answer one particular question on my mind. I decided to leave a note if he was out but, fortunately, I caught him just as he was about to leave to visit a patient. Not wishing to delay him, I asked my question at once, and he answered immediately, and without any doubt in his voice.

'No, ma'am. Mr. Fenton and the Comte were definitely not killed with the same knife. Nor do I believe they were murdered by the same man. The weapon used on Mr. Fenton had a narrow blade, and as you know, he was killed with a single thrust to his heart. Whereas the

Comte suffered a frenzied attack with a very much broader blade, and the murderer's clothes would have been covered in blood.' I thanked him and inquired if the constable had asked the same question. 'I'm afraid not, ma'am. But I will inform him of it.'

He went on his way then, and after I talked to Mudd about what the doctor had said, I rode home deep in thought. Once there I enjoyed my cold meal of bread, cheese and ham, with tomatoes from the garden, and thought about the murders. At first it had seemed to me that two men stabbed within a few miles of each other, in just three weeks, suggested there was only one murderer. But, considering what Dr. Redding had said, I did not think that was likely now. Yet, it was hard to imagine there were two murderers at large in our small community, both using knives to kill.

If, as I believed, the turncoat had killed Mr. Fenton, then who could have stabbed the Comte? For, the Comte had spent the last two years in Spain, and had only been here a few days, and was laid up in bed the whole time. So, what possible reason could anyone on the Island have had for murdering him?

I thought about what Mr. Pitt had said when Mr. Reevers and I met him in London. That he had every faith in our ability to find the man who'd killed Mr. Fenton. I shook my head from side to side, a sardonic smile on my lips. For, frankly, neither of us had any idea who the turncoat was. Nor did I know what to do next.

CHAPTER FOURTEEN

The day had started with dull skies, but the clouds had completely disappeared in the last hour and collecting a parasol I went outside to enjoy the sunshine. As I put up my parasol I saw Mr. Reevers riding towards the house. I walked over to greet him, thankful for this unexpected opportunity to discuss the Comte's murder, and our lack of progress in finding the traitor. A servant quickly took charge of his horse, and I suggested we went for a stroll in the garden. He agreed readily and I politely inquired if Mr. Morel had settled in at Norton House.

'Yes, Tom's no trouble at all. Actually he's gone to see Giles today. They worked together for a short time in Paris,' he said, and changing the subject he asked if I knew what had happened to the Comte. 'I've only had a garbled version from my groom.'

I repeated everything that Richard had told us and ended by saying, 'The constable is convinced Pink killed him, but I think it more likely that a man climbed through an open window during the heavy rain last night and stabbed the Comte. Dr. Redding said the knife used on the Comte had a much broader blade than the one that killed Mr. Fenton, and it was such a frenzied attack that the murderer's clothes would have been covered in blood.'

He murmured thoughtfully, 'Perhaps the Comte put up a fight. Although it wouldn't have been easy in his weakened state.'

'No, but he was the only one to get ashore alive when the yacht capsized in that storm.'

'A survivor,' he acknowledged. 'Only this time his luck ran out. Was anything stolen?'

'His rings. Apparently he wore four that were extremely valuable.'

'Really?' he responded, raising his eyebrows. 'The killer stole from Fenton too.' He didn't speak for a minute or two as we walked along the winding path through the flower beds. I guessed he was searching for a connection between the two murders, in much the same way as I had. But, like me, he clearly ended up with the same uncertain result, for he couldn't quite hide his exasperation when he muttered, 'Perhaps smugglers did kill Fenton after all.'

I understood how he felt. I wished the answer was that simple too, but as I told him quietly, 'The difficulty I have with that is, every instinct I possess tells me it wasn't smugglers.' Observing a faint smile on his lips, I remarked icily, 'I suppose you don't believe in a woman's instinct.'

'My dear girl, I would never be so rude. It so happens....'

'I am not your dear girl.'

'No,' he whispered softly. Foolishly, I turned to look at him, and the expression in his eyes left me in no doubt what he did wish for.

I took a deep breath. 'Mr. Reevers, working together for Mr. Pitt doesn't mean......'

He held up his hands in surrender. 'I beg your pardon. Actually I was about to explain it was instinct that saved me from the guillotine on the morning our agents were arrested.'

I glanced up at him in surprise. 'But you told me it was going for a walk that saved you.'

'That's what I've told everyone,' he admitted with a wry smile. 'But the truth is I was woken by a thunderstorm, and when I tried to go back to sleep, something kept urging me to get out of my lodging with all possible speed. In my business, you don't ignore that kind of instinct, no matter how hard it's raining. But it's not the kind of thing you admit to your colleagues.' I understood that and said so, whereupon he told me, 'And like you, my instinct tells me smugglers did not commit these murders.'

Reaching the walled garden, he opened the gate and politely waited for me to walk through first. As he followed, he observed, 'Not a soul in sight. Not even a gardener's boy.' He raised an amused eyebrow at me. 'What would your aunt say? Should I go and find a chaperone?'

I choked back the laughter rising in my throat and spluttered, 'Don't be absurd. We have to talk about these murders.'

'Must we?' he murmured provocatively. 'I'd much rather not.'

I took a deep breath. 'Mr. Reevers will you please be sensible.' I shook my head at him, cursing the tremble in my voice. The difficulty with my decision not to marry Mr. Reevers was that, when in his company, I began to weaken.

Determined to get a firmer hold on my emotions, I took a deep breath, and he, seeing I was about to give him another set-down, did as

I'd asked. 'Oh, very well, the murders it shall be. But I cannot see any possible connection between Fenton and the Comte.'

My heart sank at those words, for I had hoped he could suggest a reason why the murderer had killed both men. There had to be a connection, surely. And, again, I had that odd feeling we had missed something.

Strolling round the walled garden we talked through every detail we had learnt about the two men, including their backgrounds. 'Fenton lived in London,' Mr. Reevers said, 'but grew up in Kent. He was twenty-two, unmarried, educated at Eton and Cambridge, and had been a secret service messenger for almost a year. He was often sent to France, as he spoke the language perfectly. The Comte had a wife and son, and a large estate in the south of France, all of which he lost to the revolution two years ago. Since then he has lived quietly in Spain, until he set sail for London with two of his friends. He didn't meet anyone here except Richard, the doctor and your uncle.'

'Yes, and Fenton was killed to stop him warning you that the turncoat had betrayed all our Paris agents. But no-one knows why the Comte was murdered.'

'Or even if it was the same killer.'

In some despair, I said, 'But what was the motive? Robbery? That is the only thing that links the murders.'

'They were both stabbed,' he reminded me.

'Yes, but not with the same knife. Or even the same kind of knife. Nor were they killed in the same way. Fenton suffered a single blow to his chest, and the Comte endured a frenzied attack. Nor do they have anything in common. Mr. Fenton was a decent, brave, patriotic young man. The Comte treated his servants like slaves and was an absolute tyrant.'

'I agree, yet there must be an answer.'

That was when I told him I kept getting this odd feeling that we had missed something vital. Jago would have dismissed that without a thought, but Mr. Reevers didn't. 'In that case,' he said, 'let's go back to the beginning and check out everything carefully.'

Thus, the following day, assisted by Mudd, we made a thorough search of the area in Ledstone woods where Mr. Fenton's body had been left. The undergrowth was dry and we pulled out as much of it as we could, in the hope of finding some clue to help us. But there was nothing. We spent the next two days, with Richard's permission, going through everything in Mr. Hamerton's house with meticulous care, starting with the bedchamber the Comte had occupied. Again there was nothing. A few of the rooms were rather poky, forcing us to be in close proximity, but Mr. Reevers did not take advantage of it, much to my surprise. He appeared to be concentrating entirely on looking for anything that would lead us to the identity of the turncoat. Regrettably the whole exercise proved fruitless. And by then the Comte had been buried in Dittistone churchyard.

Spending so much time in the company of Mr. Reevers, yet having made up my mind not to marry him, I tried to behave with proper decorum. But the more I saw of him, the more I wanted to be with him, and the more I was forced to admit to myself what he really meant to me. Yet, I still refused to risk marriage.

In the beginning, when Mr. Pitt asked us to work together to solve Mr. Fenton's murder, I hadn't expected it to take long, and that Mr. Reevers would then be sent elsewhere. But we had made no progress at all. And our surveillance of Jago and Louis only showed that they had not put a foot wrong in any way. They continued to assist Mr. Arnold with the émigrés, and were so busy they asked Mr. Morel if he would help, which he kindly did for a day or two.

The following day Lucie and Marguerite had invited Aunt Thirza and Julia to Ledstone Place, to discuss ideas for decorating the nursery for the baby, as they both had a flair for such matters. Lucie also wanted to show them all the lovely things she had bought in London for the child, and to ask if they knew of a suitable nursemaid. She'd invited Lizzie and Gisele too, out of politeness, and told me I would be welcome to join them if I wished. Lizzie accepted, but Gisele did not wish to go. Fortunately, Lucie knew it was not the sort of thing I enjoyed and I was easily able to decline the invitation and thank her for being so understanding.

Mr. Reevers and I should have spent that day searching for Mr. Fenton's killer, but we were at our wits' end, unable to think of a single possibility we had not explored. It was then that an idea totally unrelated to that task, entered my head. The gathering of ladies at Ledstone Place meant that all the gentlemen would be at a loose end, and I decided to organise a picnic for them at Westfleet. When I told Mr. Reevers what I had in mind, he was most encouraging. 'That's a splendid idea. A relaxing day might help us to think more clearly.'

All the gentlemen accepted my last minute invitation, and the lovely weather we had been enjoying lately did not let us down. In fact, it was so hot I had the picnic table placed in the shade of the oak trees just beyond the end of the terrace. The servants brought out the food, which included jellies and fruit, as well as bread, cold meats and pies, wine, and jugs of freshly made lemonade.

Once everything was ready, my guests settled themselves at the table. Mr. Morel was impeccably dressed as usual, despite the heat, and as I left them to go back into the house, the others were teasing him over his amazing ability to look cool and neat in such hot weather. I was still smiling as I went inside to thank the servants for all their efforts and to suggest they had a picnic of their own, if they so wished. I was instantly greeted by Luffe, who informed me "The Times" had just arrived. And he added elatedly, 'The boy who brought it was bursting with news.' When he told me what all the excitement was about, I grabbed the newspaper and eagerly read the relevant report. It was the most wonderful news and after I'd read the thrilling account, I burst out happily, 'I must tell the others, Luffe.'

All the doors and windows were open, and even as I headed out onto the terrace, I could hear a great deal of banter about how a secret agent lived in France, their voices carrying well in the still air. I heard Giles say, 'Radleigh, do you remember that lodging I had when I first went to Paris. It was incredibly dirty, reeked of garlic, and....'

'It was a palace compared to the one I've just left,' Mr. Reevers interrupted, with a laugh, as I drew closer. 'It was down a dreadful dark alley with stinking, rotten filth everywhere. In fact, Tom --------------'

Mr. Morel broke in jovially, 'Nothing could be as bad as that ghastly place Louis and I shared when I first went to Paris.' He smiled at me as I reached the table where they were sitting, and went on, 'That was so rickety it actually fell down.'

Louis chortled, 'Luckily we weren't in it at the time.' That made the others fall about with so much laughter, tears ran down their cheeks. Tom Morel took out his pristine handkerchief and dabbed at his eyes, then he folded it with meticulous precision before returning it to his pocket.

As he did so, Jago declared, 'I don't know how any of you could bear to live in such absolute squalor. I insisted on something half decent.'

'You always were far too fastidious,' Louis joked, and told the others, 'Jago lived in clean lodgings, told everyone he was an artist, and only ever mixed with lawyers, doctors and other artists. While I got all the dirty jobs, wearing those ghastly sans-culottes clothes so that no-one would guess I was spying on the revolutionary leaders.'

'Well, Wickham wanted an agent to mix with professional French people who supported the revolution, and I was happy to do that. People talk a great deal when sitting for a portrait and the information I learnt proved to be most useful. Besides, there wouldn't have been any point in my wearing filthy clothing,' Jago protested. 'I mean – just look at my hands.'

'Soft and white,' Giles said, with a chuckle. 'The French would instantly have guessed you were an aristocrat, and carted you off to the guillotine in one of those appallingly grubby tumbrils.'

'My dear fellow,' Jago informed him in measured tones, 'I should have insisted on riding in one that was spotlessly clean. One must have standards, you know.'

That brought fresh shouts of merriment, and Tom Morel remarked, with slightly twitching lips, 'Louis could have persuaded his friend, Danton, to fix that for you.' Georges Danton had been a highly popular revolutionary leader.

Surprised though I was to discover that Jago had a sense of humour after all, I was even more astonished by what Mr. Morel had said about Louis. So was Richard, who instantly demanded, 'Good God, Louis. Did you really know Danton?'

'I did. Only for a few weeks though. I ran messages for him.'

'Yes,' Jago said. 'But he didn't know you could read, did he?'

Louis grinned. 'Just as well, or I would have been for the chop too.' Danton had been guillotined in April after Robespierre accused him of trying to overthrow the government. 'Those messages gave us some amazing information.'

'Very true,' Jago agreed. 'Think how much more we might have learnt if you hadn't fallen off your horse and injured your knee.'

'Don't be cruel, Jago,' Gisele protested. 'At least Louis is home for good, safe and sound.'

It was at this point that I finally got the chance to interrupt, but before I showed them the newspaper I said to Louis, 'You didn't tell me you knew Danton.'

'Well, it's not the sort of thing one boasts about in England.'

'What was he like?' I asked, out of curiosity.

'Ugly and lazy, but very witty. The people worshipped him and he was kind to me.'

Richard asked, 'How did you meet him, Louis?'.

'Oh, it was simple enough. I had a friend who knew him and he introduced me. I said all the right things about the revolution, and Danton gave me a job as a messenger. He wanted to put an end to The Terror, so there were lots of messages, but I was only with him about a month before I had my accident. Then I had to come home.'

'Just as well,' Giles said, 'or you might have been arrested and guillotined with him.'

'Louis lives a charmed life,' Jago commented. 'Always falls on his feet.' And he teased, 'He also managed to marry the most beautiful woman in London.'

Gisele blushed and made a modest, but not altogether convincing, protest that brought about a tiny break in conversation. That break finally enabled me to dramatically slam the newspaper down on the table, and announce with considerable glee, 'The Times has the most wonderful news. Robespierre is dead! He was guillotined!'

The shock on their faces quickly gave way to sheer delight. Giles grabbed the newspaper first and read out the report. The others listened intently, making the odd comment, and sat grinning happily as the list of Robespierre's associates, who were guillotined at the same time, made it clear that his reign had finally come to an end.

Everyone was ecstatic that this monster, responsible for the Terror in France, in which thousands of innocent people were guillotined, had perished in the same way as most of his victims. Terror had been the order of the day for the best part of a year. In that time anyone could be denounced for criticising the government, complaining about the lack of bread in the shops, or for failing to address their friends as "citizen." These and many other trivial things sent so many innocent people to the guillotine. But as we soon learnt, The Terror was over at last.

The meal was long and leisurely, the news putting everyone in a happy and cheerful mood. We were speculating on who would run France now when Luffe came to inform me two visitors had arrived, who wished to speak to Mr. Reevers. That gentleman immediately asked who the visitors were, but before my butler could answer, the two men appeared on the terrace and walked the few yards across to us.

Mr. Reevers drew his brows together and immediately demanded in a tone of barely disguised contempt, 'Knight? What the deuce are you doing here?'

Giles broke in, 'Just a minute, Radleigh.' Giles turned to me, 'Drusilla allow me to do the honours. Mr. Knight is one of our colleagues from the Alien Office. I'm afraid I'm not acquainted with the other gentleman.'

Mr. Knight bowed briefly and introduced his companion as Walter Brown. They were also introduced to Gisele, and then to Richard, and I was about to offer them some refreshment, when Mr. Knight looked directly at Mr. Reevers and asked if he might speak to him in private.

'Why?' was the bristling response. 'We're all friends here, Knight.' And I knew from his expression and from that of the other secret agents, that this was a man none of them liked.

The newcomer's eyes were full of malice as he said, 'Not in front of the ladies, surely?'

'Why not,' Mr. Reevers retorted. 'Best to have whatever it is out in the open, don't you think?'

'Very well.' A faint smirk of satisfaction hovered on Knight's lips. 'Don't say I didn't warn you.'

'Oh I won't. Come on then, out with it man.'

As the uninvited visitor took a letter from an inside pocket, Gisele whispered to me, 'Perhaps we should leave the gentlemen and go into the house, Drusilla.'

'You go if you want,' I said. 'I'm staying here.'

In the end she remained too and watched Mr. Knight hand the letter to Mr. Reevers. 'It's signed by Mr. Wickham,' he said, 'and confirms what I am about to say. We have been ordered to escort you back to London to face a charge of treason.'

CHAPTER FIFTEEN

'Treason?' Tom Morel exploded. 'Radleigh?' And he leapt to his feet so quickly, he accidentally jolted the table, causing the plates to jump and the one leftover melting jelly to wobble alarmingly. 'You must be out of your mind, Knight.'

'It was Mr. Wickham's decision, not mine,' Knight informed him.

'But you would have had your say,' pronounced Giles, angrier than I had ever seen him, for he never lost his temper.

Mr. Morel sat down again and I finally managed to find my voice. 'This is totally absurd. Mr. Reevers is working on a secret assignment of vital importance to our country.'

Knight turned his head slightly and looked at me as if I, as a woman, had no right to enter the conversation. 'I am aware of that,' he informed me in a dismissive manner.

Conscious I must keep calm, I inquired, 'Are you aware of what that assignment is?'

He was clearly annoyed at my making a second intervention, and pursing his lips, he answered brusquely, 'No, but Mr. Wickham is.'

It was then that Mr. Reevers got to his feet and towering over our exceedingly unwelcome visitor, addressed him in arctic tones. 'If you wish to leave Westfleet in one piece, Knight, you will treat Lady Drusilla with the greatest of respect. She is more intelligent than any man here and the country already owes her a greater debt than you could possibly imagine.' Knight did not answer and Mr. Reevers demanded, 'Do I make myself clear?' Knight glared at him, but gave a curt nod. 'Very well. Now, treason covers a multitude of things. What, in particular, am I supposed to have done?'

I admired his coolness in dealing with that awful man, for I was still far from calm, and itched to wipe the smirk off Knight's face when he asked Mr Reevers, 'Surely you don't wish me to explain the nature of the charge in front of your friends?'

'Certainly I do. I want them to hear what I'm accused of --- I have nothing to hide.' And that brought a chorus of unqualified support from his friends.

Knight glanced at his companion, who had not spoken yet, and looking round at us all in turn, he announced, 'I'm only doing my duty as ordered by Mr. Wickham.'

'And revelling in it, by God,' Mr. Morel declared, not hiding his revulsion. This brought even more fierce condemnation down on Knight, until Jago put a stop to it by urging us to let the man speak.

'Why?' Richard spluttered, his face red with fury. 'There's no greater patriot here than Radleigh. I say we tear up this letter and send these two men back to London empty-handed.'

At which Louis jumped out of his seat and clapped a hand on Mr. Reevers' shoulder. 'I'll stand with you on that. Who will join us?'

My uncle, who had sat white-faced, quietly listening, declared in a clear voice, 'No. You cannot do that, Louis. We all know this is a stupid mistake, and that Mr. Reevers is innocent, but he must go to London and answer the charge. There is no other way. If he doesn't go willingly, it will be taken as an admission of guilt.'

We all listened to what he'd said, but none of us uttered a single word in response, for as we quickly realised, my uncle was right. But being right didn't make it any easier. My uncle looked up at Knight, who was still standing, and suggested that he told Mr. Reevers exactly what he was accused of.

The sun was at its hottest by then, and the two visitors, who had stood with the rays shining straight onto their faces for a good ten minutes, were perspiring freely. Mr. Brown had mopped his brow several times with his handkerchief, and at last, Mr. Knight followed his example.

We sat in the shade provided by the trees, but it failed to reach the two men. I did not offer them a seat out of the sun, nor did anyone else. Sheer outrage at the reason they were here made us ignore their discomfort in a manner we would not have done with any normal visitor.

Knight returned his handkerchief to his pocket before pronouncing, 'Recently, Mr. Wickham was given proof that Mr. Reevers was a double agent.'

This statement sparked off such a furore of protests that Mr. Reevers was unable to speak for several minutes. When everyone had finally quietened down, he asked in a dignified manner, 'What was this evidence? And who provided it?'

'I'm not at liberty to say,' Knight retorted.

Immediately, Richard jumped to his feet and grabbed Knight by the scruff of his neck. 'We'll see about that, you little pipsqueak. I've met your kind before. You don't have an ounce of guts in your entire body. You're the type who enjoys hiding behind your orders.'

Clearly petrified, Knight blurted out in a high-pitched whine, 'Let me go at once, do you hear?' And begged his companion, Mr. Brown, to help him. But Brown was busily mopping his face again and I had the impression that he, too, detested Knight.

Before the situation got out of hand, Mr. Reevers intervened. 'I appreciate the thought,' he told Richard, with an understanding smile. 'But it won't answer. Mr. Frère is right. I must go to London.'

Knight managed to regain control of his voice and said he was pleased that Mr. Reevers had seen sense. 'I have orders to keep you under lock and key until we leave in the morning.'

A statement that finally made Mr. Reevers lose his calmness. 'Don't be ridiculous. I've said I'll come with you. Do you doubt my word?'

'My instructions are to------'

'Your instructions may go to the devil! I need time to put my affairs in order.'

Knight then took a pistol from inside his jacket, and before Richard could intervene again, Mr. Morel said wearily, 'Look, it so happens I'm staying with Mr. Reevers. Surely that will suffice?' Knight hesitated, and Mr. Morel looked him straight in the eye. 'Or do you doubt my word too?'

Knight lowered his gaze and said, 'No, sir. Of course not.'

Mr. Reevers' face lightened a little and I saw a devilish glint in his eyes as he said, 'There's an inn a mile or so down the road from my house. I have to go past it to get anywhere. You can put up there overnight.'

Giles tightened his lips slightly, for as everyone in this part of the Island knew, this was a disreputable low class inn that no gentleman would dream of entering. Frankly, I could think of nowhere better for Knight to stay.

With so little time to put his affairs in order, Mr. Reevers left at once, declining all offers of assistance, assuring us all that Tom Morel would do whatever was needed. As he said goodbye to everyone I saw him exchange a meaningful glance with Giles, who immediately engaged Knight in conversation. Whereupon, Mr. Reevers turned to me, took my hand and raised it to his lips, but instead of taking his leave of me, he murmured, 'The turncoat must be behind this. Find him Drusilla, or I'm a dead man.'

Before I could answer he abruptly turned away from me, and shortly afterwards I watched him ride off with Mr. Morel, accompanied by Knight and Brown. The rest of us sat around in a state of shock, and Gisele was so upset she kept dabbing her eyes with her handkerchief. We talked over all that had happened, our voices filled with disbelief. As we did not know what evidence they had against him, or how Mr. Wickham had come by it, no-one was able to suggest a way of helping Mr. Reevers.

Eventually Richard and Giles went home, and soon after that my aunt returned. I left the others to explain to her what had happened, while I walked in the garden. I needed time on my own to think. Mr. Wickham was an honourable man and would not have ordered the arrest unless he was convinced there was a case to answer. And I decided the turncoat must have provided the so-called evidence for the arrest, intending to see that Mr. Reevers paid the ultimate price.

I walked through the orchard with Mr. Reevers' final words ringing in my ears. But how was I to identify this traitor? And find proof of his guilt? We had already spent more than three weeks trying to pin him down, and failed miserably. Yet, somehow, I had to get to the truth on my own.

Frankly I did not know which way to turn. But if I didn't find out who he was, I would never see Mr. Reevers again. For, he could do nothing to prove his innocence while he was in prison. If I identified the turncoat, Mr. Reevers would live. If I failed, he would die, and I would have to live with that for the rest of my life.

Slipping quietly into my workroom, I added today's events to the information on the sheets on the wall. I carefully studied the facts already there, but saw nothing odd. Over dinner we talked of little else but Mr. Reevers, although my uncle did his utmost to assure me that all would be well by saying, 'He'll soon be back on the Island, Drusilla. It's utter nonsense to suggest he's a double agent.'

When we finally ran out of things to say, my aunt gave an account of the very pleasant day she had spent at Ledstone. But I only half listened, as I could not get my fears for Mr. Reevers out of my mind. I believed in English justice, but for the first time in my life I saw how skilfully faked evidence could result in an innocent man being convicted and executed.

114

The turncoat must be responsible for Mr. Fenton's murder and perhaps the Comte's too. I was absolutely convinced he'd fixed Mr. Reevers' arrest to keep him out of action while he seized Mr. Pitt and took him to Paris. That night I decided that the first thing I must do was find out what evidence had led to the arrest. And who had provided it. I considered asking Mr. Wickham, but as we'd only met once he might refuse to tell me, and I could not afford to waste time. Better by far to write to Mr. Pitt. He'd told me to contact him if I ever needed assistance, and I had never needed it as badly as I did now. With that decision made I finally fell into a dreamless sleep.

I woke a little later than usual in the morning and my first thought was that Mr Reevers would already be on his way to London. I saw too that the hot sunny days we had enjoyed for a week or more, had given way to much cooler, windier weather. Once I was dressed I walked down to the stables and sent Mudd to Norton House to ask the messenger Wickham had assigned to us, to call on me as soon as possible.

When I went into the breakfast parlour, Luffe told me Jago and the Gauvans had already eaten, and as my aunt and uncle had not yet appeared, I breakfasted alone. As soon as I'd finished I headed for my workroom and wrote to Mr. Pitt. Then I went in search of Jago and found him sitting at a desk in the library going through some papers. I explained I had an urgent letter to be taken to London and asked if my messenger could be conveyed to Portsmouth in his yacht, which was lying idle in Yarmouth.

'I have no objection,' Jago said. He clearly misunderstood who the letter was for, as he went on, 'I'm sure it will be a comfort to Mr. Reevers to receive a letter from you, but he may not be allowed to reply you know.' I considered telling him I was writing to Mr. Pitt, but decided not to, as I still did not know the identity of the turncoat. I found it hard to believe it could be Jago, but then I had not thought Toby East was a traitor either. And Mr. Pitt had decreed that no agent who had been in Paris when Toby East went over to the French was to be considered above suspicion, no matter how high his position in the secret service. And Jago's position was very high.

When I didn't answer at once he said, 'Drusilla, I must talk to you about what happened yesterday and-----' He stopped and pulled out a chair for me. 'It would be best if you sat down.'

Exasperated, I burst out, 'For heaven's sake, Jago. Stop treating me like a helpless invalid.'

He pursed his lips in annoyance. 'I beg your pardon, but I believe you should prepare yourself for the worst.'

I glared at him. 'Do you really? Well, I won't. No matter what you say.'

The expression on his face reminded me of an occasion years ago, when Mudd came to tell me my favourite horse at that time had broken his leg and had to be put down. I could take sympathy from Mudd, but not from Jago. In this mood he was insufferable, but as I turned to leave the room, he urged, 'Drusilla, I beg of you to listen to me.' He picked up a letter from his desk and in his gravest voice declared, 'You will want to see this. It lists the names of our agents who were guillotined.'

I almost snatched it out of his hand, but when I saw that none of them had escaped execution, I muttered in despair, 'So the turncoat wasn't one of our agents in Paris.'

'I'm afraid not.'

I sank into the chair he'd provided and looked at the names again. For, if it wasn't one of them, then it had to be a man I knew. And that filled me with great sadness. 'Such fine young men gone,' I said. 'The traitor has much to answer for.'

'Indeed.'

Only then did I notice the date at the top of the letter, and I instantly demanded, 'When did this come?'

'A week ago, but-----'

'A *week*?' I echoed in a mixture of exasperation and disgust. 'Why did you keep it from me? Mr. Pitt told you to inform me of everything that happened here.'

'Yes, but if I had done so, you would have realised who the turncoat was, and I didn't want to upset you, Drusilla.'

'Upset me?' I spluttered angrily. 'What on earth are you talking about, Jago?'

'If you recall, no-one believed Toby East was a traitor. Everyone thought he was a true patriot. Well, the turncoat wasn't one of our Paris agents, so he must be back in England now, and that means he will be someone we both know and like. You do see that, don't you, Drusilla?'

'Of course I do,' I snapped.

'He is also a very clever man, and-----'

116

'I know that too,' I broke in.

'In that case, you must understand why Mr. Wickham ordered Radleigh's arrest.' I gasped out loud, but before I could speak, he hurried on, 'Now all our Paris agents are dead, Radleigh must be the turncoat. There is no-one else it can be.'

'Don't be ridiculous,' I hissed. Determined not to listen to such rubbish, I jumped up and marched towards the door.

'You should hear me out, Drusilla.'

'Why?' I muttered between clenched teeth, as I reached the door and started to open it.

'Radleigh was the only agent to escape from Paris.'

'That's not true,' I retorted, opening the door wider. 'Morel got out too.'

'Yes, but he was the one who rushed back to London to warn Mr. Wickham that the turncoat had betrayed all our other agents. So it can't be him. Nor can it be Louis. I know him far too well. Don't forget Mr. Reevers was sent to Paris to seek out the turncoat, but failed to do so.' I started to protest, but he held up his hand and insisted, 'Kindly allow me to finish. There's something else I really must bring to your attention. I understand you were involved, no doubt in a minor way, in bringing about the downfall of that treacherous Fat Badger Society earlier this year. The organisation Toby East used to try to start a French-style revolution here.'

I inclined my head. I had indeed been involved, although *not* in a small way. He went on, 'I'm told that when Mr. Reevers caught up with East, only one door stood between that contemptible traitor and the King, yet Radleigh failed to shoot East.'

The memories that brought back made me swing round on my heel. I stepped back into the room and slammed the door shut so that we would not be overheard. 'Mr. Reevers and Mr. East were great friends. How would you feel if you were told a close friend was a traitor, and a few minutes later you were expected to kill him?' I demanded in scathing tones. 'Imagine if it was Louis?'

I saw a glimmer of pain in his eyes, but he straightened his shoulders and said, 'I would do my duty.'

'Yes,' I said. 'I do believe you would.'

'Duty to one's country comes first, Drusilla. The King's life was at stake, and if another agent hadn't shot East, the King would now be dead. And we could easily be in the midst of a revolution. Or perhaps you didn't know that.'

I glared at him. 'I know *exactly* what happened.' In fact I believed that, apart from Mr. Reevers and myself, only the King, Mr. Pitt, and Mr. Dundas, who was Secretary of state for the Home department at that time, knew the full details.

'Really?' he said, raising an eyebrow. 'I suppose Radleigh told you.'

'No, he did not.'

'But he must have done. I was told in the strictest confidence, so how else could you possibly have known about it?'

I walked back to the door, opened it, and swung round to face him. 'How do you *think*, Jago?' And I left the room, shutting the door quietly behind me. Whether he would work out what part I had played, I neither knew nor cared. It was utter nonsense to suggest Mr. Reevers was the traitor. I was so furious with Jago I had to go outside to cool off.

It was true that Mr. Reevers hadn't found out who had betrayed all the other agents in Paris, but he'd only been there for about two weeks. And, yes, he had escaped the guillotine, but only because he happened to go out early on the morning the others were arrested. It was nonsense to suggest such things were proof of guilt. After all, Tom Morel had escaped from Paris too, and no-one had suggested he could be the traitor.

Every one of the agents recently guillotined had been in Paris when Mr. East went over to the French. That left just four other agents who had also been there at that time. Jago, Louis, Tom Morel and Mr. Reevers. One of them had to be the traitor. Not Mr. Reevers, of course. His arrest was an appalling mistake, no matter what Jago said. But it did explain why Jago had kept very quiet when Knight appeared at the picnic.

I considered the other three agents. Only Jago and Louis had known Mr. Fenton was on the Island. Jago had not left Westfleet on the morning of the murder, but Louis had gone to see Mr. Arnold half an hour before Mr. Fenton left for Yarmouth. So he could have killed him. It was also possible for him to have murdered the Comte too. No other agent could have committed both murders. But was he really the turncoat?

Or could Jago and Louis be working together, as they had in France? In truth, I did not believe Jago was involved, but I hadn't thought Toby East was working for the French either. Therefore I had to keep an open mind.

If it wasn't one, or both of them, that only left Tom Morel. But he was in London when Mr. Fenton was killed, and we wouldn't have known the traitor had betrayed all our Paris agents if he hadn't rushed back from France to inform Mr. Wickham of that terrible event.

It was so hard to accept that one of them was the turncoat. But then, earlier in the year, I had thought of Toby East as a good friend and a true patriot. He had fooled me for a long time. Now everything pointed to Louis, although I did not have one scrap of evidence to prove it was him. I prayed with all my heart that he was innocent, but how was I to find out, when this traitor did not seem to have made a single mistake?

Again I had the oddest feeling that I'd missed something vital. But what? I tried going back to the way I had solved the murders in the Saxborough family, and those connected with the Fat Badger Society. Small clues had given me the answer in both cases. But if there were any such minor clues here, I had not spotted them.

CHAPTER SIXTEEN

By the time the messenger assigned by Mr. Wickham to Mr. Reevers and myself had arrived at Westfleet, I'd managed to calm down enough to quietly explain why I wanted him to sail on the next tide. Jago sent the necessary order to Captain Barr, and I urged the messenger to return to the Island with all possible speed, impressing on him that Mr. Reevers' life was at stake.

That afternoon, feeling the need for some fresh air, I went for a ride on the Downs, despite the ominous black clouds forming in the west. Accompanied by Mudd I instantly urged Orlando into a gallop, and when I eventually came to a halt, I had to wait for Mudd to catch up, but I felt better for the exercise, and as we made our way slowly back, I told him what had happened to Mr. Reevers. Only to find that, as usual, servants already knew what was going on.

I asked if he'd noticed anything unusual about any of our guests or visitors, but he shook his head. 'I'm afraid not, my lady.'

'Well, keep your eyes and ears open, John. If we are to save Mr. Reevers we must find the turncoat, and frankly I simply don't know where to start.'

There was no mistaking the concern in his eyes, but he said, 'I'm sure something will come to you, my lady. Murderers make mistakes and.....'

'This one hasn't.'

'Perhaps he has, my lady, but you may not have realised it yet.' Riding back to Westfleet I prayed Mudd was right. But would I realise it before it was too late?

Visitors kept me busy for the rest of the afternoon. The Tanfields, Tom Morel and Giles were so worried about Mr. Reevers they begged me to let them know the instant I had news of him, which I promised to do. Giles stayed on after the others had left and we took a walk through my walled garden.

He gazed at me thoughtfully as we strolled along the path. 'Drusilla, I may no longer be part of the secret service, but it is clear to me that you and Radleigh have been trying to discover who murdered Fenton and the Comte. I also believe, as I'm sure you do too, that the turncoat is trying to get rid of Radleigh, and has provided Wickham with false evidence he cannot ignore.'

'Yes, I am aware of that.'

'Well, if I can assist you in any way, please don't hesitate to ask.'

I thanked him and promised to do so if I needed help. I couldn't tell him all the details, of course, but as Mr. Reevers was his friend, cousin, and also his heir until Lucie produced a son, Giles would do everything he could to prove Mr. Reevers was innocent. But I did not want to involve him, not now he was married and would soon become a father. I did not want to do anything that would ruin his happy life, and I hoped I would never need to do so.

Before he left, Giles invited us all to dinner on Saturday, and added, 'The Tanfields and Tom Morel will also be there.'

'Is Lizzie included?'

'Of course.'

'Jago will be pleased,' I said. I also wished Jago had the sense to see Mr. Reevers could not possibly be the turncoat. To suggest he'd recruited Toby East, in order to start a French-style revolution in England, was absurd. For, there was no greater patriot in the whole of Britain than Mr. Reevers.

I prayed that the messenger would return on Saturday, even though many things could prevent a speedy return. Such as bad weather, Mr. Pitt being away from home, or too busy to deal with my request immediately. If he didn't return today, he would not be back until Monday. So, when Luffe informed me late in the afternoon that the messenger had arrived, I was overwhelmed with relief.

When the messenger handed me the letter, and I saw my name inscribed on it in the great man's own hand, it took all my willpower not to break the seal at once. First, however, I thanked the messenger for his efforts, inquired after his journey, and suggested he went to get some well-earned rest.

I rang for Luffe to see him out, and once I was alone I opened the letter, expecting to see the evidence Mr. Wickham had against Mr. Reevers. But the letter began in a most startling way, with an invitation for my aunt, my uncle and myself to join Mr. Pitt at Walmer Castle for a week from the first of September. And he went on to say..........................

By then, I hope to have all the information you require, and we will be in a better position to discuss the situation at length. Do not worry about Mr. Reevers, ma'am. He is quite comfortable in the Tower.

'The Tower,' I gasped out loud. Why had they taken him there? The Tower of London was where they imprisoned notorious traitors. Usually until their execution. How could anyone possibly be comfortable there?

Mr. Pitt ended by saying that he looked forward to seeing me on Monday the first of September. It was clearly a command, not a request. It was also the same week that Jago and the Gauvans would be there. Perhaps he had a reason for wanting us all to be present at the same time. But I found it immensely frustrating that he had failed to tell me what the evidence was against Mr. Reevers. For, how was I to prove his innocence without that knowledge?

Once I'd calmed down, I went in search of my aunt and uncle, as we had little time in which to prepare for such a journey, and my aunt did not care to be hurried. My uncle was sitting on the terrace, reading "The Times," and I could see Aunt Thirza in the distance, strolling through the gardens. When I reached Uncle Charles, he spoke first, informing me there was an account of the Comte's murder in his newspaper. 'It doesn't say much,' he said, passing the newspaper to me and pointing to a small paragraph reporting that the Comte de Saint Martin, an émigré from France, had been murdered in his bed at Dittistone on the Isle of Wight. And that the assassin had not yet been apprehended.

'Nothing helpful there,' I agreed absently.

He looked at me more intently. 'I can see you are full of news, Drusilla. I hope it is something good this time.'

'Well, I think so,' I said, smiling.

'In that case, I'll go and collect your aunt and you can tell us together.'

He walked off into the gardens and I watched from the terrace as he explained why he wanted her to come back to the house. Judging by the way she was waving her arms about, I guessed she didn't want to leave the garden, and I chuckled to myself that even my uncle had trouble persuading her at times. I knew how he felt, for she rarely did what I suggested. Eventually, however, he succeeded in getting her to return. When she reached me, she instantly demanded, in barely concealed irritation, 'What's this all about, Drusilla. I was enjoying watching the bees and the butterflies.'

'I'm sorry,' I said, 'but I thought you would want to know straightaway that Mr. Pitt has invited us all to Walmer Castle for a week from the first of September.'

'The first?' Aunt Thirza exclaimed. 'But that's a week on Monday.'

I smiled. 'Yes. It's exciting, isn't it? If we cross to Portsmouth next Wednesday, we can spend two or three days on the road and finish the journey on the Monday morning. We'll rest on the Sunday of course.'

It was several minutes before I was given the chance to say another word, for my aunt droned on and on about the difficulties of arranging such a journey in so short a time, but as I was quite certain she wanted to go, I knew these difficulties would be overcome. When she finally paused for breath, she asked why we had been invited.

'Oh, I imagine it's his way of thanking us for allowing Jago and Louis to use Westfleet as a base for assisting Mr. Arnold.'

Aunt Thirza accepted this without question, but I caught the look of disbelief on my uncle's face, and in the morning when he joined me for an early breakfast, he immediately spoke about our visit to Walmer. 'Am I permitted to know the real reason for this invitation, Drusilla?'

I laughed. 'By all means. Mr. Pitt said he wishes to talk to me at length.'

'About Mr. Reevers?'

'Yes. And other things.'

He grimaced when I told him Mr. Reevers was in the Tower. 'Poor fellow. Surely they must realise he is innocent.' A lump came into my throat and stopped me answering, and seeing this, my uncle reached across the table and put his hand over mine to comfort me. 'If anyone can get out of this awful situation, he can. And he will. You'll see.' He was only trying to cheer me up, for it was not easy for anyone to get out of the Tower of London. At least, not alive.

That evening we went in the carriage to Ledstone Place for the dinner party Giles was giving. It was a pleasant occasion, although rather overshadowed by our concern for Mr. Reevers. This was made worse when Marguerite learned that it wasn't only Jago and the Gauvans who had been invited to Walmer Castle.

She exclaimed in despair, 'Oh, not you too, Drusilla.'

'It's only for a week,' I pointed out. 'And it is an honour to be invited.'

Giles quickly changed the subject by asking Tom Morel what his plans were, and was told, 'Actually I'm thinking of leaving next week too, provided Mr. Arnold no longer requires my services. I'm dining with him tomorrow, so I'll know for certain then. But it's time I moved on. It'll soon be September and I haven't booked a passage home yet.'

Marguerite burst out, 'But, if you leave too Mr. Morel, there won't be any well-mannered young gentlemen left on the Island to dine with us.'

'Well, that's put me in my place,' Giles said, tongue-in-cheek, as obviously he dined with her almost every day.

Marguerite patted his hand. 'Don't be silly, I didn't mean you, Giles. You are the most well-mannered young man I know.'

'If I am, Mama, it's entirely due to you,' he teased.

The evening was clearly enjoyed by Jago and Lizzie, who spent as much time together as they could. Jago hardly took his eyes off her, which was not surprising, as she wore a pretty sky blue dress that enhanced the beauty of her eyes, figure, and hair. As Jago was leaving for Walmer on Monday I wondered if they would come to an understanding before he left, although he couldn't make her an offer until he'd spoken to her father.

I went to church as usual that Sunday morning, where my aunt eagerly spread the news about our invitation to Walmer. Everyone was most impressed, and asked so many questions that I didn't get a chance to talk to Julia and Richard alone. I decided to call on them that afternoon to make my farewells before going to Walmer, realising I would be too busy to do so over the next two days. Soon after I arrived Julia persuaded me to stay to dinner, as Richard had an engagement that evening. I was happy to agree and she sent a message to Westfleet to inform my aunt and uncle of my change of plan. It would mean a quiet evening for them as Jago and the Gauvans were dining with Captain Barr on board Jago's schooner. But a quiet evening before a long journey was not a bad thing.

I had a lovely relaxing evening too, as Julia insisted we did not mention the murders or Mr. Reevers' arrest, as everything that could be said about it had already been discussed at great length, and she wanted to spend a couple of hours talking of innocuous things. Thus, we spoke of family matters and laughed at Edward's latest exploits and the trouble he gave his nursemaid. Talking of servants led her on to ask, 'By the way, when is your maid getting married?'

124

'On the twenty-seventh of September. I will miss Gray. She's very good at her job.'

'Have you found anyone else yet?'

I shook my head. 'If you hear of anyone suitable, do let me know.'

She promised to do so and knowing Julia I felt sure she would have two or three girls lined up for me to see when I returned from Walmer. By the time I left, the weather had become so excessively blustery that Julia said, 'I'll get one of our grooms to escort you home.'

'There's no need for that, Julia.' It was only a mile. 'I'll be home in five minutes.'

She began to protest, but by then I was already in the saddle, and with a cheery farewell I set off down the hill at a sensible pace. Away from the shelter of the house, I was exposed to the full force of the wind, which had got up with a vengeance, with frequent violent gusts. Orlando was a calm horse as a rule, but he didn't like this kind of weather. Half way down the hill I leant forward to pat him and speak words of reassurance. As I did so, something whizzed past my left ear, and a second later I heard a strange thwacking noise. Quickly looking round I saw a knife sticking out of the trunk of a large tree.

At the same time the wind brought down a huge branch from an overhanging tree, which crashed across the road right in front of Orlando. He squealed in terror, rose up so quickly on to his hind legs, that I lost my grip on the reins and began to slip out of the saddle at the very moment Orlando leapt over the branch.

The instant he landed on the other side he bolted down the hill and I desperately clung onto his mane for I knew that unless I stayed on his back, this would be my last day on earth.

CHAPTER SEVENTEEN

Orlando shot down the road like a bullet, but by hanging on to his mane I was able to slowly inch myself back into the saddle. By the time we reached the sharp corner near the bottom of the hill, I finally managed to get the reins back in my hands. But even so, we flew past the parsonage and when the Manor came into sight I had only been able to slow Orlando to a canter.

Mudd, who had been to Dittistone to see his father, was waiting for me at the stables. His eyebrows shot up in alarm when he saw Orlando's flanks were soaked in sweat. He instantly wanted to know what had happened and I heard the worry in his voice, but I could not speak in that moment, for my whole body was still trembling. I looked down at him and he asked in much greater anxiety, 'Are you all right, my lady?'

Wiping the sweat from my brow I finally managed to whisper, 'Yes, thank you.' I dismounted slowly and rather shakily handed him the reins. Aware I was breathing far too quickly, I took some long deep breaths to try to calm myself. But when I told him how close I had come to being killed, he burst out, 'I should have come with you.'

'It was my decision, not yours, John,' I said quietly. 'Mrs. Tanfield offered to send a groom with me, but I refused that too. I did not think my life was in danger in this business. Clearly I was wrong.'

'Did you see who it was, my lady?'

'No. I didn't even catch a glimpse of him.' I shuddered at the thought of who it could have been, and after a moment, I said, 'Mr. Reevers can't be at Walmer now he's imprisoned in the Tower of London. Clearly the turncoat doesn't want me there either. So that must be where he plans to capture Mr. Pitt.'

Mudd agreed, but he did not suggest I shouldn't go out alone again, as most grooms would have done. For, having known me since I was three, he understood how my mind worked, and knew I would never venture out alone again after such a hair-raising episode. I was only too well aware how extremely fortunate I was to have survived that attempt on my life. Even so I did not tell anyone else about the incident. For, in two days time we would be setting off for Walmer, and I would be surrounded by people on the journey, and at the Castle.

On walking into the house I found my aunt and uncle in the sitting room reading, and learnt that Jago and the Gauvans had not yet returned from dining with Captain Barr. They appeared about an hour later, assuring us they'd had a splendid evening. As they were making an early start in the morning they soon retired for the night, saying they looked forward to seeing us all at Walmer in a week's time.

It was a clear night and not long afterwards I went out into the garden to look at the stars and enjoy the warm air. I had not gone far when, to my surprise, I saw Jago sitting on a garden bench with his head in his hands. I thought he had gone straight to bed after saying good night to us, but not wishing to intrude, I would have walked quietly away, if he hadn't heard me approaching and looked up. In the moonlight I caught a glimpse of extreme distress on his face before he quickly adopted his normal expression. Rather hesitantly I asked, 'Is something wrong, Jago?'

He shook his head, but as he liked to keep so much hidden from me and I had no idea whether this particular worry affected me or not, I retorted, 'Well, that's clearly not true. Is it something I ought to know about?'

'No,' he whispered. 'It's nothing to do with the turncoat.' He turned and looked at me, and the absolute desolation in his eyes made me catch my breath. 'It's Lizzie.'

'Oh?' I queried, not quite knowing what to say.

'I cannot marry her.'

I sat beside him on the seat and asked, 'Why not?'

'Oh, come on, Drusilla. You know why. I owe it to my family to marry someone more suitable. My father will insist on it.'

'But her family is perfectly respectable, Jago. Her father isn't in trade or anything like that. He's a gentleman.'

'Yes, but ever since we acquired the title, every duchess in our family has been a member of the aristocracy.' Putting his head back into his hands, he muttered, 'I've behaved very badly. I should never have allowed it to get this far. Only she is so enchanting, Drusilla, I cannot bear to give her up. But I have no choice. I have to do it.' He dropped his hands and looked up at me again, his face lined with anguish. 'Somehow I have to tell her. I must. I absolutely must.'

127

'Well, you can't do so yet. You're leaving for Walmer in the morning.'

'I know. I thought of writing a letter, but that's the coward's way out. I cannot do that to her. I will speak to her when I return from Walmer. It will break her heart. But my father will insist I do my duty and put my family's name before everything else.'

There was nothing I could say. I knew what life was like in the highest families in the land, and Jago wasn't a rebel. He sat staring into space for a few more minutes, then got to his feet and offered to escort me back into the house. I felt so sorry for him that, for once, I allowed him to do so.

That night I lay awake for a long time. At first I thought of Jago and Lizzie, but there was nothing I could do to help them, and then my mind returned to the attempt on my life. For, I was only too aware that if I hadn't leant forward in the saddle to keep Orlando calm in the violently windy weather, the knife would not have missed me. And, in all probability, I would now be dead.

Early on Monday Lord Elvington and the Gauvans set off for Walmer Castle. They went by sea in Jago's yacht, leaving the Island two days before us as they had to report to Mr. Wickham in London first. Jago seemed to be in command of his emotions again, remarking that he thought it a pity our invitation had come at the last minute, or we could all have gone together on his yacht. I suspected he regretted letting me see how much Lizzie Ford meant to him, so I did not refer to his dilemma, but merely said all that was proper. I did enjoy the fresh sea air, but I had never liked the fact that I could not get off a yacht whenever I felt like it. At least by travelling overland we could stop at an inn for refreshment and a change of horses, which would enable us to take a short walk to stretch our legs.

After our visitors had left, my aunt remarked that the house seemed decidedly empty, but I barely noticed, as I was still rather shaken up by the attempt on my life, and was content to remain at home preparing for our journey to Walmer.

I'd arranged for us to stay at the Rose and Crown in Cowes on Tuesday night, as we were due to leave for Portsmouth on Wednesday morning. We planned to set off in time to dine at the inn, but at around eleven on Tuesday morning, I was giving Luffe his orders for looking after Westfleet while we were away, when I saw Mr. Arnold riding up

128

to the house. I went into the drawing room and when my welcome visitor was ushered in, I begged him to be seated and offered refreshment, which he politely refused.

'I mustn't stay long, ma'am, but I promised Mr. Morel I would deliver this letter to you,' he said, taking it from his pocket and handing it to me. 'He asked me to express his deep regret for not taking his leave of you in person, but he sailed for New York on.....'

'He's gone back to America?' I exclaimed in surprise.

He nodded. 'This very morning. On the "Frederica." A lovely ship too. Very modern.'

'But I understood he was taking a leisurely tour of our country before returning home at the end of September.'

'That was his original plan, ma'am. In fact, only the other day he told me he meant to visit Devon next. With everyone at Westfleet going to Walmer, there was very little to keep him here, and he felt rather awkward about living at Norton House while Mr. Reevers was under arrest.'

'Yes, that would make anyone feel uncomfortable. But what made him return to America in such haste?'

'Well, I'd invited the captain of the "Frederica" to dine with us on Sunday. He's American, and thinking Mr. Morel would enjoy meeting a fellow countryman, I asked him to join us. When he mentioned, during the meal, that he planned to return to America soon, the captain immediately offered him the best cabin on the ship at half price, explaining it would otherwise be unoccupied, due to the sudden death of the passenger who had reserved it. Mr. Morel promised to think about it, and the captain promptly invited us both to dine with him on board last night, and he told Mr. Morel that if he wanted to accept the offer, he should bring his luggage with him. And that's what he did ma'am, having decided it was too good an opportunity to miss.'

I saw the sense of that and asked, 'What time did he sail?'

'Around daybreak. So he will be well on his way now.' When I didn't answer, he said in his kindly way, 'I can see this has come as a shock ma'am, but I feel it's only natural he should want to return home. Although I must say I will miss him. He has been most helpful with the émigrés, but thankfully the numbers have dropped considerably since Robespierre's death, and we can manage now.'

'That is good news,' I said.

'It is, ma'am. I don't mind admitting we've had a very difficult time of it. Still, I mustn't keep you chattering about my problems. You will have much to do before you leave for Walmer, but I shall look forward to hearing about the Castle and how Mr. Pitt kept everyone entertained. A great man, Mr. Pitt. A very great man.'

'Indeed he is.' I liked Mr. Arnold, but wished I could be sure that every other gentleman who had crossed the threshold at Westfleet lately was as loyal to England as he was. As he stood up to take his leave, I promised I would invite him and his wife to dine with us after our return, so that I could fulfil his wish to hear all about our trip. As soon as I was alone again I broke the seal on Mr. Morel's letter, unfolded the single sheet of paper and read what he had written the previous day.

My dear Lady Drusilla,

I am writing to you in some haste as I am leaving for New York on tomorrow's early morning tide. My original intention, as you know, was to go home next month after I'd toured this beautiful country. But, as Mr. Arnold will have explained, I was unexpectedly offered the most expensive cabin on the "Frederica" at half price. What with that and the weather looking set fair, it seemed too good an opportunity to miss, especially as I regret to say I am a poor sailor.

I am sorry to be leaving when Mr. Reevers is still under arrest, but I hope, and believe, the matter will soon be happily resolved.

Please accept my sincere gratitude for the hospitality you have offered me during my stay. It has been a delight and a real pleasure, ma'am, to have made your acquaintance, and that of your aunt and uncle. Should you, or Mr. and Mrs. Frère, travel to America at any time, I would be delighted to reciprocate with true American hospitality.

I beg you to forgive me for not taking my leave of you in person, but time is short and I have a mountain of letters to write.

I remain,
Your servant, ma'am.
Tom Morel.

I sat for some time, thinking about all that had happened in the past week. It began with the Comte's murder, then Mr. Reevers was arrested, and someone had tried to kill me as I rode home after dining with the Tanfields. Nor was that the end of our troubles for, when Mr. Pitt was at Walmer, I was certain the turncoat planned to abduct him.

130

I was still staring unseeingly out at the garden when Aunt Thirza came in and demanded to know what I was doing lounging about when there was so much to be done before we set off for Cowes. In answer I showed her Mr. Morel's letter, and her response to the fact that he'd failed to take leave of us personally did not surprise me. 'Well, it's no more than I expected,' she said. 'Americans have no manners.'

The crossing from Cowes to Portsmouth the next day was rather tedious, as there was very little wind. That night we stayed at the George Inn, and after breakfast we began our long journey to Walmer in hired carriages. Mudd drove our carriage, of course. The second, which conveyed our maids, my uncle's valet, and much of the baggage, was driven by Jenkins, one of my other grooms at Westfleet.

Our route was decided by my aunt's wish to call on an old friend who lived near Hastings. When we arrived two days later, her friend, a charming widow, insisted that we stayed at her house that night, which made for a pleasant, and most relaxing, interlude. The house had substantial grounds and I was able to take a good long walk, accompanied by my uncle, leaving my aunt and her friend to indulge in the kind of long conversation they used to enjoy when they had both lived in London.

In the morning, after a leisurely breakfast, we set off for Folkestone, which was about fifteen miles from Walmer. It was another long drive, but thankfully we arrived without suffering any mishaps. My uncle procured rooms for us at "The Ship," and my aunt said that with tomorrow being Sunday, we could enjoy a rest from travelling. I couldn't help but agree. After dinner I was eager to go for a walk, and my uncle was happy to accompany me, although Aunt Thirza insisted that our first task was to find a suitable church where we could attend morning service. Meanwhile, she lay on her bed to recover from a severe headache brought on by so much travel.

'Will you be well enough to go to church tomorrow?' my uncle asked her in concern.

'Of course,' she retorted. And so it proved. We chose the nearest church, but it turned out to be too modern for my aunt's taste, and in her opinion the parson was far too young to use his sermon to lecture his congregation on the proper way to treat those not as fortunate as ourselves.

The afternoon was spent exploring the town, and after dinner, Aunt Thirza insisted on having a quiet evening, followed by an early night, as we were to leave for Walmer immediately after breakfast. Thus we all retired at ten, much earlier than was my usual custom, and after my maid had gone to her own bed, I sat in the chair by the window, thankful for some peace and quiet.

On our long journey there had been little else to do but talk, and my aunt never seemed to run out of things to say. It was only when I was alone at night that I'd had time to think about who had tried to kill me, and the huge difficulties I faced in finding this murderer by myself, when Mr. Reevers and I had failed to do so together.

Mr. Reevers, of course, had never been out of my thoughts. I did not know how prisoners were treated in the Tower, but it could not be a pleasant experience. I feared he might be in some dark dungeon, with perhaps only straw to sleep on. Far worse than the Paris lodgings he had spoken of on the day of the picnic. But I could hardly wait to get to Walmer, where I expected Mr. Pitt to finally tell me what evidence had led to Mr. Reevers' arrest, and who had provided it.

Although Louis was the only agent who'd had the opportunity to murder both Mr. Fenton and the Comte, if he actually was the turncoat, my aunt and uncle would be utterly devastated. And I dreaded to think how Mr. Pitt would feel, for he was very close to the Gauvan family. Yet, so much evidence pointed to Louis, in particular his connection with Georges Danton. Although guillotined in April, Danton had been highly popular with the people of France. When he was on the Committee of Public Safety, Louis had spent a few weeks running messages for him. In such circumstances, even an Englishman could have his head turned. Louis had spent virtually his whole life in England, but the fact of his being born in Paris might matter much more to him than anyone realised. Jago had not left Westfleet the morning Mr. Fenton was murdered, but he and Louis had worked together in France for two years and were close friends. I thought about that for some time.

During the picnic I'd organised at Westfleet on the day Mr. Reevers was arrested, I recalled the hilarious banter about Jago's refusal to disguise himself in filthy sans-culottes clothes, or to live in appallingly dirty lodgings. I felt some sympathy for him in that, and wondered how the others could bring themselves to do such a thing. In conversation they talked as if it was all some sort of a game, vying with each other over who had endured the worst kind of abode. Jago had not suffered their kind of hardship, yet they all seemed to trust him. The picnic had been such fun until that awful man, Knight, appeared. And I could not stop thinking of Mr. Reevers last words to me. "Find the double agent, or I'm a dead man."

At breakfast the following morning, those thoughts continued to prey on my mind. If it was Louis, or Jago, or both, neither of them appeared to have put a foot wrong. Either they were totally innocent, or extremely clever. But, if it wasn't them who else could it be? It couldn't be Mr. Reevers, no matter what Jago said. He had not been in his lodgings in Paris when the other agents were arrested, and had not shot Mr. East when he ought to have done, but that did not make him a double agent. Jago was wrong.

Again I had that odd feeling that I'd missed something vital. As I tucked into my ham and eggs, I was so deep in thought, trying to work out what I could possibly have missed, I didn't realise my aunt was speaking to me, until she put her hand on my arm and asked in concern, 'Drusilla, are you quite well?'

I looked up in surprise. 'I'm sorry, did you say something?' And I added quickly, 'I was thinking about Mr. Reevers.'

My uncle instantly urged me not to worry. 'I'm sure they will soon realise they've made a terrible mistake.'

'I wish I had your confidence,' I said. 'I believe someone wants him out of the way. For good.'

CHAPTER EIGHTEEN

My aunt and uncle were rather excited about visiting Mr. Pitt at Walmer, as I would have been too if I hadn't been so worried about Mr. Reevers.

None of us had been to Walmer Castle before. We knew it to be one of three fortresses Henry V111 had ordered to be built between Sandwich and Dover, to defend the east coast from the very real threat of invasion at that time. When the castle finally came into view, my aunt, who had visited many other castles, exclaimed in obvious disappointment that it looked rather small.

'Well, my dear,' my uncle declared, 'that may not be a bad thing. For my part, if it means I won't have to climb up one of those everlasting circular staircases to be found in most castles, I will be delighted. I find them tiring, tedious, and to be frank they make me feel a trifle dizzy. The truth is,' he admitted sorrowfully, 'I'm getting too old for that sort of thing.'

Aunt Thirza protested that was nonsense and listening to their courteous arguments over who was right and who was wrong, I smiled to myself, and looking out of the window, I commented, 'I hadn't realised the castle was so close to the beach.'

'Forts often are,' my uncle teased.

I laughed and said, 'I suppose so. Well, we will be able to enjoy some good long walks in the sea air here.'

'We can do that on the Island,' my aunt pointed out.

'That's true,' I said. 'But I do like exploring new places.'

When we arrived at the castle my aunt was thankful to see a reassuring number of cannons facing out to sea. Cannons that would play a vital role in repelling any French invasion force on this part of the coast.

We were soon ushered into the drawing room, while our servants were directed to their quarters. Within a few minutes Mr. Pitt came to greet us, and after enquiring whether we'd had a good journey, he informed us that Jago and the Gauvans had not arrived yet. They planned to sail on to Walmer after reporting to Mr. Wickham in

London, but it was never easy to predict how long a sea journey would take. Our host then took us on a tour of the main rooms in the castle, before showing us to our bedchambers. Where he informed us, 'There's a cold nuncheon awaiting us in the dining room. Do join me when you are ready.'

Although my bedchamber was not large, it was perfectly adequate, and the decor was a relaxing shade of blue. Once I had washed my hands and face and my maid had assisted me with changing my clothes and seeing to my hair, I made my way to the dining room, where I complimented Mr. Pitt on the elegant furniture and a number of very charming paintings. My aunt and uncle appeared a few minutes later and conversation over the meal was light-hearted, enabling us to relax after our long journey. Afterwards, my aunt said that she would like to rest for an hour, if that would be convenient, as it had been a rather tiring drive.

Mr. Pitt was all smiles. 'By all means, ma'am.'

Aunt Thirza went off to her bedchamber, and our amiable host turned to me clearly expecting I would follow her example, but I assured him I did not need to rest. 'Actually sir, I rather hoped you would show me round your grounds, if you have the time.'

He beamed at me. 'Nothing would give me greater pleasure, ma'am.' My uncle politely declined an invitation to join us, being aware I wished to speak to Mr. Pitt alone, and asked if he could browse through the castle library. Once he was happily settled in the library, I went outside with Mr. Pitt, where we took the path that ran beside the kitchen garden. A gardener was busy digging up potatoes and I waited until we were well out of his hearing before I asked Mr. Pitt, 'Sir, would you kindly tell me what was the evidence that led to Mr. Reevers' arrest?'

'I will do so, Lady Drusilla,' he said in an understanding voice. 'But it must be kept strictly between ourselves.'

'Yes, of course,' I said, and waited as he gathered his thoughts together.

'Well, there were three reasons for his arrest, and although it grieves me to admit it, the facts do fit with what we know of him. First, Mr. Reevers was our only agent in Paris who was not arrested at the time of the betrayal. To the Alien Office that means he must be the one who betrayed the others to the French. Secondly, the turncoat put East in charge of the traitorous Fat Badger Society, and those two gentlemen were believed to have been good friends. And, as we know, Mr. Reevers and East were extremely good friends. The third, and most damning reason, is what happened when East attempted to assassinate the King and start a French-style revolution here. When Mr. Reevers finally caught up with him, only one door stood between East and the King, and he should have shot East there and then, but he failed to do so.'

'Sir, that was just minutes after he'd learned Mr. East was a French spy, and shooting a close friend cannot be easy.'

'I accept that, but if you hadn't dealt with the situation, the King would now be dead and we would probably be in the middle of a revolution.'

To hear such accusations made against Mr. Reevers, who had given years of his life defending our country, left me so angry I stopped walking, turned to face Mr. Pitt, and swept aside the other two reasons he'd given me. 'Mr. Reevers and Toby East were close friends, but if Mr. Reevers was the traitor he would be incredibly stupid to betray every other agent in Paris, knowing that the finger would then point at him.'

'I understand how you feel, Lady Drusilla. I, too, have always thought Mr. Reevers to be extremely brave and patriotic. Nevertheless, in the opinion of those whose job it is to make these judgements, there is no other agent it can be. Of course, Mr. Reevers denies it all, as you can imagine.'

I took a deep breath. 'Is – is he allowed a degree of comfort?'

'He's not sleeping on the floor, if that's what you mean.'

'I'm thankful to hear that, sir.' Mr. Reevers had been under arrest for thirteen days, and he could be kept in the Tower indefinitely, as Habeas Corpus was suspended at present. This was due to the unrest caused by the Corresponding Societies, who were campaigning vigorously for all men to be given the vote. Another thought occurred to me. 'You didn't mention Mr. Fenton, sir. Mr. Reevers can't have killed him, as he was in France at the time.'

'According to Elvington, smugglers murdered Fenton.'

A wasp began to buzz around my head, and I flapped my hand at it, as I absolutely detest wasps. In fact I was almost as irritated with the wasp as I was with Jago, and I pronounced in a firm voice, 'Lord Elvington is wrong, sir.'

Lashing out at the wasp must have stunned it a little, as it landed on the ground just in front of us. Mr. Pitt instantly trod on it and I couldn't help wishing that the turncoat was as easily eliminated. We walked on again and he urged, 'Now tell me ma'am, why do you think Elvington is wrong?'

'It's to do with Mr. Fenton's horse, sir.' I explained the arrangements Louis had made with the Yarmouth inn, where agents and messengers about to sail to France, could leave their horses at the Dog and Duck stables, at any time of the day or night. 'Mr. Fenton's horse was left there after he was murdered, although no-one actually saw it being brought in. Believe me sir, no smuggler would go to that much trouble to cover his tracks. Yet, it is *exactly* what the turncoat would do, so that we would believe Mr. Fenton had definitely gone to France.'

'Yes, I do see that. Tell me, is Lord Elvington aware of your opinion, ma'am?'

'He is, sir. But he believes he is right and I am wrong. I regret to say he considers himself to be infallible.'

'Does he indeed?' he murmured. 'Well, it is largely due to Elvington that Mr. Reevers is believed to be guilty. He put forward his reasons, expressing his utmost regret, but said he saw no other possibility.'

I ground my teeth quietly, realising I must answer sensibly and coherently, for anger would get me nowhere. 'Lord Elvington is a perfectly pleasant gentleman, but if evidence appears to point in one direction, he never looks at any other possibility. He's convinced Mr. Fenton was murdered by smugglers for the money he had on him. But, when I told him smugglers would never have carried the body fifty yards from the track, or covered it up carefully, and then returned Mr. Fenton's horse to the Yarmouth stables, he just shrugged, as if my opinion was of no importance. The fact is sir, he has a total disregard for my judgment on any subject, because he's utterly convinced that no woman can possibly be as intelligent as a man.'

His lips twitched. 'Then he has a lot to learn, ma'am.'

That made me smile, and I went on, 'There is one other thing, sir. On the day before we left for London, I visited friends who only live a mile from Westfleet. When I was riding home alone, a knife flashed past my head, missing me by a whisker.'

He stopped walking and the concern I saw in his eyes brought a lump into my throat. He demanded, 'Did you see who it was?'

'No sir, but Mr. Fenton was killed with a knife.'

'And you think it was the turncoat?'

'I'm sure of it, sir.'

'What day was this?'

'Five days after Mr. Reevers was arrested.'

'I see. If you're right, then he cannot be the turncoat.' And his brow furrowed in deep thought. 'Ma'am, if it isn't Mr. Reevers, who do you think it is?'

So much pointed to Louis, but as I was only too aware of Mr. Pitt's close friendship with the whole Gauvan family, I could not bring myself to mention the facts that suggested it could be him. Instead I shook my head and said, 'I simply don't know, sir. I haven't found any evidence at all. Not a single thing.'

We walked on again and he said, 'Don't despair, Lady Drusilla. I believe you will soon find out who this traitor is.'

'You are very kind sir, but unlike Lord Elvington, I don't consider myself to be infallible.'

His lips twitched again. 'Did you tell him about the attempt on your life?'

'No, sir. I've told no-one, except my groom. I dare not trust anyone else.'

'You don't think Elvington is the turncoat, surely?'

'I can't rule anyone out, sir. The turncoat clearly knows I'm trying to identify him.'

'And that's why he wanted to kill you?'

'Actually sir, I think he wanted to make sure I wouldn't be in Walmer, so that I could not possibly stop him taking you off to Paris.'

Mr. Pitt stood still and stared at me. 'But surely, Lady Drusilla, we can forget that French threat now that Robespierre is dead. The Terror has abated since he was guillotined, and I----'

'I cannot agree, sir. According to the newspapers the Committee of Public Safety continues to pronounce you to be the Order of the Day. We're still at war with France, and they want to get rid of you. I believe that------'

I stopped abruptly, having observed a servant hurrying towards us. He handed Mr. Pitt a letter, informing him quietly, 'The messenger says it is very urgent and he is waiting for an answer, sir.'

Mr. Pitt promised to deal with it immediately, and having apologised for the interruption, he offered to escort me back to the castle. I thanked him but said I would rather like to explore the grounds.

'By all means, ma'am. Although I fear you will be most disappointed.'

I had barely noticed our surroundings as we had talked, for my mind was entirely fixed on what was happening to Mr. Reevers. But as Mr. Pitt returned to the castle, I very soon saw he was right. There were a few trees and shrubs dotted around, but apart from the kitchen garden, the grounds were rather barren. The lack of a beautiful garden did enable me to concentrate on the reasons Mr. Pitt had given me for Mr. Reevers' arrest.

I thought back to that terrible day two months ago when Toby East attempted to assassinate the King. It was also the day he told me the man who'd recruited him to set up the Fat Badger Society, was a Frenchman working for us. Only it seemed he'd lied to me, for Mr. Wickham had since learned the traitor was English.

I was still deep in thought when I came to the chalk pit at the end of the grounds. I turned and headed back towards the castle, and had reached about half way when I saw my uncle coming in my direction. As I soon learned he'd come to inform me that Lord Elvington and the Gauvans had now arrived. Back at the castle we all greeted each other cheerfully, and I asked Gisele if she'd enjoyed her time at sea. She responded with a happy smile, 'It was wonderful, Drusilla. Fortunately I seem to be a good sailor.'

'Well, that does help,' I agreed light-heartedly.

'Jago was very kind too. He showed me how to sail the yacht.' He would, I thought. To his mind, Gisele acted as a woman of her class should. Eager to allow a man to show her the ropes. In her case, quite literally.

Louis said proudly, 'Gisele could sail the yacht by the time we reached London.'

Gisele sighed, 'Wouldn't it be nice to have our own yacht one day.'

Mr. Pitt soon came to greet them and after they had rested and changed their clothes, he took them on a tour of the castle. Dinner that evening proved to be a highly jovial occasion, with everyone in a happy mood. The conversation flowed, jocular remarks and banter abounded, with Mr. Pitt very much the convivial host. During a momentary lull in conversation, Jago casually inquired if Tom Morel had set off for Devon yet.

'Well, he has left the Island,' I said. 'But not for Devon. He's gone back to America.'

'America?' Louis gasped. 'What ---- already? When did-------?'

'He sailed early on Tuesday,' I said.

Louis sighed and shook his head. 'Well, that is a shame. We were going to spend a week or two with Tom in London before he left.'

Gisele asked why he'd left so suddenly, and I explained about the offer of the half price ticket for the most luxurious cabin on the ship. Before she could respond, Jago said, 'Well, surely that explains it. Only a fool would turn down a chance like that.' And he then changed the subject by asking Louis when he was going to see the Fencibles.

'Tomorrow. First thing, if I can. Would you care to come with me?'

Jago accepted at once and they went on to discuss how best to train these brave men to defend our shores to the death, should the French invade.

Later, I managed to have a quiet word with Jago, asking how the sea trip had gone, and he told me, 'Very well. The weather was in our favour.'

'You saw Mr. Wickham in London?'

'Indeed.' I could tell from his expression that was all he meant to tell me, and I ground my teeth quietly, infuriated by his patronising manner. But I managed to curb my annoyance in order to ask the one question I was desperate to have answered. 'Do you have any news of Mr. Reevers?'

CHAPTER NINETEEN

'They are still questioning him,' he informed me abruptly and immediately turned to speak to my uncle so that I couldn't ask him any more questions without behaving in the kind of rude manner I detested in others. I was left quietly fuming, and became even more so when I failed to find another opportunity to talk to him again that evening. Frankly, I feared Jago's reticence meant he was trying to shield me from what he considered was better for me not to know. Regrettably he did not realise that keeping things from me made my imagination run riot.

That night, I could not stop thinking about what it was Jago didn't want to tell me, and I began to picture the most terrifying possibilities. Aware how foolish this was, I gritted my teeth and forced myself to concentrate on how I was to identify the real traitor. If I failed to do so, Mr. Reevers would never leave the Tower alive. Jago, being in charge of the secret operation to find the turncoat, had told me why he believed it was Mr. Reevers. But I was still very shaken by Mr. Wickham's acceptance of that conclusion.

Mr. Reevers had been in France when our agents were betrayed. And he had still been there when Mr. Fenton was murdered. Jago had provided the evidence for Mr. Reevers' arrest, and I had long believed that whoever offered that proof, must be the turncoat. But it seemed I was wrong. For, Jago was at Westfleet when the betrayal took place, and I had been with him in the breakfast parlour when Mr. Fenton was murdered.

I couldn't sleep for thinking about what would happen to Mr. Reevers if everyone believed he was the turncoat. I tossed and turned until sheer exhaustion got the better of me just as it was getting light. Consequently, I woke up later than usual and by the time I went down to breakfast, Jago and Louis had already gone into the village to visit the Fencibles. Mr. Pitt was still at the table however, talking to my aunt and uncle about this worthy group of men. My uncle asked him, 'Could these brave men fight off an invasion?'

'I pray they can, Mr. Frère. They would fight to the very last man, however an invasion is not as easy to carry out as one might imagine. Soldiers crossing the channel may suffer from sea-sickness, then there's the weather, tides and currents to contend with, and on this coast they could easily get caught out by the Goodwin Sands.'

Looking up from buttering my toast, I asked, 'Are the Sands really as dangerous as everyone says, sir?'

'Indeed they are, Lady Drusilla. A large number of ships have run aground there over the centuries. If a ship becomes stuck overnight in a bad storm, the continual battering by huge waves can actually break it up so badly that, by morning, the ship may have completely disappeared.'

'Entirely?' I asked, stunned that such a thing could happen overnight.

'Yes,' he said. 'It does happen. In fact the Sands are known locally as the "Great Ship Swallower." And it has....'

Aunt Thirza broke in. 'What about the people on board? Are they ever rescued?'

'Rescue is a hazardous business, ma'am. Yet, thankfully, lives are saved at times. If the ship's cargo is thought to be particularly lucrative, local fishermen and smugglers will rush off to the scene, each one hoping to reach the wreck first. Willing, it seems, to risk their lives for rich rewards.'

He leant back in his chair and told us some hair-raising stories of shipwrecks. We hung onto his every word, learning of cargo totally lost in the Sands, of would-be rescuers who had drowned, of fit and healthy men who had been stranded on the Goodwin Sands in a storm and never seen again. All of which made me thankful that we had travelled here by carriage, for I had not realised how truly horrendous it would be to run aground during a storm in this notorious area.

Glancing out of the window I saw Gisele standing outside dressed for riding, and guessed she had breakfasted early too. She stood there tapping her crop impatiently against her riding boots, even though she could see Roche approaching with her horse. I smiled to myself, for I had noticed she could be rather volatile at times. She was always polite when in company, but here in Walmer, the Gauvans' bedchamber was next to mine and I had heard her shouting at her maid several times.

After breakfast my aunt and uncle expressed a desire to explore the local area, and I joined them on their walk. We set off along the coast, in the direction of Deal, observing there were a large number of ships at anchor. Yesterday had been fairly calm, but overnight very strong gusts of wind had made conditions unsuitable for sailing. I was very thankful, as it meant Mr. Pitt would be safe until that changed, for the turncoat would need reasonable weather to get him to France.

My aunt, however, did not complain about the blustery weather, for the sun was shining from a clear blue sky, and she was enjoying exchanging pleasantries with the local walkers. Traffic was light, with just the occasional gig, or horseman, but this change of scene and faces did lighten my own mood a little.

When we returned to the castle I stopped by the stables to have a word with Mudd. He was grooming one of our hired horses, and as I wished to go riding that afternoon I asked him to have our horses ready at two. I was about to leave when Gisele rode into the courtyard, accompanied by her groom, Roche.

Her outing in the fresh air had left her looking decidedly rosy-cheeked and after she had given her horse into Roche's care, we walked back to the castle together. I asked if she'd enjoyed her ride and she responded happily, 'Yes, I did, Drusilla. It was just what I needed.'

A slight silence ensued and trying to think of something to say, I asked if she was disappointed that Tom Morel had gone back to America.

'Oh no. He couldn't pass up an opportunity like that.'

I suggested, 'Perhaps, one day, you'll be able to visit America.'

'That's what Louis said, and I would love to go. Tom says it's a wonderful country.'

'Has he never considered returning to France to live? I mean, when the war is over.'

She shook her head. 'He won't do that. All his relatives are dead.'

'All of them?' I repeated in surprise. I recalled him saying his parents and siblings had died, but there would be cousins and so on.

'I'm afraid so. It was truly awful, Drusilla. They all died of starvation.'

That bald statement made me gasp out loud. When Mr. Morel had spoken of his family's demise I'd assumed the cause had been some kind of epidemic which, regrettably, was all too common. Greatly shocked by her words, I stopped walking and turned to her. 'How did such a terrible thing come about?'

'He didn't say. He didn't want to talk about it.'

143

'Which part of France does he come from?'

She gave a shrug. 'Somewhere in the south.'

When we parted company she went to change, and I set off for a walk in the grounds. I wanted to be alone for a while, as I was utterly sickened by what she'd said.

I was not as well acquainted with Tom Morel as I was with the others. In fact after I left London I had not expected to see him again, and I was absolutely astonished when Mr. Reevers and I came across him on the Downs that Sunday morning. He had been stunned too, but also overjoyed to find Mr. Reevers had not lost his life on the guillotine along with the other agents, as he had feared.

He'd worked with Jago, Louis, Giles and Mr. Reevers in Paris, and said he came to the Island to say farewell to them. That I could easily understand for, once he'd returned to America, he would not expect to see them ever again.

At that moment I stopped to watch the progress of a tortoiseshell butterfly fluttering nearby, and noticed a moth too. Moths always made me think of Mr. Hamerton. He'd loved them, and had told me that some did appear in daylight.

A sigh escaped me, for the loss of Mr. Hamerton still filled me with sadness. I admired his bravery in going to France to try to rescue his sister and bring her back to the Island. How I wished he'd succeeded. But I was immensely thankful that he had managed to warn me about the plot to abduct Mr. Pitt.

I thought of his lovely house up on the hill at Dittistone, and how Richard, in good faith, had allowed the Comte to use it to recover from the injuries he'd received in that horrendous shipwreck. The fact that the Comte had been murdered shortly afterwards was something I could not wish on any man, but in his case, I did not feel sorry for him either. From the way he had treated Mr. Pink and the other servants who looked after him on the Island, he had obviously been one of those aristocrats who failed to alleviate the suffering of the peasants who worked the land he owned.

Whereas my father and I had always believed that the families who rented our land should live in good conditions and be happy with their lives. In France peasants' lives had been notoriously hard. They had to pay taxes, whereas the rich did not. They not only paid rent to the owner of the land they farmed, but also had to give him a proportion of their produce, and spend some days working for him without being

144

paid. Some peasants also had to use the landowner's bread oven, mill and wine press, and pay for the privilege.

Countless people ended up in dire poverty as a result, and some, like Mr. Morel's family, had starved to death. Many French aristocrats had treated their workers in the cruellest manner, and some lost their heads on the guillotine as a result. Others, like the Comte, escaped that fate by getting out of France quickly.

A cloud blotted out the sun at that moment, cooling the air instantly. The tortoiseshell butterfly landed on a rather dilapidated looking statue nearby, and I stood staring at it, unseeingly. For, it had suddenly struck me, with all the force of a mighty thunderbolt, that there could be another reason why Tom Morel had come to the Isle of Wight. And I shuddered, although not from the coolness of the air.

Was such an incredible coincidence really possible, I asked myself? For, the thought that had entered my head did seem utterly unbelievable. Yet the unbelievable did actually happen at times. And the more I thought about it, the more convinced I became that I could be right. That the real reason Thomas Morel had come to the Island was to kill the Comte.

CHAPTER TWENTY

I stood absently watching leaves swirling around, caught up in a whirlwind, rather like my mind was at that moment. The Comte and Thomas Morel both came from the south of France. The south covered an enormous area and I had never, not even for one second, imagined they could have lived in the same village. The chances of that were far too remote. But I began to imagine it now.

According to Gisele, Tom Morel's family had died of starvation. When he learnt what had happened to them, the distress and rage he felt must have been overwhelming. If the Comte had been the landowner in that village, and done nothing to help them, I could not blame Morel for taking his revenge. I did not have one shred of evidence to prove that's what had actually happened, yet I still believed I could be right, for it all made sense.

I considered the difficulties Morel would have encountered in finding the Comte, and the triumph he surely felt on catching up with him. Working for the Alien Office enabled him to check the records of every émigré who came to London. But the Comte had gone straight to Spain, and stayed there for two years before leaving for England. If he hadn't been shipwrecked in Dittistone Bay on his way to London, and if the disaster hadn't been reported in the newspapers, Morel might never have found him.

As I wandered on, with my mind totally engrossed with Morel, I began to see other possible hair-raising consequences of what I now believed to be the true reason for the Comte's murder. These thoughts made me lose all sense of time, and I almost forgot about the mid-day meal. When I hurried into the dining room, everyone was there except our host, and Jago told me, 'Mr. Pitt sends his apologies, Drusilla. He has some urgent business to attend to, and is having his meal on a tray in his study. On no account are we to disturb him, and he'll see us at dinner.'

We all understood, of course, and although we missed his presence, Jago and Louis were full of everything they had learnt about the local

146

Fencibles that morning. Jago told us, 'They are very much looking forward to Mr. Pitt's inspection tomorrow.'

Louis enthused, 'If the French invade on this coast they will fight to the death. They are true, brave Englishmen. Every one of them.'

My uncle took a sip of wine and said, 'I should very much like to meet them.'

'And so you will,' Louis assured him. 'Mr. Pitt has invited the officers to dinner on Thursday.'

I tried to push Morel from my mind, and did my best to take part in the conversation, for I was certain the brave Walmer Volunteers would do everything possible to withstand the onslaught of the French army, should an invasion ever come. An invasion, however, was not easy to accomplish, when tides and currents, wind direction, sudden squalls, and soldiers suffering from sea-sickness, had to be taken into account. Nevertheless I asked Louis, 'Do you think the French will invade?'

He chewed at his lip. 'I don't know. Mr. Pitt believes it could happen and is determined to ensure that everything possible is done to prevent them landing.'

'The French are a rabble,' muttered Jago, cutting into a thick slice of ham. 'They won't get far. Since the revolutionaries took over, their fighting men have become the scum of the earth.'

'I think you underestimate them, Jago,' my uncle remarked quietly.

Louis nodded. 'So do I.'

At which point Gisele chose an apple from the dish and cut in, 'Could we please talk about something other than this wretched war?'

The gentlemen instantly apologised for being so thoughtless and Louis sat grinning at her, 'What would you like to discuss, my love?'

'Well, no-one ever seems to talk about this wonderful castle? And I do think it is truly beautiful, don't you?'

He instantly responded, 'I expect it gets very cold here in the winter, especially when the wind is from the east.'

I sat back, smiling, enjoying my glass of wine. It was obvious that Louis adored Gisele, but before she could answer, Aunt Thirza remarked, 'An easterly wind is particularly unpleasant. It has a tendency to make all the chimneys smoke.'

In an attempt to stop her recounting all the houses she'd visited that had smoking chimneys, I quickly mentioned the rather barren state of the grounds, and suggested that some rose bushes would make quite a difference. 'Oh, it would,' Gisele declared at once. 'We had some beautiful roses in the garden where I grew up.' Tears threatened to overcome her and she whispered, 'I expect it's quite different now.'

Louis quickly explained, 'The house belongs to another family.' And he immediately changed the subject by admiring the gown my aunt was wearing. This led to a discussion about the latest fashions, which along with other light-hearted subjects lasted until the end of the meal.

That afternoon I went for a ride, accompanied by Mudd, to explore the pleasant local countryside. Sheep abounded here, as they did on the Isle of Wight, and I had little doubt that some farms close to the coast gained extra income from smuggling. After we'd enjoyed a good gallop we came across a wood on a hillside and rode into it. On reaching the highest point we dismounted to give the horses a well-earned rest.

It was my habit to keep Mudd up to date with what was going on. Then, if anything happened to me, he could relate all that I'd told him. Ever since I'd become involved in solving mysteries and murders, he had willingly assisted me, with no thought for his own safety. And I had never kept anything from him, for if he was to help me he needed to know every piece of information I had.

Of course, no murderer had ever imagined Mudd knew what was going on. To them he was just a groom. But he wasn't just a groom to me. He had a good deal of common sense and intelligence – in fact my father had taught him to read and write, and I passed on our newspapers to him, as he liked to know what was going on in the world. Even so, he assured me he was happy with his life at Westfleet, for he loved working with horses and never wanted to do anything else.

As we walked along I reminded him of what he'd said to me a week or two ago, when I couldn't see any way of solving the murders and identifying the traitor. 'You said you were sure something would come to me.'

'I remember, my lady.'

'Well, I think you may be right.' And I told him, 'I may have discovered who killed the Comte.' His eyebrows shot up and I explained, 'This morning Mrs. Gauvan told me that when Mr. Morel returned to France, he learnt that his whole family had died of starvation.'

'All of them?' he repeated in horror.

'I'm afraid so. It is truly appalling, for the owner of the land rented by his family, clearly did nothing to help them. I knew that the Comte

148

and Mr. Morel both came from the south of France, and incredible though it seems, I now believe they lived in the same village.'

'Really, my lady?' he responded, and I could detect a slight doubt in his voice.

I smiled and said, 'Yes I realise how unlikely it sounds, John. But if I'm right, and the Comte was the landowner, then Mr. Morel killed him out of revenge.'

Mudd stared at me, clearly taking it all in, and after a minute or two, he said, 'I see what you mean, my lady.'

'But you don't think I'm right?'

'I don't know, my lady. But it does seem a little –er-----'

'Far-fetched?' I suggested.

'Er - yes, my lady.'

'Well John, I cannot prove it, but frankly I don't see who else it could be. The only people on the Island who met the Comte, were Doctor Redding, Mr. Tanfield, my uncle, and the servants who looked after him in Mr. Hamerton's house. The butler was the only man there, and the Comte did treat him very badly.'

'It can't be Mr. Pink, my lady. He won't kill anything bigger than a fly. The cook has to get rid of the spiders and mice herself,' he informed me with a grin.

I couldn't help smiling. 'I didn't know that. Well, I'm quite certain it wasn't him, but I cannot prove it was Mr. Morel. When we saw him on the Downs that Sunday morning, he said he'd only arrived in Cowes at breakfast time. If that's true, then he is innocent. But if he was the murderer, he must have arrived on Saturday.' And I suggested, 'If it was him, he probably rode down to Dittistone, stayed at an inn, and killed the Comte in the night. Dr. Redding said the murderer would have been covered in blood. But, if Mr. Morel returned to the inn to wash and change, he would have had to wait until the servants were up to provide him with hot water. And after that, he would need breakfast.'

'He could have washed the blood off in the sea, my lady.'

'Yes, that's quite possible. But he is also the kind of gentleman who would not have left the inn until he'd had a proper wash and shave, and looked absolutely immaculate in every way.' And I went on, 'When we saw him on the Downs I believe he was actually *returning* to Cowes.'

Mudd thought for a moment and said, 'But if he'd murdered the Comte, my lady, why would he set off for Cowes that late in the morning? Wouldn't he want to leave the Island as soon as he'd had breakfast?'

That had puzzled me too, for I also thought a sensible man would escape at soon as possible. But as I mulled it over in my mind, the answer suddenly shot into my head. 'I know why, John. If he'd left after breakfast, he risked bumping into one of his friends out riding.' I often went for a ride early on Sundays, before church, and so did Giles. 'I think he decided it would be more sensible to leave when he expected all his friends to be in church. Therefore, if none of us saw him on the Island, no-one could ever have known he'd murdered the Comte. And it would have worked too John, if I had not gone riding with Mr. Reevers when everyone else was in church.'

'That's true, my lady.' He hesitated briefly before asking, 'Do you believe Mr. Morel murdered Mr. Fenton too?'

'No,' I said. 'He couldn't have done. Mr. Wickham happened to mention that Mr. Morel was at the Alien Office every day after he returned from France.'

On arriving back at the castle, I changed my riding habit for a dark green gown suitable for walking in the grounds. I needed time on my own to think about Morel, but as I was about to go outside, my aunt and uncle returned from a long walk in the countryside. They were so eager to tell me about the birds they'd seen, and the people they'd spoken to, that I had no choice but to listen. My aunt described everything in so much detail that when she finally ran out of things to say, it was time to dress for dinner.

Mr. Pitt was in great form that evening, entertaining us all with amusing stories of events in his life, and the people he'd met. Consequently it wasn't until I climbed into bed late that night that I was finally able to think about Morel. At first I began to seriously doubt myself. Was I really right about him? For, I had no proof whatsoever. Or was I doing what Jago did? Fitting it all together in the way I wanted it to go.

But, by going over everything I knew of Morel I became even more certain he was guilty. And that brought other thoughts rushing into my mind. Thoughts that made me shiver. For any Frenchman who learnt his whole family had starved to death, would want the aristocrats to pay with their lives. Such a man would support the French revolution with every breath in his body. And he would spy for France, not England.

150

I got out of bed, slipped on my dressing gown and began to pace up and down the room, as walking invariably helped me to think. Was Morel really a French spy? After all he was the man who told Mr. Wickham that the turncoat had betrayed all our Paris agents to the French. Proof, in all our minds, that Morel could not possibly be the traitor we were desperate to identify.

On the other hand, I could not imagine a more perfect alibi. As perfect as the one I believed he'd devised after killing the Comte. And that would have worked too, if Mr. Reevers and I had both gone to church that Sunday morning.

If he really was the turncoat, then he was the man who had recruited Toby East to set up the Fat Badger Society, and he must also have tried to kill me the evening I rode home after dining with the Tanfields.

As I began to count the reasons why I now believed he was the turncoat, a blood-curdling scream suddenly broke the silence.

CHAPTER TWENTY-ONE

I ran to the window and hurriedly drew back the curtains. A little moonlight showed through the clouds, but I couldn't see anyone outside. At that moment there was a knock on the door, and I heard my uncle call out anxiously, 'Are you all right, Drusilla?'

I quickly crossed the room and opened the door. In the light from the candle my uncle carried I saw how relieved he was at finding me unharmed. He asked, 'Was it you who screamed?'

'No. I think it came from outside.'

By then Aunt Thirza had joined us in the corridor and she blurted out, 'Thank goodness you're safe, Drusilla.'

My uncle said to her, 'Drusilla thinks it was someone outside, my dear. Now, if you will both stay here, I'll go out and take a look.'

'Oh no, Charles. Not on your own. Please........'

At that point Mr. Pitt appeared, carrying an oil lamp, and the two gentlemen were about to investigate together, when we heard a woman sobbing. Mr. Pitt swung his lamp around the dark corridor and we soon saw the woman was Gisele. On seeing us, she gave a huge heartfelt sob and threw herself into Mr. Pitt's arms. My uncle quickly relieved him of his lamp, enabling Mr. Pitt to pat Gisele on the back in a rather embarrassed fashion. 'There, there,' he murmured awkwardly, gently removing her arms from his neck. As he put her a little distance from him, he begged her to tell him what was wrong.

'It's Louis,' she whimpered, mopping her eyes with a handkerchief. 'He – he went out just before midnight and----------'

'Went out?' Mr. Pitt repeated. 'At that time of night?'

'He thought I was asleep.' And she began to twist her handkerchief in her hands. 'You see, he's been acting rather oddly lately, and I---' Tears began to run down her cheeks again. 'I thought he was seeing another woman. So I followed him.'

We all looked at each other, and my uncle asked quietly, 'Was there another woman?'

She shook her head. 'It was much worse than that.' And another sob escaped her. 'He went straight down to the beach. There were two men waiting for him and I heard them talking. They were French and looked like smugglers. Louis----' She stopped, took a deep breath and blurted out, 'Louis gave them a letter and told them to get it to Paris as soon as possible.' Not one of us spoke; we were all too shocked. In fact Mr. Pitt reached out and put a hand on a small side table, as if to steady himself.

'What did you do, Gisele?' I asked gently.

'I didn't know what to do, Drusilla. I went back into the grounds and walked about, trying to think. Then I saw Louis hurrying towards the castle. I called out to him, and he rushed over to me, demanding to know what the devil I was doing outside. I told him what I'd seen, and he said --- he said.....' She put her hands over face and started sobbing again.

'Go on,' I urged.

When she removed her hands, I saw tears rolling down her cheeks as she told me, 'He said he was spying for France. And that he'd killed that nice Mr. Fenton.'

My aunt gasped and Mr. Pitt exclaimed, with a discernible shake in his voice, 'Louis said that?'

'I couldn't believe it either,' Gisele whispered. 'But it's true. I was very angry with him for being so stupid, and I threatened to tell you, Drusilla.' She gave a shudder. 'That's when he grabbed hold of me and said he'd see me dead first. He had a knife and-------'

'A knife?' I repeated. Words that I feared would only confirm Louis was the turncoat. And it filled me with utter despair, for I had hoped and prayed all along that it wasn't him. The distress this was causing my aunt and uncle, and Mr. Pitt, left me feeling utterly helpless. For there was nothing I could say, or do, that would alleviate their feelings. And the horror of it all would stay with them for the rest of their lives.

But did that mean Louis had killed the Comte too? My mind was in a complete whirl and I no longer knew what to think. An hour ago I'd believed Morel was the turncoat. And now Gisele had shown me how very wrong I was.

'I didn't know Louis had a knife,' she insisted, unable to keep the fear out of her voice. 'I was so terrified I pushed him away from me as hard as I could, and he fell backwards down some stone steps. I didn't even know the steps were there.' She took a long deep breath. 'He must have hit his head. There was blood everywhere.' She began to cry again. 'It was horrible.'

153

'Where is he now?' I asked.

'He's still there.' And she wailed, 'I think he's dead.'

Still no-one spoke. The enormity of it all was too great. My uncle tried to comfort her by putting his arm round her, and she immediately turned towards him, weeping into his shoulder. It was then that Mr. Pitt took charge, saying to us, 'If you will all kindly go into the drawing room, I will deal with this. Gisele, you must take me to Louis.'

'I'll come with you,' my uncle insisted.

Distraught though she still was, Gisele did as she was bid. I wanted to go too, but I couldn't leave my aunt alone, she was far too upset. Thus we went into the drawing room to wait for the gentlemen to return. 'I do not believe Louis is a French spy,' my aunt declared rather shakily, as we sat beside each other on a sofa. 'His whole family detested everything those dreadful revolutionaries stood for. Louis is such a nice, kind, gentle man. It can't be true, Drusilla. It can't be.'

I found it as hard to believe as my aunt did, yet Gisele said he'd met French smugglers on the beach and given them a letter to take back to Paris. We were all aware that smugglers on both sides were used as messengers and spies, whether we were at war or not.

Thankfully it wasn't too long before my uncle returned. 'Louis is alive,' he told us. 'But he's unconscious.'

Aunt Thirza closed her eyes in immense relief. 'Thank goodness,' she whispered. 'Has the doctor been sent for?'

'Yes, a groom rode off a few minutes ago, and Mr. Pitt had two strong servants carry Louis to his bedchamber. Gisele is making him as comfortable as possible, and her maid, Gussie, is with her in case she needs anything.'

'Did he really have a knife?' I asked quietly.

My uncle admitted reluctantly that it was true. 'It was on the ground near him.'

I sighed. 'I did so hope Gisele was wrong.'

There was nothing we could do until the doctor arrived, which he did very speedily. He spent a long time examining Louis before coming into the drawing room where we had all congregated. He looked so grave I feared the worst. Naturally he addressed his findings to Mr. Pitt, saying, 'Well sir, incredibly there are no broken bones. He has suffered a severe blow to the head, which has left him deeply unconscious.'

'Will he recover,' Mr. Pitt asked anxiously.

'Frankly the odds are against him, but he's young and strong, so there is always a chance.' He looked round at us all. 'I have given Mrs. Gauvan instructions on how to nurse him and I'll call again first thing in the morning. If there should be any change don't hesitate to send for me.' Mr. Pitt expressed his gratitude and walked outside with him, no doubt to quiz him further on Louis' chances.

My aunt, who was an excellent nurse, said she would offer to help Gisele. Now she had something definite to do she was more like her usual self, and when she'd left the room to go and speak to Gisele, Uncle Charles said to me, 'If he does recover he'll be tried for treason, and there can be only one outcome to that.' He shook his head from side to side. 'I still can't believe it, Drusilla. I always thought Louis was as true a patriot as I am.' I understood how he felt, but I prayed Louis would recover, for that was the only way we could ever be certain of the truth.

Aunt Thirza came back a few minutes later to tell us that she would be assisting Gisele overnight for, as she rightly said, 'The next few hours will be the most critical time. Gisele's maid knows a lot about nursing, and has offered to help, so I've told her to come back in the morning. We will be in need of sleep by then, and it is essential that someone with experience of nursing is with Louis all the time.'

She advised us all to go to bed, as there was nothing more we could do to help. We took her advice, but I didn't think I would be able to sleep, and I did lay awake for some time going over all that had happened. For I no longer knew what to think about Morel. It looked as if I had got it dreadfully wrong. Was Louis the real traitor? Or could they have worked together? They were such great friends I feared that might be the answer.

Eventually, I did fall asleep, but woke again just after seven. I rang for some hot water, as a wash always made me feel very much better. After my maid had seen to my hair I walked into the breakfast parlour just in time to hear Mr. Pitt ask Jago if he'd slept well last night. He had not joined us at any point during the night, and we soon discovered why, for he answered cheerfully, 'I slept like a log.'

No-one else was there, not even the butler, at that moment, and Mr. Pitt inquired, 'Did you hear anything at all?'

Jago shook his head. 'No. Not a thing.' Looking rather puzzled, he asked, 'Why? Should I have done?'

155

As Mr. Pitt began to explain what had happened to Louis, I watched the colour drain from Jago's face. But when he heard Louis had admitted to Gisele that he was the turncoat, the normally calm and collected Jago uncharacteristically exploded, 'Louis – a traitor?' He shook his head vehemently from side to side. 'Never. I worked with him in Paris for years. Gisele is wrong. It's quite impossible.' When Mr. Pitt finished relating all that Gisele had said, Jago burst out again, 'That's absolute nonsense. Louis is not the turncoat.' He hurriedly swallowed the remains of his coffee, thrust his chair back, and announced, 'I'm going to see him for myself. If you will excuse me.'

Once we were alone, Mr. Pitt said, 'I find it hard to believe too, Lady Drusilla, but if he admitted it to Gisele ----------' He shook his head, unable to go on and I could not speak either, for my feelings were totally in accord with his. That it just did not seem possible.

After breakfast I looked in on Louis too. Jago was still there, gazing at his friend, his brow deeply furrowed. Louis' face was as white as the bandage round his head, and I could see he was breathing, but that was the only sign of life. Gisele, who looked pale and weary, told me, 'The doctor came an hour ago, but there's nothing more he can do. He promised to call in again later.'

When I saw how tired Aunt Thirza looked too, my conscience forced me to say, 'Would you like me to take over for a while?'

My aunt smiled in a mixture of gratitude and understanding of why I'd made such an offer. 'That is kind of you, Drusilla, but we've already worked out a system. Gisele's maid will arrive shortly, so there will always be two of us here. Gisele is going to get some rest now, and later I will.' A statement I greeted with relief, and a little guilt, but my aunt knew full well that I had no aptitude for nursing, and that I hated it above all things. The little I'd been forced to do in the past had driven me mad with boredom, and left me feeling totally inadequate, for I never seemed to know what to do for the best in those circumstances. To my surprise Jago offered to stay with Louis while Gisele and my aunt had some much needed breakfast. An offer my aunt accepted, and of course, I said I would stay too until the maid, Gussie, arrived.

When they left the room, Jago looked at me, shock still evident in his eyes. 'Drusilla, I'm absolutely certain Louis isn't the turncoat.'

'I understand why you say that, but why else would he admit such a thing to Gisele? Or give those smugglers a letter to take back to Paris?'

'I don't know,' he blurted out in despair. 'But there has to be some other explanation.' He sat staring into space for a minute or two, before he quietly asked, 'Tell me honestly, Drusilla. What do *you* think?'

That he should actually ask my opinion, something he had never done before, told me how desperate he was to prove Louis was innocent. I felt truly sorry for him, but there was nothing I could say to lessen his distress, for as I told him, my mind was reeling as much as his. It was entirely possibly for Louis to have murdered Mr. Fenton, and he could easily have killed the Comte too. He was also one of the very few people who knew exactly where all our Paris agents were lodging, and he could, therefore, have betrayed them.

Louis was French born, and he'd worked for Danton, the highly popular revolutionary leader, earlier in the year. Perhaps the charismatic Danton had won him over to the revolution.

Gussie, Gisele's maid, came in a few minutes later, and I thanked her for being so kind as to assist in looking after Mr. Gauvan. But Jago instantly demanded to know what experience she had of nursing, as if he doubted her ability to look after Louis. I said nothing, for I understood how very worried he was about Louis. Gussie seemed to understand that too and told him gently, 'Sixteen years ago I started as a lady's maid, sir. Nine months later my mistress became rather sickly, and as she slowly got worse over the years I learnt how to deal with all kinds of situations. I was very fond of her, but she died two months ago.'

Seeing tears in her eyes I said, 'I am sorry to hear that, Gussie.'

She thanked me and said Mr. Gauvan has seen how upset she was when she first went to work for Mrs. Gauvan, and he had been very kind to her. 'So I will do everything I can to help him, my lady.'

Before I could say anything, Jago asked rather sharply, 'Why are you called by your Christian name?' For surnames were normally used.

'Well sir, my grandfather was Russian, and his name is very long and not easy to pronounce.'

'What nonsense. Surely we would soon become used to it. Tell me what it is.'

She did so and it was very long, with five syllables, and not easy to say. Jago stared at her and finally admitted somewhat grudgingly, 'Yes, very well, I see it would be difficult. Make sure you look after Mr. Gauvan properly,' he ordered, as he rose to his feet and headed towards the door. As he opened it, he turned and warned her, 'And don't go to sleep.'

'I won't do that, sir,' she said in a serene voice.

When my aunt returned I decided to go for a walk. The strong gusty winds had moderated overnight to a pleasant breeze, and I returned to my bedchamber first to put on a hat, and as I left my room, my uncle came out of his bedchamber. He was dressed for going outside and on seeing me, he asked, 'Drusilla, my dear, are you going for a walk too? May I join you?'

'Of course,' I said, with a smile.

There was only one topic of conversation that morning as we walked through the grounds. After making a few desultory comments on the situation, my uncle pronounced in a firm voice, 'Drusilla, I don't believe Louis threatened to kill Gisele. He worships the very ground she walks on.'

'I know, but why would she lie?'

He lifted his shoulders in a helpless fashion. 'Maybe they had a terrible row and that's how she came to push him down those steps. She thought he was dead, and your aunt is convinced she made up the story about his being a traitor so that she wouldn't be arrested for murder.'

I shook my head at that. 'Why would she concoct something that devious? I mean, if she needed an excuse, she could easily have said he'd tripped and fallen down the steps.'

'Yes, you are quite right.' And he sighed. 'Do you really believe Louis is a traitor?'

'I don't know what to think, Uncle. I really don't.'

If Louis was guilty, then I was wrong about Morel. But why would Louis kill the Comte? And if he really was the turncoat who planned to abduct Mr. Pitt, Louis could not do so now. Yet, as I thought it all over, that same instinct started nagging at me again – that I had still missed something vital.

CHAPTER TWENTY-TWO

When my uncle and I returned to the castle, Mr. Pitt called us all together and quietly announced, 'I've told the servants that Louis couldn't sleep last night and he went outside for a breath of air. And in the darkness he tripped and fell down those old stone steps.'

'Good idea, sir,' Jago said. 'That should keep them quiet. We don't want any gossip, and you know what servants are like.'

'Well, I trust it will do the trick. There's nothing more we can do for Louis at present. He's being well looked after, and I think we should all carry on as normal. In any case I must inspect the Volunteers today as arranged.'

Jago and my uncle offered to accompany him, for which I was immensely thankful. After the gentlemen had left for the inspection, I looked in on Louis. When Aunt Thirza said there was nothing I could do to help, I went for a ride, accompanied by Mudd. I was immensely thankful to be out in the open countryside and after a most enjoyable good long gallop, we continued along a bridle path at a walk to give the horses a well-deserved rest. Where I took the opportunity to ask Mudd what was being said about Louis in the stables.

My question caused his brows to rise a trifle, for it clearly told him that the incident was not as simple as he had been led to believe, but he answered me with all his usual calmness. 'Roche said Mr. Gauvan had missed his footing in the dark and fallen down some steps.'

'Roche said all that?' I remarked in surprise. 'That was a long sentence for him, wasn't it?'

Mudd grinned. 'It was, my lady. But he didn't speak of it at all until I asked him what had happened.'

'Oh, I see. Well, that is the official explanation, but I'm afraid the truth is rather different.' And I repeated what Gisele had told us.

He was every bit as shocked as I'd expected and he asked, 'Will he recover, my lady?'

'I don't know, John. The doctor said it could go either way.'

A little later, we were riding down a quiet lane, on our way back to the castle, when a man in seafaring clothes, who was walking towards us, suddenly strode straight into the middle of the lane, right in our path, his arms akimbo. He was tall and fairly slim, and wore his hat well down over his eyes. There were a fair number of sailors and fishermen in Walmer, and I had no doubt some were smugglers too. Nevertheless, I did not expect to be accosted in this rude manner by a common seafarer, and I demanded imperiously, 'What the devil......?'

But Mudd was ahead of me, however when he started to reprimand him, the man said in a cultured voice that made my heart leap. 'Don't you recognise me, John?'

Mudd stared at him. 'Mr. Reevers?'

'The very same,' came the answer, and removing his hat, he swept me a long low bow.

I was so thankful to see him alive and out of prison that, for a moment, I couldn't speak. He came closer, looked up at me and smiled. 'I'm sorry to have given you such a shock, but I must speak to you.'

When I found my voice I asked fearfully, 'You haven't escaped, have you?'

He burst out laughing. 'No. They let me go.' A wicked gleam made his eyes dance. 'Although I must say my being imprisoned in the Tower will be a good story to tell our grandchildren.'

A little gasp escaped me, and I informed him brusquely, 'We won't be having any grandchildren.'

'Really? I didn't know you could see into the future.'

Somehow I choked back the laughter bubbling up inside me, and as I tried to regain control of my emotions, he turned to Mudd and said, 'John, would you look after the horses while I talk to her ladyship. I have something vital to discuss.'

'Yes sir, of course.'

I dismounted and once I'd handed the reins to Mudd, Mr. Reevers suggested we took a walk in a small copse nearby. 'You won't want to be seen talking to a ruffian like me in the middle of the street,' he said, grinning.

'Certainly not,' I agreed light-heartedly. 'Tell me, why are you dressed like that?'

'I'm in disguise, of course,' he replied with an irrepressible chuckle.

'Like you were in France?'

'True. But these clothes are clean.'

'I'm very glad to hear it,' I murmured in appreciative amusement. 'Where did you get them?'

'Mr. Wickham procured them for me.'

I stopped and looked at him in disbelief. 'Mr. Wickham did? But he was the one who had you arrested.'

'Ah – well, that wasn't quite as simple as it seemed at the time. In my last report I told Wickham our investigation was getting nowhere. He received my report on the same day as he heard from Jago, who informed him that now all our Paris agents had been guillotined, there were only four other agents it could be. He insisted it had to be me, as it wasn't Louis, or himself, and it couldn't be Morel because he'd given Wickham the news of the betrayal, and no traitor would do that.'

'Yes,' I muttered as we walked on. 'Jago told me that too. His way of thinking is entirely due to a lack of imagination.'

'How very true,' Mr. Reevers agreed with a grin. 'But, as Jago is in charge of the turncoat operation, Wickham decided to act on his findings. Of course I knew nothing of this until I reached London. Fortunately, Wickham was convinced Jago was wrong, however he thought if he had me arrested and put in the Tower, the turncoat would feel so safe he might make a significant mistake. But as that hasn't happened, Wickham sent me here to find him, so it's essential that I go about as the kind of low individual he would never notice. That's why I'm in disguise.'

I laughed. 'Well your disguise fooled me.'

'So I observed. I trust it will fool the turncoat too.' I didn't respond at once, but something in my expression made him inquire, 'Or have you already discovered who the traitor is?'

I related all that had happened last night, beginning with Gisele's blood curdling scream. He listened intently, his eyes widening when I told him that Gisele said Louis had admitted to killing Mr. Fenton. And I added, 'If you remember, during the picnic at Westfleet Louis said he'd spent several weeks running messages for Danton.'

'That may well account for it,' Mr. Reevers agreed sadly. 'Louis was young and impressionable when he met Danton, and he could easily have been influenced by such a highly charismatic and popular revolutionary leader. But if he is the turncoat then we need no longer worry about Mr. Pitt being taken off to Paris.' I did not answer and raising an eyebrow at me, he inquired, 'You don't agree?'

'It ought to make sense, but------'

161

When I stopped, he urged, 'Go on--------'

'Well --- I still keep getting the feeling that we've missed something vital.'

Strolling on, we talked it over for a few minutes, but failed to come to any reasonable conclusion, and in the end Mr. Reevers asked, 'Do you think Louis murdered the Comte too?'

'I don't know. I can't think of any reason why he would. I can, however, see a possible reason why Mr. Morel would.'

'Tom?' he exclaimed in surprise. 'What makes you say that?'

The sun was making me feel rather hot, and I suggested we stood in the shade of an oak tree. 'Mr. Morel said he came from the south of France. And that's where the Comte came from too.'

'Well, y-e-s,' he said, giving me a sceptical look. 'But the south covers a very large area. In any case why would Tom want to kill the Comte?'

In answer I told him Morel's whole family had died of starvation, and that I now believed the Comte had been the landowner in their village. 'If I'm right, the Comte could have saved them, but chose not to. This is what I think happened, although I must admit I cannot prove it.'

Mr. Reevers ran a hand round his chin before declaring, 'That does seem rather improbable, Drusilla. The chances of them both coming from the same village is extremely remote.'

'I realise that. But it is *not* impossible. We may, however, never learn the truth, as Mr. Morel has gone back to America. The night before he sailed, he dined with Mr. Arnold and the ship's American captain. The captain, hearing Mr. Morel was returning home soon, offered him the best cabin at half price, which was available due to the sudden death of the wealthy passenger who had reserved it.'

Mr. Reevers nodded in appreciation. 'Well, if Tom did kill the Comte in an act of vengeance, then a swift return to America was very sensible.' He gave an indulgent chuckle. 'Tom will revel in all that luxury. It will make a delightful change from that ghastly room he had in Paris. Although, to be fair, his wasn't as bad as mine.'

I shook my head at him. 'I'll never understand how you could all bear to live in such squalor.'

'We didn't all do so. Jago absolutely refused to.'

'So I heard at the picnic,' I said, smiling at the recollection.

162

'Tom wasn't too keen either. He's not as fastidious as Jago, but walking down that dark stinking alley where I lived absolutely disgusted him.'

'Well, at least that shows he--------' I stopped abruptly, as something Mr. Morel had said about Mr. Reevers when we first met at the Alien Office in London, suddenly shot into my mind. And it took my breath away. I looked up at Mr. Reevers and managed to whisper, 'Are you saying Tom Morel came to the room where you were lodging?'

'Yes. He called on me a couple of times.'

'When was that?'

'Early in July. Just after I got back to Paris.'

'July of *this* year?'

'Yes, of course.'

I was so stunned by what Mr. Reevers had said, and what I knew it meant, that for a few seconds, I simply stared at him, and he inquired in concern, 'Is something wrong, Drusilla?'

Taking a long deep breath I said, 'When I met Mr. Morel at the Alien Office, I asked him why he hadn't warned you that the French were about to arrest all our Paris agents, as he must know you could not possibly be the turncoat. He said, at that particular time, he'd been out of Paris for three weeks and thought you were still in London.'

Mr. Reevers was clearly startled. 'That was a bad mistake,' he murmured softly. 'I didn't think Tom made mistakes.'

'I did ask him what the chances were of you escaping arrest, and he said he was afraid it was most unlikely. I expect that's why he thought it safe to lie to me.'

'Well----I always did think Tom was more intelligent than the rest of us.' He ran a hand through his dark curls. 'And by telling Wickham about the betrayal, he ensured nobody would ever suspect he was the man who had actually betrayed us all.'

'And he was right, wasn't he? No-one did.'

'That's true.' He shook his head in disbelief, and put his thoughts into words. 'So it was Tom who betrayed all our Paris agents to the French, and he recruited Toby East to assassinate the King and start a revolution in England.' He took a deep breath. 'Thankfully, Toby failed. But if Louis murdered Fenton, then he must be Tom's accomplice.'

'I suppose so,' I said. It did make sense, for they were very good friends and had worked together in Paris.

163

'But with Louis out of action, only Tom can capture Mr. Pitt and take him to France. In which case, I don't believe he's really gone back to America.'

'I don't think so either. He definitely dined on board with Mr. Arnold and the American captain. The ship did sail around daybreak, but he could easily have gone ashore during the night and his absence wouldn't have been noticed until the ship was well out at sea.'

Mr. Reevers clapped his hands together. 'Of course, that's exactly what Tom would do. In the hope it would hoodwink us all. That means he must have a boat here in Walmer. The weather is ideal for sailing right now, but there's no guarantee it will be tomorrow, and on Saturday Mr. Pitt returns to London. Where is he now?'

'He's inspecting the local Volunteers. Jago and my uncle are with him.'

'Well, he should be safe enough there. But when he gets back it is imperative that you make sure he doesn't leave the castle grounds again.'

I bit my lip. 'That may not be as easy as you think. He might not listen to me.'

'He will, Drusilla. He has a great admiration for you, you know. Tell him the truth. Tell him he is in more danger today than on any other day in his entire life. That should do it.' And he went on, 'Now I must go and find Morel.'

As he escorted me back to where Mudd was waiting with the horses, I asked, 'If I need to contact you, where----'

'I'm staying at the "Rattling Cat."'

'The *what?*' I said, amused.

'The "Rattling Cat." It's an inn on the Dover road, and is fitting accommodation for a humble sailor like me. Smugglers use it too. I'm told there are tunnels and rooms underground.'

'It's a very odd name.'

'The owner uses his cats to warn him when strangers are coming towards the inn. Strangers are usually excise men. He attaches bits of bone to cats' collars, and they always run indoors if a stranger approaches. Running makes the bits of bone rattle.'

I laughed. 'I've never heard of such a thing. Guards cats, indeed. Smugglers are incredibly inventive.'

'Indeed.' And he added, 'Oh, by the way, no-one knows I'm here, except Wickham. Not even Pitt. So Morel cannot hear of it.'

Once he'd gone on his way, I told Mudd why we must keep Mr. Reevers' presence secret, and added, 'Mr. Morel must have a boat at Walmer. Mr. Reevers has gone to seek him out, while I have to make sure Mr. Pitt stays safely within the castle grounds. So, if you see, or hear, anything odd, tell me at once, John.'

When we arrived back at the castle, I went to see Louis. My aunt told me the doctor had called at about three, and there was a change in Louis' condition.

CHAPTER TWENTY-THREE

The news about Louis was encouraging. My aunt told me, 'The doctor said there was a very slight improvement.'

'I am so glad,' I said. 'Have you told Gisele?'

'Not yet, Drusilla. She's asleep and I don't want to disturb her.'

At that moment I happened to glance out the window and when I saw Mr. Pitt and the other gentlemen were returning from their outing to inspect the Walmer Volunteers, I gave a huge sigh of relief.

I continued to talk to my aunt and a few minutes later the door opened and Gisele came into the room. Aunt Thirza got up and took Gisele's hands in her own. 'My dear, I have some good news. The doctor said Louis is a little better.'

Gisele's jaw dropped and almost at once her eyes filled with tears, and it was a minute or two before she could speak. 'That's wonderful,' she whispered. 'Does the doctor think he will come round soon?'

Aunt Thirza answered in a gentle tone. 'Not today. He said, possibly tomorrow.'

'Tomorrow?' She looked at me, and I saw her tear-filled eyes were full of hope, and she said, 'I do so pray he is right.'

As Gisele wasn't due to take over from my aunt until after dinner, she left then saying she had some letters to write. I soon followed her and went straight to my bedchamber. I had half an hour to spare before I needed to dress for dinner and I took the opportunity to go over all that had happened today, knowing I would not be disturbed.

I was immensely thankful that Mr. Wickham had the intelligence and good sense to release Mr. Reevers from the Tower and send him to Walmer to find the turncoat. Morel only had forty-eight hours in which to carry out the abduction, and I felt very much happier now that Mr. Pitt was safely back at the castle. All I had to do was make sure he did not leave again until he returned to London. I prayed he would listen to me.

Glancing out the window I saw Roche riding off, no doubt on some errand for Gisele, as he frequently did. Mr. Pitt had told her she was welcome to stay at the castle as long as she wanted, and it seemed to me that Louis would not be well enough to leave Walmer for quite some time. But I could not help wondering what the future held for them. If Louis really was a traitor, there could only be one possible outcome for him. Gisele was naturally upset by what had happened last night, yet she was still standing by him, and I admired her for that, as it couldn't be easy for her.

I began to pace up and down the room, trying to make sense of all that had happened. The half hour I had to myself positively flew by, and all too soon the clock above the fireplace showed it was now time to dress for dinner. I was about to ring for my maid, when I saw Gisele and Mr. Pitt walk out of the castle into the grounds. She had taken his arm and I wondered why they were going for a walk now, when it was beginning to get dark, and when they should be dressing for dinner too. Perhaps she wanted Mr. Pitt's help in saving Louis from the gallows, but I did not believe that such a thing was possible.

I watched as they gradually disappeared into the gloom, and when I could no longer see them I still stood at the window, gazing unseeingly into the growing darkness. All along instinct had warned me I was missing something vital. When I finally realised that Morel was the turncoat, and it looked as if Louis was the accomplice who murdered Mr. Fenton, that instinct had still not gone away. Yet, as I stood there I had the oddest feeling that the answer to everything that had puzzled me was now within my grasp. I bit my lip in frustration, for I still could not see the answer to it all.

Only Jago and the Gauvans had known Mr. Fenton was at Westfleet, and Gisele said Louis had admitted killing him. I found it so hard to believe Louis had done such a terrible thing, for he was the nicest of men. Somehow, it just didn't seem possible. Could Gisele have lied? But why would she do that? After all, if it wasn't Louis, then who-------? In that instant the answer struck me like a dazzling bolt of lightning. If Louis wasn't Morel's accomplice, it had to be Gisele.

I could hardly believe what I was thinking. Was I being stupid? Could a woman really be helping Morel to betray our country? She couldn't have murdered Mr. Fenton and dragged his body fifty yards into the undergrowth. Then I caught my breath. But Roche could have, and he'd do anything for Gisele. Including murder. If she was helping Morel, and Louis had found out, that could be the real reason she'd pushed him down those steps.

As these thoughts raced through my mind, I stared out into the gloom, still puzzling over why Gisele and Mr. Pitt had gone for a walk in the grounds at such an inconvenient time. Suddenly I gripped the window ledge and gasped out loud, 'Oh my God.' Mr. Reevers had said that Mr. Pitt was in more danger today than on any other day in his entire life. And he was right.

For, in that moment, I knew exactly where Gisele was taking him. They hadn't gone for a walk in the grounds. She was leading him to Morel's yacht, which must be moored within easy reach of the beach. And I had foolishly thought Mr. Pitt was safe when he was at the castle.

I had to stop Gisele, and despite being close to the beach, I saw instantly that it would be quicker and wiser to go on horseback. What's more I couldn't rescue Mr. Pitt on my own. I was still wearing my riding dress, and lifting up the skirts a little so that I could run, I raced out into the corridor. Jago and my uncle would be dressing for dinner now. Jago would be no use. He wouldn't believe what I told him, and my uncle was not fit enough to chase after a murderer. Mudd was the person I needed.

Running out of the castle and down to the stables, I was immensely thankful to see him going about his duties. He immediately hurried over to me. 'Is something wrong, my lady?'

'Saddle the horses,' I burst out, gasping for breath. 'Mr. Pitt is in trouble.'

Without wasting a second he called out to Jenkins, who had driven the servants' coach to Walmer, to assist him. I hadn't noticed Jago's groom, Cooper, standing in the shadows, until he asked, 'Can I help, my lady?'

'Thank you,' I said gratefully. There was no point in worrying about keeping secrets now. We had to save Mr. Pitt from the guillotine. Never had horses been saddled faster, and at the same time I quickly explained what was happening to Mr. Pitt, and told Jenkins to find Mr. Reevers. 'He's staying at the 'Rattling Cat' on the Dover road----'

'I know it, my lady,' Jenkins said as he leapt onto his horse.

'Tell him about Mr. Pitt and ask him to come to the beach straightaway.'

'Very good, my lady.'

As he left I told Mudd and Cooper, 'Mrs. Gauvan must be taking him to the beach.' And the three of us rode off through the grounds at a reckless speed.

Morel was a highly intelligent man, able to devise devious plans when necessary, or a simple one if that would work best. Today he'd settled for a simple plan, in which Gisele was to use her feminine wiles to get Mr. Pitt to the beach, where he would be waiting. Once Morel had Mr. Pitt on his yacht, he'd take him to France for a show trial and a highly public execution. It would be one of the greatest catastrophes in the entire history of our country.

When we reached the beach there was still just enough light to make out what was going on, and as smugglers were very active in this area, no-one would think it odd to see a yacht heading out to sea at this time. Even less would anyone imagine that Mr. Pitt was, at that very moment, being taken off to France. I couldn't see how to stop them. Only that, somehow, I must.

As we brought the horses to a halt, I heard someone sobbing. Looking around, I saw two people standing a few feet from where the waves were crashing onto the shore. It had been calm earlier, but the wind was definitely getting up now.

It wasn't difficult to guess who the heartrending sobs were coming from. It was Gisele, of course, and her companion had to be Roche. Dismounting quickly, I handed the reins to Mudd and quietly told him to wait there while I spoke to Mrs. Gauvan.

As I walked towards her, I realised her attention was entirely focused on a yacht that was starting to move forward in the water. When I was close enough for her to hear me, I called out, 'Gisele, where's Mr. Pitt?' She turned round and burst into even louder tears. On reaching her I grabbed her by the shoulders and shook her hard. 'Where is he? *Tell* me.'

She pointed at the moving yacht. 'Out there. On that boat.' There was no satisfaction in her voice, only despair. The yacht didn't seem to be making much progress, even though the wind was beginning to strengthen. 'Tom promised to come back for me. He *promised*,' she screeched, stamping her foot, incandescent with rage.

'Well, he can't now, can he,' I declared, being deliberately provocative. 'You brought Mr. Pitt to him, so he has no further use for you. That's why he's not coming back.'

At which she let out an almighty scream. 'I'll kill him. I will. I'll-----'

I didn't wait to hear what else she meant to do. I ran the short distance back to the grooms, pointed out the boat to them, which was still moving very slowly, and told them it was the vessel taking Mr. Pitt to France. Seeing the horror on their faces I said to Cooper, 'We need Lord Elvington to chase after them in his schooner. If you tell him Mr. Pitt has been abducted, will he believe you?'

'Yes, my lady, he will. I've been with his lordship a long time. I was in France with him.'

'You went to France?' I repeated in surprise.

'I did, my lady. I enjoy a bit of excitement, and Lord Elvington doesn't like looking after himself.'

As Cooper leapt onto his horse and galloped back to the castle, I turned to Mudd and indicating at two rowing boats on the shore, asked him to row out to Jago's yacht and tell them Lord Elvington wanted to leave as soon as possible. 'Tell them why John, and then row back here. We'll need the boat when Lord Elvington arrives.' I was sure Captain Barr would do as requested. Mudd had delivered several messages to him when the yacht was moored at Yarmouth.

By the time I'd tethered the horses to a nearby tree, Mudd was well on his way. There was nothing more I could do then, except wait. Gisele was still in a rage, stamping her feet and screaming at the moving boat. Roche did nothing. He simply stood still and watched her.

When Gisele saw me returning she pleaded with me to help her. 'Tom swore he'd take me to America if I helped him capture Mr. Pitt. He promised we would live in a big mansion with lots of land and horses. That's all I want. I hate that poky little house in London,' she muttered with a scowl. 'All my life I've lived in big houses until------'

'Until your grandfather married again?'

She picked up a large stone and threw it with all her might at an approaching wave. 'The house should have been mine,' she burst out. 'But his new wife made him change his Will.'

Ignoring her continuous ranting, I demanded, 'Did you push Louis down those steps?'

She gave an uncaring shrug. 'I had to. He was going to give me away.' She grabbed me by the arm, her eyes wild with panic. 'You're going to catch up with that yacht, aren't you?' I didn't answer and she begged, 'Let me come with you. Then I know Tom will take me to America.'

I ignored that and asked, 'What's the name of that boat?'

'I don't know. He didn't tell me.'

Roche broke the ensuing silence. 'It's "The Dover Lady."'

I looked at him. 'How do you know?'

'Mr. Morel told me.'

'What else do you know about it?'

'Nothing,' he muttered, in his habitual surly manner.

I turned back to Gisele. 'How did you get Mr. Pitt to come here with you?'

'Oh, that was easy. I told him I needed a breath of sea air after being cooped up in the castle looking after Louis. I asked him to go with me because I'm afraid of the dark.' Even in the shadows I could see her smirking. 'He didn't even hesitate. Men are such fools.'

'What happened when you got here?'

'Tom and two Frenchies were waiting with a rowing boat. Tom told Mr. Pitt to get in, but he refused point blank. He said they'd have to shoot him first. So one of the Frenchies sneaked up behind and hit him on the head with something. It knocked him out, and they carried him onto the rowing boat. That meant there wasn't room for me, but Tom promised to come back for me.'

I could see Mudd rowing back now, and I asked, 'Didn't you feel even a little bit guilty for helping the French to capture the man running our country?'

She shrugged. 'How else was I to get to America?' And she added miserably, 'Otherwise I'd have to live in that poky little house in London for the rest of my life.' She stamped her foot again. 'And I *won't.*'

Words failed me, but I was thankful to see Mudd coming ashore then. He told me the yacht was being made ready to leave and I gave a sigh of relief. A moment later I heard horses approaching and turned to see Jago and his groom riding towards us. I prayed with all my heart that Jago believed what Cooper had told him. For Mr. Pitt's life depended on it.

CHAPTER TWENTY-FOUR

'W'hat the deuce is going on, Drusilla?' Jago demanded in unbridled exasperation. 'Cooper says Pitt's been captured by the French.' Clearly he thought it was utter nonsense, but informed me he had come to see for himself as his groom did not normally urge him to go on a fool's errand.

'Cooper is right, Jago. Mr. Pitt is being taken to France at this very moment. They mean to guillotine him. In public, of course.' And I quickly explained to him what had happened.

'Good God,' he whispered. Thankfully, I saw that he did believe me, for his eyes were wide with shock. 'Who did this terrible thing?'

'Morel.'

'Tom?' he gasped. 'I don't believe *that*.'

'Don't you? Well, you see that yacht moving out there,' I said, pointing my finger at it, for it was still just in view.

'Yes,' he said. 'I can see it. Why is that so important?'

'That's where Mr. Pitt is right now. He refused to go with them and said they'd have to shoot him first. So a Frenchman knocked him out, and Morel was seen taking him in a rowing boat out to "The Dover Lady." Now do you believe me?' He stared at me, but didn't answer and watching the yacht slowly disappearing from sight, I hurried on, 'We'll need your schooner to rescue him, Jago. It's our only chance. Will you do it? Is your boat fast enough to catch them?'

'It's the fastest schooner in all England,' he assured me, tight-lipped.

'Good,' I said. 'I knew you would want Captain Barr to be ready to sail, so I sent Mudd with a message to that effect. I suggest we get out there right now.'

'We?' he repeated in his most haughty manner.

'I am not staying here, Jago.'

'Drusilla ---- now look ------- you really must be sensible. If what you say is true, this will be a highly dangerous venture. And that is no place for a woman.'

'We don't have time to argue,' I said, and quietly told Mudd to push the rowing boat back into the sea. I wished Mr. Reevers was here too, but I assumed Jenkins hadn't found him at the "Rattling Cat." Or he would have reached us by now.

I said to Jago, 'If Cooper takes our horses back to the stables he can tell my aunt and uncle what is happening. At least they will know where we are then.'

'Very well,' he said stiffly. As he gave Cooper his orders, Mudd assisted me into the boat. Jago followed, strong disapproval written all over his face. He hadn't noticed Gisele and Roche standing in the shadows by the horses. But when she climbed into the boat too, quickly followed by Roche, he peered at her in the darkness. 'Gisele?' he queried, as if he couldn't believe his eyes, and demanded of me, 'What is she doing here?'

'I'll explain later,' I said, as I indicated to Mudd to start rowing.

Jago had once told me that, when he went sailing, he always took over from Captain Barr, despite the captain being a first rate seaman. Wherever he was, Jago liked to be in total control, as I had learnt only too well.

As soon as we were all on board the schooner we set off in pursuit of "The Dover Lady." I stood beside Jago, well away from Gisele and Roche, and told him that they had helped to seize Mr. Pitt. 'That's why I let them come with us. If we'd left them on the beach they would have collected their belongings and disappeared out of our lives. We can't let that happen. Gisele deliberately led Mr. Pitt to the beach where Morel was-------'

'Gisele did?' he echoed, shaking his head in disbelief. 'A woman? Oh, surely not.' I could see it was hard for him to take it all in.

'Women can be traitors too,' I admitted regretfully.

He immediately pointed out rather huffily, 'I did tell you Louis wasn't the turncoat.'

'And you were quite right.' I let that faint praise sink in before saying, 'But you were wrong about Mr. Reevers.'

'Yes, I accept that. I am very glad it wasn't Radleigh.'

'Well, I hope your schooner can catch up with Morel's yacht. For, you are the only man who can save Mr. Pitt from the guillotine.'

That brought him to his senses and I soon saw he was indeed a most able yachtsman, who knew precisely how to make good use of the wind that was definitely becoming stronger. Watching the waves being

173

whipped up, I remembered Morel suffered from sea-sickness, and I prayed he would soon be badly affected.

Thankfully, Jago's beautiful schooner was much faster than Morel's yacht, and it wasn't too long before clear skies and a rising moon brought "The Dover Lady" clearly into view again in the distance. Jago kept urging me to go down into the cabin, but I refused, for I did not trust him with the task of rescuing Mr. Pitt. I had faith in his ability to catch up with Morel, but I feared he wouldn't be able to outwit him. 'I'm staying here,' I said. 'You needn't worry. I have my pistols with me.'

'Pistols?' he echoed, horrified. 'Surely you don't mean to use them? You should leave that kind of thing to me and my men.'

'I like to be prepared. You never know what might happen.'

He sighed and shook his head. 'I shall never understand you, Drusilla. Don't you want me to keep you safe?'

'Not if it means letting Morel take Mr. Pitt to France.'

'I shan't let that happen,' he insisted pompously.

Captain Barr came over to warn him we were getting close to the Goodwin Sands. Jago responded testily, 'Yes, I know. Just look at those stupid Frenchies. They seem to be heading straight for the Sands. Don't they know they're dicing with death?'

I might not trust him to rescue Mr. Pitt, but I did believe he would keep us off the Sands. As we gradually drew nearer to our quarry, moonlight enabled us to see there were three men on the deck of "The Dover Lady." Quite suddenly they began to rush around in obvious panic, and I guessed they had just realised how close they were to those dangerous Sands.

A small cloud obscured the moon for a few minutes, and we could no longer see what they were doing. When the moon became visible again there were only two men left on deck. The third, I assumed, had gone down to the cabin where they must be holding Mr. Pitt. I was fairly sure that Morel was one of those on deck. Jago must have thought so too, as he shouted out, 'Give yourself up, Morel. You can't get away now.'

Whether Jago could be heard above the wind, I don't know, but Morel obviously recognised the schooner, for he fired a shot at us. Seeing the other Frenchman was about to fire too I threw myself flat on the deck. I heard the bullet crash into something near me, and when

I looked up, knowing they had to re-load, I saw that the two vessels were now only yards apart.

Jago shot at them but missed, his aim ruined by a giant wave hitting the yacht. Gisele ran as close to their boat as she could and yelled at Morel. Gunfire from Jago's men, along with the strengthening wind made it impossible for me to hear what she said, but I saw Morel take careful aim at her, and shout what sounded like a warning. She ignored that and screamed back at him, waving her arms about in great agitation. Within seconds I heard another gunshot and saw Gisele drop to the deck like a stone.

Roche rushed to her side, and a moment later, an eerie agonised cry reached my ears. He held Gisele in his strong arms, rocking backwards and forwards on his heels, his grief-stricken groans rising above the noise of the waves and wind made it very clear she was dead. I was not sorry. Anyone willing to lead Mr. Pitt to the guillotine deserved to die.

Roche laid her gently on the deck and took a pistol from his pocket. He stood up and fired at Morel, who rapidly fired back, but both shots missed. Roche threw his pistol aside and pulled a knife from his pocket. I saw it glinting in the moonlight. And that confirmed to me that he had murdered Mr. Fenton. He threw it with deadly accuracy at Morel, who was re-loading his pistol. I thought the movements of the yachts would cause the knife to miss, but in those few seconds the weather seemed to assist Roche, as for one brief moment there was a slight lull in the fierce winds and heaving waves.

The knife struck Morel right in his chest. He slowly staggered to the side of the boat, and just as he reached it, a huge wave crashed onto his yacht and washed him over the side, swallowing him up in those dark turbulent waters.

Only one Frenchman remained on the deck, and he had two pistols. More shots were exchanged between the yachts, and I saw Roche fall. Within seconds Captain Barr and his men eliminated that particular Frenchman. But there was still no sign of the third one, and I prayed with all my heart that he hadn't gone down to the cabin to murder Mr. Pitt.

Mudd came to tell me that Roche was dead, and a moment later I heard the captain shout, 'My God, their yacht has run aground.'

Jago's undoubted skill had kept his schooner at a safe distance from the Goodwin Sands, but now "The Dover Lady" was stuck I hoped Jago would be able to board their vessel. But, as I soon found out, it wasn't going to be as easy as that. Jago seemed to be leaning against the side of his schooner, gazing at Morel's boat. I went up to him and asked, 'Will you be able to get Mr. Pitt off that yacht?'

'What?' he mumbled, his usually loud voice becoming strangely faint. 'I'm ---' He slumped against the side of the schooner and slithered to the deck, where he lay motionless.

Kneeling beside him I saw blood seeping from his head. Mudd immediately took out his handkerchief and mopped it up, enabling us to see that a bullet had grazed down one side of his head, leaving a scorch mark. He soon started to come round, but was too dazed and incoherent to be of help. The captain came to see what was wrong, and immediately ordered two men to take Jago to his cabin. As they did so I asked Captain Barr how we were to rescue Mr. Pitt.

'Well ma'am, it won't be easy. We could wait for the tide to re-float the yacht off the Sands, but there's always a risk it won't come off at all. In my view, the wind is still strengthening and we'll soon be in the teeth of an extremely severe gale. If I'm right the yacht will be pounded by heavy seas and is likely to break up. And Mr. Pitt will not survive the night.'

'Good God,' I muttered, remembering the tales Mr. Pitt had spoken of at the dinner table the other night, of how some ships trapped on the Sands had completely disappeared overnight. 'We must get Mr. Pitt off that yacht now. Before that third Frenchman murders him.'

'Yes, ma'am. That is my fear too. Therefore I will go.' He spoke with quiet dignity.

'You?' I said, astounded.

'Of course. As captain it is my duty to do so. I'll take one of my men with me.'

'Your duty captain, is to keep this schooner off those treacherous Sands.'

He protested, 'But there is no-one else, ma'am. Lord Elvington is clearly not in a fit state.'

'That is true.'

Mudd, who was standing near me, said quietly, 'I can do it, sir.'

The captain took a good long appraising look at my groom and said, 'But you can't go alone.'

'Of course he can't,' I said. 'I will go with him.'

The captain gasped out loud. 'You, ma'am? You can't possibly.........'

'As you pointed out Captain, there is no-one else, and we must get Mr. Pitt off that yacht, or they might kill him. Besides, it is only a very short distance away.'

He didn't answer, but stood there wrestling with what was an impossible situation for him. If he went, the schooner might well end up stuck on the Sands too. Yet his natural chivalry made him protest at allowing me to go in his place. Chivalry and a dread that Mudd and I would fail to save Mr. Pitt's life.

Then Mudd spoke up informing the captain most respectfully, 'If Mr. Pitt is still alive sir, I will see he gets back here safely.' I smiled to myself, certain that Mudd's modest but determined manner would do the trick. And so it proved.

'Very well,' the captain said, and immediately gave the necessary orders regarding the schooner's small rowing boat. Within minutes we were on our way, equipped with a lantern, ropes, two pistols, and an axe with which to break down any locked doors in our way.

The wind seemed far more ferocious to me in that small boat, for we were much closer to the water, and Mudd had to use every ounce of his strength to row through those terrifyingly high waves. I knew he would never give in to any danger he encountered in this rescue, no matter what the odds were, or how bad the weather was. He would get Mr. Pitt out, even if it cost his own life.

The spray from the waves soaked us both, but thankfully we soon ground to a halt on the Goodwin Sands. Mudd jumped out at once and helped me to clamber out into the shallow water. Then he pulled the small rowing boat up onto the exposed sand and lashed it to "The Dover Lady."

Mudd did not waste time. He simply climbed up onto the yacht, taking the axe, the lantern, and a rope with him. Then he tied the rope round his waist and dropped the other end down to me. As I grasped it, a huge gust of wind almost bowled me over. It whipped off my hat, sending it sailing into the sea, but I clung on to the rope. Mudd pulled me up, and I landed on the deck in a rather undignified manner, cursing the hindrance of my sodden skirts.

'Now I know how a beached whale feels, John.'

He grinned at me. 'I knew you'd do it, my lady.' And he told me, 'There's a lot of noise coming from the cabin. Perhaps Mr. Pitt is trying to break out.'

I could hear it now too, and was enormously relieved. 'Thank heavens he's still alive, John. I was terribly afraid he might not be. Come on, we must get down there.'

As we discovered, there were two doors in our way. Mudd had no trouble breaking down the one at the top of the gangway. The cabin door, however, was much stronger. Just as I raised the lantern so that Mudd could see what he was doing, the yacht was rocked by a sudden tempestuous wind, causing the lantern to sway from side to side as we struggled to stay on our feet. But the swinging of the light showed us a key hanging on a hook near the door. I removed it and handed it to Mudd. 'Be careful, John. I think the other Frenchman must be with Mr. Pitt, and he'll be armed.' And I took a pistol from my deep pocket.

He nodded, quietly unlocked the door and kicked it open. We stood on either side of the open door, and raising our lantern I saw Mr. Pitt stretched out on a bunk. Standing beside him was another man, but he wasn't French. The sight of him made me gasp in sheer disbelief, and I burst out, 'Mr. Reevers? How on earth did you get here?'

CHAPTER TWENTY-FIVE

I was absolutely dumfounded to see Mr. Reevers, but he merely grinned at me and said, 'I'll explain everything later. It's a long story.....' and he asked, 'Where's Morel and the other Frenchman?'

'They're dead.' And I briefly explained what had happened to them and to Gisele.

'What about Jago?' he asked in concern.

'He's injured. That's why we're here.'

'Well, we must get out quickly, Drusilla.' And he immediately turned to Mudd. 'Will you help me with Mr. Pitt, John? He's still a little unsteady from the blow he received on the head.'

Together they assisted him up the gangway, and once he was safely down onto the Sands they helped me down too, hampered as I was by soaked skirts. The receding tide had left more sand exposed, which meant Mudd and Mr. Reevers had to haul the rowing boat some twenty yards across the Sands to the water's edge. "The Dover Lady" sheltered us from the wind, and I stood with Mr. Pitt for a moment, to enable us to gather our strength before we followed them.

Mr. Pitt apologised for being such a nuisance. 'I'm afraid I'm still a trifle dizzy.'

'Don't worry about that, sir. Just hold onto my arm and we'll soon have you on Lord Elvington's schooner, where you can get some rest.'

'Thank you, Lady Drusilla, I am most grateful to you. Frankly I thought those Frenchies were going to get away with it. They would have done too, if it hadn't been for Mr. Reevers' bravery, and your courage in coming to rescue us.'

'I did very little, sir. It's Mudd you should thank. He did all the hard work.'

'Mudd's a fine fellow.'

'There's none better, sir.'

Mr. Pitt took my arm and we battled our way across the sands, fighting against violent winds that threatened to sweep us off our feet with every step we took. Miraculously we reached the water's edge safely, where Mudd and Mr. Reevers assisted us into the small rowing boat. It took all their strength to row us back to the schooner, the wind having increased even more in the last hour. I insisted that they got Mr. Pitt on board first and once he was safe two men reached down to help me up, just as a particularly vicious gust of wind hit the schooner.

I thought my last moments on earth had come. That I'd either drown in the raging sea, or be crushed to death between the two boats. But, to my undying gratitude, they managed to cling on to my hands and haul me up onto the schooner, where I landed unceremoniously face down onto a wet deck for the second time in an hour. Before I could scramble to my feet, a huge wave crashed right over my whole body, soaking me to the skin and leaving me gasping for breath. Mr. Reevers got me to my feet and shouted above the wind. 'It's only a squall. It'll soon pass.'

At that precise moment, rain carried by the fury of the wind, lashed viciously at my face, and I started to laugh a little hysterically. In the last few minutes I could have drowned, or been smashed to pulp, or swept away in the small rowing boat that was now adrift and being tossed around like a cork in a mass of gigantic seething waves. My clothes were so wet I could not stop shivering, and I found it almost impossible to stay on my feet in terrifying winds that made the schooner pitch and roll alarmingly. To me it was a horrendous nightmare, but to Mr. Reevers it was just a squall that would soon pass. And he shouted in my ear, 'Now everyone is safely on board there's nothing more to worry about.'

But he was wrong. For we were suddenly caught up in another wild and ferocious squall, that made the first one look like a pleasant breeze. Captain Barr shouted orders in a voice that told me we were in the greatest danger. And almost at once the schooner gave an odd lurch and a kind of a judder, followed by an ominous grating sound. 'What the devil's that?' I blurted out.

Mr. Reevers didn't answer for a moment, and then he said in a much more serious tone, 'I rather think we've run aground.'

Despite all Captain Barr's valiant efforts, that second terrifying squall had finally driven us on to the Goodwin Sands. He tried everything he knew to get us off, but it made no difference. We were stuck fast on an ebbing tide.

Again I remembered the tales Mr. Pitt had told us of ships being caught on the Goodwin Sands and pounded to bits by violent waves, or swallowed up by the Sands, ending with much loss of life. There was, however, nothing to be gained by thinking about that, and I tried to concentrate instead on the more immediate need of finding some dry clothes. Jago emerged from his cabin, still looking rather pale, but he offered Mr. Pitt the use of his cabin in order to change out of his wet clothes and have a decent rest.

Meanwhile, Captain Barr kindly suggested that the rest of us should make good use of the clean clothes in his cabin. The gentlemen urged me to go in first, and for once I did not argue. Thankfully the captain was close to my own height, and although it felt strange to don a shirt and pantaloons, I was very grateful to get out of my wet things and into clothes that finally stopped me shivering.

The gentlemen could barely hide their amusement when I came out of the cabin in the captain's apparel, but I did not mind. At least it gave them something to smile about in this awful situation. As they went into the captain's cabin to find something dry to put on, I made my way to the area used for dining, for I was feeling decidedly hungry. Jago was seated at the table eating some bread and cheese, and he assured me he was feeling much better.

'I'm pleased to hear that,' I said, as I sat down opposite him.

He cut me some bread and passed the cheese, and praised my efforts in saving Mr. Pitt and Mr. Reevers. 'I can't imagine how you did it, Drusilla. You are an amazing woman.'

'Mudd did the difficult part, Jago. You should praise him. But it looks as if it will all be for nothing, now we're stuck on the Sands.'

'You mustn't give up, Drusilla.'

'I shan't,' I said.

And I didn't, but over the next few hours the wind continued to strengthen and when the tide eventually began to come in again, great waves began to batter the schooner. Despite the huge efforts made by Jago and Captain Barr, they failed to float the schooner off the Goodwin Sands. It was so firmly stuck it seemed we were all doomed to a watery grave.

The gentlemen tried to remain cheerful for my sake, but even Mr. Reevers could not totally hide his unease. We still hoped for a miracle, praying that the winds would drop, or the schooner might, somehow, float off the Sands. We did not discuss the terrible situation we were in, for there was nothing more we could do about it. But neither could we sit around in silence, so we talked about how Gisele had tricked Mr. Pitt into going with him.

181

'It will be a sad blow for Louis, if he recovers,' Mr. Reevers remarked.

'Even more so,' I said, 'when he hears she intended to leave him and go to America with Morel.'

'Well, she's dead now,' Jago muttered. 'Perhaps it is as well.'

I found it most odd to be talking as if we expected to be able to tell Louis of her treachery, when it was far more likely that none of us would survive the night. Yet it did not dim my curiosity as to how Mr. Reevers came to be on "The Dover Lady." In a slight lull in the conversation I asked the question, and he gave a very full account, which helped to keep our minds occupied.

He began by saying, 'Jago's schooner was conveniently moored near to Walmer Castle, and Morel's yacht also had to be close, if he was to get Mr. Pitt on board. I rowed round the area, checking out the boats as best I could, when I had the immense good fortune to catch a glimpse of Morel leaving "The Dover Lady" in a rowing boat that headed straight for the beach. It was beginning to get dark and I rowed into a position where I could see what he did once he was on shore. I thought he might be going to an inn, but when he reached the beach, he got out of the boat and stood waiting. The boat did not return to the yacht, therefore he was expecting to take someone back with him. It wasn't too difficult to guess that the passenger was to be Mr. Pitt.'

The schooner creaked and groaned in the howling wind, and seemed to shift in the Sands into an angle that caused objects on the table to roll across it. We all looked at each other, but no-one spoke, and Mr. Reevers went on with his story, as if nothing had happened.

'Morel had two men with him, and I could only see one other person on the yacht, which was ideal for their purpose, being a fairly small and inconspicuous vessel. It was then I saw people arriving on the shore, so I hurriedly climbed onto their yacht. I dealt with the one remaining sailor and slipped his body over the side, hoping that, in the darkness, Morel would not realise I wasn't the man he'd left on the yacht.' He paused briefly, but no-one spoke, and he went on, 'Their rowing boat was fast approaching the yacht, and when they got Mr. Pitt on board, I saw he was unconscious. Morel shouted at me in French to pull up the anchor and get moving. As there were three of them, I obeyed.' He turned to me and asked, 'Lady Drusilla, were you one of the riders I saw arrive on the beach?'

'I was. I had Mudd and Cooper with me.'

'I wish I'd known,' he said with a rueful smile. 'Then I would have been certain you would raise the alarm and come after us. As it was, I had to assume I was on my own. Morel and one of the men stayed in the cabin with Mr. Pitt. The other one came up to help with the yacht, but I quickly disposed of him and sailed, as slowly as I could, directly for the Goodwin Sands. It was all I could think of that would delay us. When we ran aground, Morel and the remaining Frenchman dashed up on deck, and ran about trying to see how we could get off the Sands. That's when they realised I'd taken the other man's place. I tried to fight them off, but they soon overcame me and I was locked in the cabin with Mr. Pitt.'

While we talked, Captain Barr and his men remained on deck, to be ready for any chance to refloat the schooner. Mr. Reevers took them some brandy, there being plenty on the boat, and as he said, there was no point wasting it. He reported that the rain had stopped and the skies were clear again. But the wind continued to howl and rock the vessel, and I feared that it might easily fall on its side, leaving us in an even more perilous state.

Now that Morel, Gisele and Roche were dead, the threat to kidnap Mr. Pitt was at an end. He had escaped the guillotine, but not a violent death. For, in these weather conditions I could not see how we were to survive the night. And like so many others who had found themselves stuck on the Goodwin Sands, there was nothing we could do about it.

A few minutes later Mr. Pitt joined us, saying he felt much better now, but was rather hungry. After he'd eaten some bread and cheese and washed it down with a glass of port, he finally spoke of the kidnap. 'I see how foolish I was to go with Gisele,' he admitted with a wry smile.

I said, 'You couldn't have known what she meant to do, sir.'

'Perhaps not, but Morel soon made the whole plot crystal clear.' And, even in the dire circumstances in which we now found ourselves, Mr. Pitt managed to make us all smile by saying, 'When Mr. Reevers joined me in the cabin, it raised my spirits considerably. For, at least then I knew I would be in good company on the way to the guillotine.'

CHAPTER TWENTY-SIX

We were still laughing at Mr. Pitt's jocular remark about being in Mr. Reevers' good company on the way to the guillotine, when the cabin door burst open and Captain Barr announced in tones of barely concealed euphoria, 'There's a brig close at hand.' We all gazed at him, hardly daring to hope. Not one of us spoke, fearing this unexpected chance of survival would be dashed to the ground by his next words. He grinned at us and said, 'They've launched a boat and it's heading this way.'

Everyone jumped up, eager to see the boat for themselves. Jago asked me to stay with Mr. Pitt while the gentlemen went on deck, and for once I didn't argue with him. If there was to be a chance of rescue, it was the physical strength of the gentlemen that would be needed; the kind of power I did not possess.

Mr. Reevers was first to return to the cabin. 'I'm told it's a local brig,' he said. 'So the Goodwin Sands won't hold any surprises for them.' Addressing Mr. Pitt, he said, 'There's a large rowing boat approaching with four men, sir. If you come up on deck, we'll get you into the boat first.'

'My dear sir,' Mr. Pitt protested indignantly, 'I could not countenance such a notion. Lady Drusilla will go first, as is only right and proper.'

I cut in quickly. 'Not in this instance, sir. You are far more important to the country than I will ever be.'

'Nonsense,' he reiterated in a firm manner. 'Importance has nothing to do with it. What kind of a man do you think I am? There are no circumstances in which I will agree to leave this vessel before a lady.'

Mr. Reevers responded in his calm way, 'Very well, sir.' He held out his hand to me and smiled. 'Allow me to assist you, ma'am.'

When we went up on deck, the sight that greeted me almost made my legs give way. My hair quickly became saturated once again by the spray from the waves, and began to lash across my face like a whip. Due to the incoming tide there was no longer any sand to be seen, and the boat carrying those incredibly brave men was being tossed around

184

the mountainous seas like a piece of flotsam. As it approached the schooner the wind blew with such fury I had to cling onto Mr. Reevers' arm to stop myself from being swept overboard.

'There's nothing to fear,' Mr. Reevers assured me calmly, as he tied a rope round my waist. 'I won't let you fall. It's a simple matter of slipping over the side of the schooner and into the boat. The men will catch you.'

It seemed far from simple to me, but I took a firm hold of myself. This was my only chance of survival. I had to do it or perish. My greatest fear was that I would fall into the water, for no-one could live in that seething cauldron of tumultuous waves.

When the rescue boat reached us, Mr. Reevers held the rope while I slipped over the side, with my heart thumping so loudly it drowned out the sound of the vicious wind. A surging wave between the schooner and the rowing boat suddenly shot up and struck me full in the face, taking my breath away. Sea water blasted up my nose and into my throat, and I was still choking when two of the four men in the boat reached out to me. Somehow I grabbed their hands, and they hauled me to safety.

The boat was bouncing up and down like a piece of cork, but the men undid the rope round my waist, and Mr. Reevers pulled it up ready for the next person. The men settled me onto a seat and told me to hang on tight. Which I did, gratefully clutching the side of the boat, as it swept up high on the crest of a wave, only to be dashed down into a deep trough.

Then a huge wave crashed right over the boat and soaked me to the skin again. I began to shiver and one of the men handed me something to bail out the water in the boat. This I did, clinging to the side of the boat with one hand, and using the bailer with the other. The activity warmed me a little, and gave me something to do, for which I was grateful.

Mr. Pitt was next on the boat. He came down as I had, with the rope tied round his waist, and within a few minutes was sitting beside me. Jago and Mudd followed but there was no room for anyone else. Mudd took over the bailing and as those remarkable men rowed us through those terrifying waves towards the brig, I looked back at Mr. Reevers, who was standing on the deck of the schooner watching us. 'Don't worry, ma'am,' one of the men shouted above the wind. 'We'll go back for the others.'

I prayed with every fibre of my being that it would be possible. Naturally I wanted Captain Barr and his men to be saved too, but my fears for Mr. Reevers tore at my heart in an entirely different way. His calm attitude to danger had given me the confidence to do precisely what he'd said. But, leaving him on that deck, not knowing if I would ever see him alive again, was the hardest thing I'd ever had to do. Common sense told me he could not have come with me, but that didn't make it any easier. I desperately longed for him to be safe too, for I could not bear the thought of life without him.

Time and again spray from the gigantic waves soaked us, and I knew that if the boat overturned in these mountainous seas there would be no chance for any of us. Yet, thanks entirely to the skill of our rescuers we made it back to the brig. Climbing out of the boat onto the brig was almost as hard as getting off the schooner, but we managed it without any mishap. Then we saw those brave men set off again to save more lives.

The skipper of the brig took us below, where he introduced himself as Sam Froggatt. When he saw us all in the light of the cabin, his eyebrows almost shot up into his head. 'Mr. Pitt? Is it really you, sir?'

'I'm afraid so,' came that gentleman's rueful response.

'How did you come to be out in this awful weather, sir?'

'Well, Lord Elvington here,' he said, indicating Jago, 'invited me to go for a trip on his schooner. When we set off earlier there was only a light breeze, but on our way home we were caught in a terrible squall and ran aground on the Sands.'

'Well, I never,' he exclaimed, as if it wasn't possible for that kind of thing to happen to someone as important as Mr. Pitt. 'Still, you are safe and sound now.'

'Indeed. I cannot thank you enough for stopping to rescue us. I've never seen such bravery as your men showed in getting us off the schooner in those terrifying treacherous conditions.'

'Well, we're local fishermen, sir. From Walmer. We couldn't just leave you there.'

'You're from Walmer?' Mr. Pitt echoed in surprise.

'Yes, sir. In fact my daughter Jane works in the kitchens at the castle.'

'Jane? The girl with the shy smile. She's your daughter, is she? I'm told she's a good worker.'

'She is, sir. She'll never let you down,' Froggatt said, his face breaking into huge grin. 'Now, once we've got the other men on board, we'll head for Walmer and see you all safely ashore.' He turned his attention to me, and his eyebrows shot up once again as he realised I was a woman wearing a man's shirt and pantaloons. When I told him I'd borrowed these clothes after my own become saturated, he said how sorry he was to see a lady caught up in such terrible weather.

I expressed my heartfelt gratitude to him for coming to our rescue, as did Jago and Mudd. Froggatt grinned at us and said he was glad to be of help, and went on, 'It's a bit cramped in here, but if you would all like to take a seat, I'll pour you out a drop of brandy. It will warm you up after your terrible ordeal.' Without more ado he placed some glasses on the table, opened a full bottle, and poured us all a good measure.

It was an hour before Mr. Reevers and the others joined us. The longest hour in my life. If I ever had any doubts about my feelings for him, these last few terrible hours had made it all too plain.

Captain Barr told us, 'We didn't get off the schooner a minute too soon. I was last, of course, and the pounding of the waves had already started to break up the vessel. I don't think there will be much left by morning.'

We all commiserated with Jago at the loss of his schooner, but he assured us that it could easily be replaced, and what mattered most was that we were all safe. Something that had not seemed possible a few hours ago. Nevertheless I was really surprised at him uttering such a touching remark.

Sam Froggatt continued to be so generous with the brandy, I knew we must be on a smugglers' boat. They admitted to being local fishermen, and no doubt, like fishermen on the Isle of Wight, they supplemented their income with smuggling. A way of life Mr. Pitt wanted to stamp out.

Now that everyone was safely on board, the brig set off for Walmer. At first the gales made sailing hard going, but we gained a little shelter on reaching the "The Downs," the area of sea between the coast and the Goodwin Sands. Where vessels often waited for suitable weather in which to sail.

We were all feeling relaxed and immensely thankful to be alive, when we heard some shouting going on up on deck. Mr. Reevers went to see what was happening, and soon came down again, a huge grin on his face. 'It's a revenue cutter,' he said, with a chuckle. 'Some of their men are on board now.'

Before he could say another word a revenue officer entered the cabin. The officer stared at the First Lord of the Treasury as if he couldn't believe his eyes. 'Mr. Pitt, sir,' he gasped. 'May ---- may I inquire as to what you are doing on a smugglers' boat?'

'A smugglers' boat?' Mr. Pitt questioned, feigning considerable surprise. 'I know nothing about that, Mr. Allington. What I do know is, that I owe my life to these brave men.' He explained to the rest of us that he'd met Mr. Allington at the Fencibles inspection earlier that day, and then addressed that gentleman again. 'When I returned to the castle after the inspection, Lord Elvington suggested we took a trip on his schooner. Unfortunately, we stayed out rather longer than we meant to, and on our way back a sudden squall drove us onto the Goodwin Sands, where we became stuck fast. The captain of this fine brig,' he went on, indicating Sam Froggatt, who stood beside him, 'stopped to rescue us. I have never seen such bravery in all my life. As you can imagine, I am extremely grateful to Mr. Froggatt and his men.'

'I see, sir,' Allington said, a rather sour expression on his face. 'I hardly know what to say, except I've been trying to catch this rogue red-handed for months and I------'

Mr. Pitt broke in, 'Today he was employed in saving lives.'

Allington glanced at the glasses on the table, and then at the bottle, before asking Mr. Pitt, 'Sir, may I inquire where that brandy came from?'

As the great man told me later, he lied without a moment's hesitation. 'I brought it with me from the schooner.'

'Is that so, sir?' The revenue officer did not hide his scepticism.

'Well, there was no sense in leaving it behind.'

'I see,' he said, with a resigned sigh. 'Nevertheless, it is my duty to search this brig.'

Sam Froggatt spread his hands out wide. 'By all means, Mr. Allington. Look where you like. But you won't find anything except cod and some mackerel.'

The two men went off together and after the door had closed, Jago said, 'They probably heaved the goods over the side while they rescued us, and sunk it below the surface. Then they'll pick it up whenever it suits them. Allington will know that, of course, but even if he found the goods in the sea, he couldn't prove it belonged to Froggatt.'

'Poor Allington,' Mr. Pitt said. 'He has a difficult job, and normally I would do what I could to help him. But I couldn't stab those brave men in the back.'

'Of course you couldn't, sir,' I said, and we finished off the brandy with a toast to the smugglers.

We were put ashore in Walmer just as the sun began to rise over the horizon. A few hours ago that was something I had not expected to see ever again. As we set off for the castle, Jago told us quietly that the dead bodies on his schooner had all been swept away by the waves. 'It was the best thing that could have happened to them,' he said.

Mr. Reevers agreed and suggested, 'I think that when we are asked what happened to Gisele and Roche, we should simply say they were swept overboard in the storm. No-one will question that. It's happened to many other people before. And as Morel was believed to have returned to America we need not mention him at all.'

He was right, of course. It was the sensible thing to do. I would tell my aunt and uncle the truth, but make it clear that Mr. Pitt intended to stick to the story that he'd gone out on Jago's schooner and run aground in the storm.

It was then that I thought of Mr. Hamerton, who had warned me of the French threat to take Mr. Pitt to Paris. His information had been right, and it was extremely fortunate that he'd lived long enough to pass it on to me, or Mr. Pitt's fate would have been very different. Nevertheless that whole terrible episode was now at an end. For which I was immensely grateful. I would, however, never forget what we owed to Mr. Hamerton.

CHAPTER TWENTY-SEVEN

The storm had finally passed, leaving clear blue skies and a gentle breeze, and the birds were singing joyfully as we walked the short distance to Walmer Castle. I revelled in the delightful sounds that, only a few hours ago, I had feared I would never hear again. Mudd, who Mr. Pitt had shaken by the hand and thanked with genuine heartfelt gratitude for his part in the rescue, went off to his quarters. As he did so, my uncle came rushing out to greet us, followed by my aunt at a more sedate pace. She never hurried.

They were shocked to see me in Captain Barr's clothes, but as we stood outside soaking up the glorious sunshine, I quickly explained how that had come about. Cooper, Jago's groom, had done as I'd asked and told them of Mr. Pitt's abduction and of our determination to rescue him. When the weather deteriorated into one of the worst gales they had ever experienced, they had spent a terrible night waiting and worrying.

Naturally they wanted to hear the whole story, but urged us to change our clothes first. That made good sense and it wasn't long before we were all gathered together in the breakfast parlour, and as we enjoyed a much needed meal, we recounted everything that had happened overnight. They were profoundly shocked by Gisele's treacherous part in the French conspiracy. 'Louis will be dreadfully upset,' Aunt Thirza said. 'But perhaps it is as well she's dead.'

I gazed at her, hardly daring to hope that Louis was now well enough to be capable of being upset. 'Aunt, are you saying Louis is conscious?'

'He came round a few hours ago,' my uncle said.

Jago breathed a huge sigh of relief. 'That is good news.'

'He's still very sleepy,' my uncle went on. 'Nevertheless, the doctor is hopeful that he will not suffer any lasting damage.'

'Is someone with him at the moment?' Mr. Reevers asked.

My uncle said, 'Gisele's maid, Gussie, who had nursed him during the day, offered to do so at night when she saw how worried we were about you.' And he added, 'Do go to see him if you want but, for the moment, I think we should keep Gisele's death from him.'

I thought so too, although Mr. Pitt said, 'Won't he wonder where she is?'

'We can tell him she's unwell,' my aunt suggested.

After breakfast, Jago and I looked in on Louis, but he was asleep. Gussie was still sitting with him, and I quietly asked Jago if he would take her place for a few minutes, while I told her what had happened to Gisele. He nodded in understanding and Gussie came out of the room with me.

When I told her Gisele was dead, she went rather pale. 'I am very sorry to hear that, my lady.' Gisele's death meant that she would have to find another place of employment, and I immediately thought about my need for a new maid. Of course she already knew that Gray was getting married at the end of the month, and I took the opportunity to talk to her to see if she would be suitable for me. I began by asking if she had enjoyed staying at Westfleet.

'I did, my lady. Westfleet Manor is a beautiful house. I was happy in London, but I really love the Island. It's so nice being near the sea and the countryside too.'

Taking into account her kindness in nursing Louis, I talked to her for some time. I liked her cheerful manner and her calm positive attitude to life. It wasn't long before I decided I would offer her the job, but thought I should give her a day or two to recover from Gisele's sudden death first. When I did ask her later, she accepted at once, and did so happily.

On joining the others again, Mr. Pitt reminded us that the officers from the Fencibles were dining with us this evening. 'But I won't mention our adventure to them.' And he gave a hearty chuckle. 'Imagine what the newspapers would make of it if they found out the French intended to put me on public trial, and then force me up the steps to their guillotine! If that got out it would cause a sensation.'

'It certainly would sir,' I said. 'There would be quite an uproar too if people heard you had been caught on a smugglers' brig by the revenue men.'

Mr. Pitt chortled, 'It would indeed, ma'am. But I had a quiet word with Sam Froggatt and Mr. Allington while we were on the brig. They both understood how vital it is to keep such news quiet. I find that if you explain things in the right way, most people will do as you ask.' I prayed he was right. Smugglers were certainly accustomed to keeping secrets, and Mr. Allington was a man of the highest principles.

Everyone went to get some rest then, and when I woke several hours later I was so thirsty I made my way to the dining room as soon as I'd washed and dressed. Mr. Reevers was seated at the table, partaking of a light, rather late nuncheon, but he immediately rose to his feet, selected a chair opposite his own, and held it out for me. Once I was seated he offered to help me to some cold meat. I thanked him but refused. 'I have a fancy for some plain bread and butter, and some tea. I'm positively parched.' Having poured myself some tea I drank half of it straightaway and felt better for it. As I buttered a slice of bread, I asked if any of the others were up.

'Mr. Pitt is, but I haven't seen your aunt and uncle.'

'I'm not surprised. It must have been awful for them, not knowing if we were alive or dead.'

A faint smile quivered on his lips. 'Well, it wasn't much fun for us either.'

I laughed. 'True. It's not an experience I wish to repeat.'

'Nor me. You were very brave, Drusilla. Not many women would have coped as well as you did,' he said in quiet approval.

Before I could answer, Jago joined us and said he had just been to see Louis again. 'But he was still rather sleepy, and we only exchanged a few words. I'll go along later.'

After I had finished my meal Mr. Reevers inquired if I would care to join him for a walk in the gardens. 'Some fresh air would do us good,' he said.

Recalling the vast amount of violent fresh air we had endured on the Goodwin Sands, I couldn't help smiling as we set off for our walk. The sun was still shining and we strolled through the rather barren grounds counting our blessings. We watched the blackbirds scurrying in and out of the occasional shrub, admired the butterflies on a small clump of Michaelmas daisies, and the bees on a patch of lavender. Enjoying to the full some of the little things in life that we usually took for granted.

After a while I reminded Mr. Reevers of what we owed Mr. Hamerton, and pointed out, 'If he hadn't warned us of the plot to abduct Mr. Pitt, the French might have succeeded in guillotining one of our greatest leaders. Imagine what that would have done to our morale. It might even have led to us losing the war.'

'Perhaps,' he admitted. 'Although Pitt won't see it that way. Hamerton was immensely brave, but his actions would have come to nothing if you hadn't seen Gisele and Pitt going off together, and realised what was happening.'

'I was lucky.'

'That wasn't luck, Drusilla. That was intelligence and sheer good sense. Thank God it was you who saw them and not Jago. He would not have realised there was anything odd about it.' I had to admit that was true. He would have assumed they were simply taking a short walk before dinner.

We spent a most delightful couple of hours in this carefree mood, enjoying the glorious sunshine. When we eventually went back into the castle, we looked in on Louis. He was awake, but rather drowsy, so we did not stay long, nor did we speak of anything important.

Dinner that evening with the officers from the Fencibles was a delightful affair. Mr. Pitt was on top form and his entertaining stories made us laugh a good deal. That took our minds off the trauma we had endured. The officers were full of praise for the Walmer Volunteers who had sworn to fight to the death to prevent a French invasion. Mr. Pitt expressed his heartfelt admiration for such outstanding courage, and his sentiments were echoed by everyone around the table.

I slept very well that night, and in the morning while we were all together at breakfast, Mr. Pitt told us, 'I have to return to London tomorrow, but I beg of you to stay here as long as you wish, or at least until Louis is well enough to go home.'

My aunt and uncle agreed immediately, and as I could not go back to Westfleet without them, naturally I went along with it. When Mr. Reevers said he would stay too, I was delighted, for I could think of nothing I would rather do than spend time with him at this fascinating castle. Jago leant back in his chair and declared, 'Well, in that case you won't need me here any longer.' Addressing Mr. Pitt, who sat opposite him, he went on, 'If you have no objection sir, I would like to leave later this morning. I have some urgent personal business to attend to.'

'By all means,' Mr. Pitt responded. 'But first you must allow me to express my gratitude for your part in saving me from that wretched French guillotine.'

'It's Lady Drusilla and Mr. Reevers you should thank, sir. But for them, no-one would have known you had been abducted.'

I immediately pointed out, 'Yes, but without your schooner Jago, we could not have caught up with "The Dover Lady."'

'Lady Drusilla is right,' Mr. Pitt declared. 'Don't be so modest, Elvington. Believe me, I am very grateful to you all. If it hadn't been for your brave efforts I would now be in the hands of those cut-throat French revolutionaries. I can never thank you enough.'

When breakfast was over, Jago accompanied me out of the room, and as we strolled along the corridor, he said, 'Everything seems to be settled now, Drusilla. The traitors are dead and as Mr. Arnold no longer requires our assistance with the émigrés, we won't need to use Westfleet Manor again. I am most grateful to you for allowing us to stay for so long,' he ended politely.

'I was glad to be of help,' I responded with equal civility. 'If you do mean to visit the Island again, you-----------'

'As a matter of fact, that's where I'm going now.'

'Really?' I said. 'To see Lizzie?'

'Yes. But I mean to call on her father first.' I stopped walking and looked at him in considerable surprise, and his face turned a delicate shade of pink. 'I intend to ask her to marry me, Drusilla. But, of course, I must have her father's permission first.'

Only a day or two earlier he'd said he could never marry Lizzie as she was not a member of the aristocracy. 'What made you change your mind, Jago?'

'The sheer terror we endured last night,' he said. 'Facing what looked like certain death, I thought back over my whole life, and my greatest regret was that I would never see Lizzie again. I found that so unbearable, I decided that, if by some miracle I did survive, I would never let her go. And I won't. I want to live the rest of my life with her. And that is what I am going to do,' he ended joyfully.

'Good for you, Jago,' I exclaimed. 'But your father won't like it.'

'No, he won't,' he agreed in his calm way. 'Nevertheless, I won't change my mind.'

'I'm glad. I wish you good luck.'

He thanked me and when he came to take his leave of me shortly afterwards, he said, 'I've just looked in on Louis, but he was asleep, so I didn't disturb him, Drusilla. But I would be grateful if you would keep me informed of his progress.'

'Of course I will,' I said. I did not doubt now that Jago would marry Lizzie before the year was out. And I was right. He did.

I watched him set off and a little later I went to see Louis, and found him awake. He was alone, there being no need now for someone to be with him the whole time. He was still rather pale, although he spoke easily enough.

'Where's Gisele?' he demanded quietly, as I sat in the chair beside the bed. 'Mrs. Frère insists she is unwell, but I think she's lying.' I hesitated, uncertain if he was well enough to be told the truth, but he soon put me right. 'I know she and Morel are working for the French. You see, when she sneaked out into the garden after midnight, I followed her. The click of the door woke me up, and when I went outside I overheard her scheming with Roche on how to abduct Mr. Pitt. I was so angry I instantly accosted them. That's when I learnt she was leaving me to go to America with Morel. She also said she intended to tell Pitt that I was the turncoat. I stood there, reeling with shock, and that's when they pushed me down those stone steps. They meant to kill me, Drusilla. So don't spare me any details.'

I did as he asked, explaining that Gisele had persuaded Mr. Pitt to escort her to the beach, and how Morel had taken him onto "The Dover Lady." 'Thankfully,' I said, 'Mr. Reevers climbed onto that yacht and ran it aground on the Goodwin Sands.'

'Good for Radleigh,' he said. And he then asked, 'Drusilla – where is Gisele now?' When I hesitated he urged, 'For heaven's sake, *tell* me.'

I took a deep breath. 'I'm sorry Louis, but I'm afraid she's dead.'

Despite the enormity of the crimes she had committed, his eyes filled with tears. He brushed them aside, as if annoyed with himself for allowing his emotions to show. 'What happened to her?' he whispered.

I told him the truth as gently as I could and that Morel and Roche had died too. 'We were caught up in a tremendous storm and I'm afraid their bodies were washed overboard.'

He did not speak for a few minutes, and then he wanted to know if we had rescued Mr. Pitt. I assured him that we had and said, 'He's quite safe now.'

He didn't ask any more questions at that time, but of course I would give him all the details when he wanted them. I felt so sorry for him. He was a good, kind, decent man and I hoped that, one day, he would marry someone who truly loved him. I left him then, so that he could grieve for Gisele.

Walking back into the hall I saw my aunt and uncle returning from a stroll in the grounds. Greeting them, I said that I'd just spoken to Louis. 'He wanted to know the truth about Gisele, so I've told him. It seemed the right thing to do. He said Gisele and Roche had deliberately tried to kill him by pushing him down those steep stone steps.'

My aunt closed her eyes momentarily and then murmured, 'Poor Louis. I'll go to him as soon as I've removed my hat.'

She went off to her bedchamber, and as I stood talking to my uncle, Mr. Reevers came into the hall and asked if I would care to go for a ride. Before I could answer, my uncle urged, 'Do go, Drusilla, a ride will put some colour back into your cheeks. I'm going to see Louis too, so you need not worry about him.'

My spirits rose at the very mention of a ride, but my uncle's remark made me turn to Mr. Reevers and ask, 'Do I really look pale?'

'A little,' he said. 'What happened yesterday was enough to take the colour out of anyone's cheeks.'

He suggested taking a picnic with us, so that we could stay out as long as we liked, and I was happy to agree. For it was a glorious morning with clear blue skies, warm sunshine, and only the faintest of breezes coming in off the sea. A beautiful, balmy day and this was to be only the first of several days we were to spend at Walmer Castle. That thought made me give a long deep sigh of contentment. It was wrong of me to spend the day with him when I'd decided there could be no future for us together, but I simply could not resist it.

My excuse to myself was that we still had much to discuss concerning the French conspiracy. But the truth was, that after our narrow escape from death on the Goodwin Sands, I could not think of anything more delightful than spending a day in his company.

Naturally we were accompanied by Mudd, who followed at a discreet distance. Once we were well out in the countryside we enjoyed a good long gallop, coming across more sheep than people.

I didn't know it then, but it was to be a day I would remember all my life.

CHAPTER TWENTY-EIGHT

Later on, when riding at a walking pace through some very pretty woods on a gentle hillside, we decided it was time to have our picnic and give the horses a well-deserved rest. We settled for a place that had a bank to sit on, and where the sun was breaking through the trees. Once Mudd had made the horses comfortable, he brought the picnic basket over to us and laid out the food.

While we all tucked into the delightful repast supplied by the Castle's cook, Mr. Reevers and I talked to Mudd about his part in rescuing Mr. Pitt. Aunt Thirza would have had a fit, seeing us 'hobnobbing,' as she called it, with a servant. But John Mudd was much more than a servant to me. Without him, Mr. Pitt and Mr. Reevers might never have escaped from "The Dover Lady." Mudd denied it, of course, insisting in his modest way that, if it had been necessary, Captain Barr would have gone in his place.

After we'd finished our meal, Mr. Reevers and I took a stroll through the woods. Mudd followed with the horses and before long we emerged from the trees, to find we were about half way up the hill, and made our way to the top, where there was a most pleasant view of the surrounding countryside. Sitting on the dry grass in the sunshine, we pointed out nearby villages and their churches, and talked of many things. Like the pleasures of living on the Isle of Wight, of Giles and Lucy and Marguerite, of Richard and Julia Tanfield, of Westfleet, and so much more. I also learnt a great deal about his life as a secret agent, the funny incidents as well as the sad.

We spoke too of the terrible sadness that had turned Morel into a double agent, and how Gisele had willingly assisted him to abduct Mr. Pitt. Thankfully, that was all over, and I asked Mr. Reevers what he would do now. He didn't answer at once and I went on, 'I mean, Robespierre is dead, and the Terror seems to be over.'

'Yes, but we are still at war. I can't see any sign of that ending.'

At that moment a wasp began to buzz about my head, and I waved my hand at it irritably and declared, 'I loathe wasps.'

He grinned at me. 'So I see. Keep still and it will go away.'

'I've tried that before,' I declared acidly. 'It never works.' I flicked a hand at it again, and almost at once it was joined by a second wasp.

Mr. Reevers was greatly amused. 'Clearly it sent for reinforcements.'

I jumped to my feet, removed my hat and used it to lash out at the wasps. They buzzed even more furiously, which made Mr. Reevers laugh out loud. 'It is not funny,' I muttered huffily, and I began to walk down the hill, hoping the wasps would leave me alone. But they didn't and as I tried to ward them off with my hat, I stumbled over a large clump of grass, right at the steepest part of the descent. Suddenly I found myself tumbling down the hill out of control. I tried grabbing at the grass, but it just slipped through my fingers.

Although the hill was rather steep, it wasn't very high, and I knew I would soon come to a halt at the bottom. Unfortunately I hadn't realised there was a smallish tree directly in my path, and I crashed into it, catching my head against the trunk. It must have knocked me out, for when I came to my senses I was being lovingly cradled in Mr. Reevers' arms.

The gentle kisses he planted all over my face felt so wonderful I did not move an inch. I kept my eyes shut and gave myself up to the bliss of those glorious breathtaking moments. 'Don't leave me, my darling girl, I beg of you,' he whispered, his voice choking up. 'I can't live without you.'

His lips brushed my hair, my forehead, my nose, and briefly touched my lips, his loving words continuing to overwhelm me with joy. Obviously he thought I was still unconscious, and was only too aware that a blow to the head could be fatal. The way he was reacting to that terrifying knowledge, finally removed the one biggest worry that had been on my mind ever since he'd made it clear he wished to marry me. All along I had feared he was only after my fortune. The way he was reacting now to his fear that I might not recover, told me how very wrong I was. And that made me deliriously happy. For it changed everything. Absolutely everything.

I'd refused to marry him, convinced his declarations of love weren't genuine. For I knew that if we married, and then I found he did not care for me at all, I could not have borne it. Nor could I have done anything about it for, the moment I became his wife, Westfleet, my estates and whole fortune would automatically become his. That was the law. I would be left with nothing of my own. That was a risk I had not been prepared to take. But now he'd swept away all those fears. For, there was no mistaking the tenderness and sincerity in his voice.

Suddenly the delightful kisses and adoring murmurings of love stopped, and I heard Mudd ask Mr. Reevers anxiously if I was all right. 'I don't know, John. She's unconscious,' Mr. Reevers said, with considerable disquiet.

With regret, I decided it was time I showed signs of coming round. I opened my eyes slowly and saw so much relief and love in his dark eyes that I could barely speak. But, somehow, I managed to mumble dazedly, 'Oh ....my head....what happened?'

'You crashed into a tree,' he explained softly. And with great gentleness, he set me down so that I could lean back and rest against the tree. Sitting beside me he asked how I felt. I reached up, touched the growing lump on the back of my head, and winced, but assured him I would soon be better, if I could just rest for a few minutes.

Mudd, who I could see was worried about me, inquired, 'Is there anything I can get you, my lady. Some wine, perhaps?'

'That would be splendid, John. Thank you.' He'd left the picnic basket in the shade of the trees, near the horses, and he hurried off to fetch it. In an effort to show Mr. Reevers I was indeed recovering quite quickly, I asked, 'What happened to the wasps?'

His eyes began to dance. 'Oh, they disappeared the minute you fell over.'

I knew I had been silly, and I expected him to tell me so, yet he didn't. Feeling a little embarrassed I said, 'I'm not afraid of wasps. I just find them immensely irritating.' I gave an involuntary shudder. 'Wretched, loathsome things.' He grinned at me but didn't comment, and I carried on, making even more of a fool of myself. 'My aunt hates mice, and with Lucie it's spiders. There must be something you can't stand too.'

'Ah, that would be telling.' he teased, but changed the subject so quickly I decided I must be right. I was surprised, for it was hard to imagine that anything would bother him. But as I soon saw, he was concentrating on working out the best way to get me back to the castle, for we were a considerable distance from it. 'I'll send Mudd to fetch a carriage,' he said. 'Then we-----'

'There's no need for that,' I assured him. 'I'm feeling much better now. It's only a bump on the head. I can ride back at a walking pace. That will be better than being shaken around in a carriage.'

199

'Perhaps,' he murmured doubtfully.

Mudd arrived with the wine, which did much to revive me. When I decided to get to my feet, Mr. Reevers assisted me, and asked if I felt dizzy. 'Not in the least,' I said. 'I'm sure I can manage. After all I have you and Mudd to look after me.'

Mudd fetched the horses and Mr. Reevers helped me up into the saddle. The slow ride back to Walmer Castle through the woods and country lanes must have taken at least two hours, but I barely noticed the time. The euphoria of knowing Mr. Reevers truly loved me totally outweighed everything else.

On the way back, Mr. Reevers insisted on sending for the doctor to take a look at me, but when we reached the castle, the doctor was already there, visiting Louis. He came to see me afterwards and having thoroughly checked me over, said he couldn't see any cause for alarm.

I rested for the remainder of the day and slept surprisingly well that night. When I woke in the morning I sat up and felt the bump on my head. It was very tender, and I was aware of a few bruises brought about by rolling down the hill, but I was too happy to care about any of it. In any case, bruises would heal in a few days. Sinking slowly back onto the pillows, I revelled in the recollection of every single moment when Mr. Reevers had cradled me in his arms. The wonderful loving words he'd uttered and the extreme anxiousness in his voice when he feared I might be badly hurt. Or worse.

The fact that I was to spend the next few days with him at Walmer sent a delicious thrill through my whole body. And I spent a considerable time thinking of what it would be like to live the rest of my life with the man I loved. That made me give a long deep happy sigh, and I stretched my limbs in a leisurely fashion, like a well satisfied cat.

Marriage would change everything, and I was certain now that it would be absolutely marvellous. Only then did I remember I'd told Mr. Reevers, in no uncertain terms, that I would never marry him. But I was so happy I soon dismissed that from my mind, convinced that such difficulties would be easy enough to overcome.

Now I knew what his true feelings were, all those worries had disappeared. Revelling in anticipation of my future life with a man who truly loved me, I threw back the covers, jumped out of bed and danced round the room.

Then I looked out of the window at the gardens bathed in the early morning sunshine. It was going to be another beautiful day, and as I stood there with joy in my heart, my maid came in carrying a note from Mr. Reevers.

I took it and could barely wait for her to leave the room before I opened it. Eagerly I began to read it, but as I did so, my heart sank.

I had hoped to have the pleasure of your company here for the next few days, but Pitt had an urgent message from London last night that ruins such a delightful prospect. I have to return to France at once. I will be crossing the channel early this morning, and I do not know how long I will be away.

I only hope you will regret my absence as much as I do. You are always in my thoughts.

He'd signed it quite simply as Radleigh.

I threw on my clothes, ran out of my bedchamber, and on seeing the butler I asked if Mr. Reevers had left yet.

'Yes, my lady. Some twenty minutes ago.'

I thanked him and raced down to the beach. A yacht was just putting out to sea, and a tall figure stood on the deck watching the shore. I waved, and he waved back. The ache in my heart brought tears to my eyes, but I watched until the yacht disappeared over the horizon.

He'd already spent years in France and knew Paris well. It was quite true that The Terror had passed, but he was still an English spy. Who, if caught, would be sent to the guillotine. I knew he felt it his duty to go, and I believed it to be his only source of income too. But I wished with all my heart that he was still here at Walmer, safe from the revolutionaries.

There was no way of telling how long he would be in France, and his presence there would, without question, be a constant worry to me. I had so hoped that what had happened yesterday would soon lead us to a long and happy future together. I gave a sad sigh, for there was nothing I could do now, except pray for his safe return. Thus I straightened my shoulders determinedly, turned away from the sea, and walked slowly back to the castle.

THE END

201

If you enjoyed my book, I would be most grateful if you would kindly put a review on Amazon. *Thank you.*

Printed in Poland
by Amazon Fulfillment
Poland Sp. z o.o., Wrocław

54861154R00125